# THE THREE EVANGELISTS

Fred Vargas

# The Three
# Evangelists

TRANSLATED
BY
Siân Reynolds

Harvill Secker
LONDON

Published by Harvill Secker, 2006

6 8 10 9 7

First published with the title *Debout les morts* by
Éditions Viviane Hamy, Paris, 1995

First published in Great Britain in 2006 by
HARVILL SECKER
Random House, 20 Vauxhall Bridge Road,
London SW1V 2SA

Random House Australia (Pty) Limited
20 Alfred Street, Milsons Point, Sydney,
New South Wales 2061, Australia

Random House New Zealand Limited
18 Poland Road, Glenfield,
Auckland 10, New Zealand

Random House South Africa (Pty) Limited
Isle of Houghton, Corner of Boundary Road & Carse O'Gowrie,
Houghton 2198, South Africa

The Random House Group Limited Reg. No. 954009
www.randomhouse.co.uk

Maps and illustrations drawn by Emily Faccini

A CIP catalogue record for this book is available from the British Library

ISBN 1 84343 089 4

This book is supported by the French Ministry of Foreign Affairs, as part of the
Burgess Programme headed for the French Embassy in London
by the Institut Français du Royaume-Uni

**ĩi institut français**

Ouvrage publié avec le concours du ministère français chargé
de la Culture – Centre National du Livre

This book is published with support from the French Ministry
of Culture – Centre National du Livre

Papers used by Random House are natural, recyclable products made
from wood grown in sustainable forests; the manufacturing processes conform
to the environmental regulations of the country of origin

Typeset in Minion
by Palimpsest Book Production Limited, Polmont, Stirlingshire
Printed and bound in Great Britain by
Clays Ltd, St Ives plc

*To my brother*

# PARIS

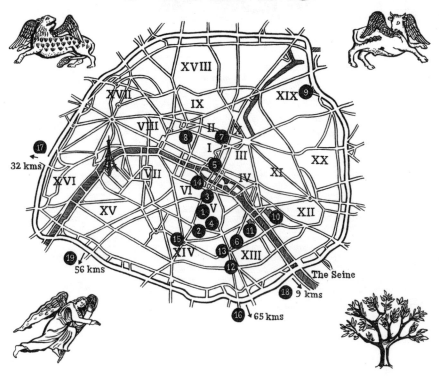

1. Rue Saint-Jacques
2. Rue du Faubourg Saint-Jacques
3. The Sorbonne
4. The Val-de-Grâce
5. Métro Châtelet
6. Rue Chasle
7. Rue Saint-Denis
8. Métro Opéra
9. Rue de la Prévoyance
10. Gare de Lyon
11. Gare d'Austerlitz
12. Métro Maison-Blanche
13. Avenue d'Italie
14. Saint-Michel fountain
15. Place Denfert-Rochereau
16. Fontainebleau forest
17. Marly forest
18. Maisons-Alfort
19. Dourdan

Rue Chasle is on the Left Bank in the southeast corner of Paris, in the *13th arrondissement*, but so quiet a street as to be difficult to locate.

*The Three Evangelists* is set in the mid-nineties.

# I

'PIERRE, SOMETHING'S WRONG WITH THE GARDEN,' SAID SOPHIA.

She opened the window and examined the patch of ground. She knew it by heart, every blade of grass. What she saw sent a shiver down her spine.

Pierre was reading the newspaper over his breakfast. Maybe that was why Sophia looked out of the window so often. To see what the weather was like. That's something you do quite often when you get up in the morning. And whenever the weather was dull, she would think of Greece, of course. These sessions standing at the window had, over time, become full of nostalgia, which swelled inside her some mornings to the point of resentment. Then it would pass. But this particular morning, something was wrong.

'Pierre, there's a tree in the garden.'

She sat down beside him.

'Pierre, look at me.'

Wearily, Pierre raised his face towards his wife. Sophia adjusted the scarf around her throat, a habit she had kept since her days as an opera singer. Protect your voice. Twenty years earlier, on one of the stone terraces of the open-air Roman theatre in Orange, Pierre had proposed to her with a cascade of protestations of love and undying certainties. Just before a performance.

Sophia cupped in her hand the gloomy face of the newspaper reader.

'What's eating you, Sophia?'

'I just told you something.'

'You did?'

'I said: "There's a tree in the garden".'

'I heard you. That's pretty normal, isn't it?'

'There's a tree in the garden that wasn't there yesterday.'

'Well, what about it? Am I supposed to react or something?'

Sophia was not feeling calm. She didn't know whether it was because of the newspaper, or the weary look, or the business about the tree, but it was clear that something was not right.

'Pierre, explain to me how a tree can turn up in a garden all by itself.'

Pierre shrugged. He really could not care less.

'What's the problem? Trees reproduce themselves. A seed, a cutting, a graft: that's all it takes. They grow into mighty forests in this climate. I imagine you know that.'

'It isn't a cutting. It's a tree! A young tree, standing up straight, with branches and everything, planted all by itself a metre or so from the end wall. How did it get there?'

'It got there because the gardener planted it.'

'The gardener's been gone two months and I haven't found a replacement. So, no, it wasn't the gardener.'

'Well, it doesn't bother me. Don't expect me to get worked up about a little tree standing by the end wall.'

'Don't you even want to get up and have a look? Can't you just do that?'

Pierre heaved himself to his feet. His reading had been interrupted.

'See?'

'Yes, of course I can see. It's a tree.'

'It wasn't there yesterday.'

'Maybe.'

'Not maybe. It wasn't there. So what are we going to do about it? Any ideas?'

'Why should I have?'

'That tree frightens me.'

Pierre laughed. He even put an affectionate arm round her. Briefly.

'I'm not joking, Pierre. It frightens me.'

'Well, it doesn't frighten me,' he said, sitting down again. 'In fact, having a tree turn up is quite nice. You just leave it in peace and that's that. And you might perhaps give *me* a bit of peace about it. Someone got the wrong garden, I dare say. Their problem, not ours.'

'But it was planted during the night, Pierre!'

'All the more likely someone got the wrong garden. Or perhaps it's a present. Have you thought of that? One of your fans wanted to honour you discreetly on your fiftieth birthday. Fans get up to all kind of tricks, especially those mouse-type fans, the obsessive ones, who won't give their names. Go and see, there might be a message.'

Sophia thought for a bit. The idea wasn't entirely ridiculous. Pierre had decreed that her fans fell into two camps. There were the mouse-type fans, who were timid, agitated, silent, but unshakeable. Pierre had once known a mouse transport a whole bag of rice into a rubber boot over the course of a winter, grain by grain. That's the way they are, mouse-fans. Then there are the rhino-type fans, equally to be dreaded in their way: noisy, loud-mouthed, very sure of themselves. Inside these two categories, Pierre had developed masses of sub-groups. Sophia couldn't remember them all. Pierre despised the fans who had come before him and the ones who came after him, in other words, all of them. But maybe he was right about the tree. Possibly; not certainly. She heard Pierre go into his 'Bye-see-you-tonight-don't-worry-yourself-about-it' routine, and then she was alone.

With the tree.

She went to take a look. Gingerly, as if it might explode in her face.

No, of course there wasn't a message. At the foot of the young tree was a circle of freshly dug earth. What sort of tree was it? Sophia walked round it a few times, grudgingly, feeling hostile. She was inclined to think it was a beech. She was also inclined to uproot it now, to tear it out, but being slightly superstitious, she dared not attack a living thing, even a plant. The truth is that few people would tear up a tree that had done them no harm.

It took a long time to find a book that would help. Apart from opera, the life of the donkey and Greek myths, Sophia had not had time to become expert on anything. A beech tree, perhaps? Hard to say without seeing its leaves. She went through the index of the book, to see if there were any trees called *sophia*-something in Latin. It could be some sort of disguised homage, the kind of convoluted thing a mouse-type fan might think up. That would be quite reassuring. But no, no *sophias*. Well, perhaps a species by the name of *stelios* something. That would not be nice at all. Stelios was nothing like a mouse, or a rhino. And he did worship trees. After the cascade of declarations by Pierre on the terraces in Orange, Sophia had wondered how she was going to leave Stelios, and had sung less well than usual. And the immediate reaction of her mad Greek had been to try and drown himself. They had fished him out of the Mediterranean, gasping for breath and floating like an idiot. When they were teenagers, Sophia and Stelios used to love to go out of Delphi along mountain paths with donkeys and goats, playing at being 'Ancient Greeks', as they called it. And then the imbecile had tried to drown himself. Luckily there was the cascade of declarations by Pierre. Nowadays, Sophia was still trying to locate a few trickles of it. Stelios? Was he a threat? Would he do something like this? Yes, he might. When he had been pulled out of the Mediterranean, he had been suddenly galvanised, and started screaming like a madman. Her heart beating too fast, Sophia made an effort to get to her feet, drink a glass of water and look out of the window.

The view calmed her down at once. What had come over her? She took a deep breath. Her habit of creating a whole terrifying logic out of nothing was exhausting. It was almost certainly just a beech tree, a sapling, and it didn't mean a thing. But how did whoever planted it get into the garden, with their blasted beech tree? Sophia dressed quickly, went outside and examined the lock on the garden gate. Nothing to notice. But it was such a simple lock that anyone with a screwdriver could undoubtedly open it in a moment and leave no trace.

It was early spring. The day was damp, and she was getting chilled, standing there defying the beech. What might it mean? Sophia tried not to think. She hated it when her Greek soul got carried away, especially twice in one morning. And what was she to think if Pierre wouldn't take any interest in this tree? Why didn't he? Was it normal that he should be so unconcerned?

Sophia had no wish to stay alone all day with the tree. She picked up her handbag and went out. In the street, a young man, well thirty-something, was looking through the gate of the house next door. 'House' was perhaps putting it too grandly. Pierre always referred to it as 'that tumbledown disgrace'. He thought that in this privileged street, where the houses were all desirable residences, that barn of a place, which had for years lain empty, let the side down. Up to now, Sophia had never imagined that Pierre might become stupid with age. The notion now crossed her mind. This is the first sinister effect of the tree, she told herself without really meaning it. Pierre had even had the side wall of their garden built higher to prevent them from having to see the so-called 'disgrace'. You could only see it now from the second-floor windows. This young chap, on the other hand, seemed to be looking admiringly at the façade with its broken windows. He was skinny, with black hair, black clothes, chunky silver rings on the fingers of one hand, and a bony face; his forehead was pressed between two bars of the tall, rusty gates.

Exactly the kind of person Pierre could not stand. Pierre was a defender of moderation and sobriety. And this young fellow was elegant, both rather austere and rather showy. The hands gripping the gates were beautiful. Looking at him, Sophia felt a little comforted. No doubt that was why she asked him if he could identify the tree. The young man moved his head away from the gate, flecks of rust now in his straight black hair. He must have been standing like that for some time. Without showing surprise or asking any questions, he followed Sophia, and she pointed to the tree, which could be seen quite clearly from the street.

'That's a beech tree, Madame,' the young man said.

'Are you sure? Forgive me, but it is quite important.'

The young man looked again carefully. With his dark and as yet unclouded eyes. 'Absolutely sure, Madame.'

'Thank you, Monsieur. You're very kind.'

She smiled at him and walked away. The young man walked off in the other direction, kicking a small stone with the toe of his shoe.

She was right, then. It was a beech. Just a beech.

Dammit.

# II

THAT WAS HOW IT STARTED.

He had been down on his luck – for how long now? About two years.

And then finally, a gleam of light at the end of the tunnel. Marc kicked a pebble, sending it about five metres up the street. It's not so easy on the pavements of Paris to find a pebble to kick. In the country, yes. But who bothers in the country? Whereas in Paris, you sometimes really need to find a pebble and give it a good kick. Sod's law. And, like a little ray of sunlight in the clouds, he had had the good luck, about an hour ago, to find a very suitable pebble. So he was kicking it along and following it.

His pebble had now taken him all the way to rue Saint-Jacques in the Latin Quarter, not without one or two problems. You're not allowed to touch it with your hand, it's strictly feet only. So, anyway, the bad luck had lasted two years now. No job, no money, no woman in his life any more. And no way out in sight. Except, perhaps, the house, or if you prefer, the 'disgrace'. He had seen it yesterday morning. Four floors, counting the attics, plus a bit of garden, in an out-of-the-way street, and all in a totally tumbledown state. Holes everywhere, no central heating, an outside lavatory with a wooden door and latch. If you screwed up your eyes, it looked fantastic. If you opened them properly, it looked like a disaster area. On the other hand, the landlord was willing to let it at a peppercorn rent, in exchange for the tenant doing it up a bit. This house might help him get out of the hole he was in right now. What was more, there would be room for his godfather. Somewhere near the house, a woman had asked him an odd question. What was it now? Oh yes. The name of a tree. Funny how people know absolutely nothing about trees, yet they can't live without them. But maybe they're right. After all, he knew the names of plenty of trees and where had that got him?

The pebble went off-piste in rue Saint-Jacques. Stones don't like going uphill. It had rolled into a gutter right by the Sorbonne, what was more. Well, farewell the Middle Ages. Farewell all those monks, lords and peasants. Marc clenched his fists in his pockets. No job, no money, no woman and no more Middle Ages. How pathetic. Skilfully, Marc propelled the pebble out of the gutter and back onto the pavement. There's a trick to doing that. And he knew all about the trick, just as he knew all about the Middle Ages, it seemed to him. Don't even think about the Middle Ages. In the country, you never have to confront the challenge of getting a pebble back onto a pavement. That's why one can't be bothered to kick a stone in the country, even though there are tons of them there. Marc's pebble sailed smartly across rue Soufflot and manoeuvred without too much difficulty into the narrow part of rue Saint-Jacques.

Two years, then. And after two years of that, the first reaction of someone down on their luck is to look out for someone else down on their luck. Seeing friends who have succeeded, when you have made a complete mess of your life, aged thirty-five, only makes you bitter. At first, OK, it's interesting, it gives you ideas, and encourages you to try harder. But then it begins to get on your nerves and makes you bitter. Well-known fact. And Marc wanted at all costs not to become bitter. It's pathetic, and even dangerous, especially for a medieval-ist. Dispatched with a solid thump, the pebble reached the Val-de-Grâce.

There was someone else who was in his position, or so he had heard. According to information recently received, Mathias Delamarre was very seriously down on his luck, and had been for some time. Marc liked him, liked him a lot in fact. But he had not seen him for the last two years. Maybe Mathias would come in with him and rent the disgrace. Because even if it was a peppercorn rent, Marc could only manage about a third of it. And the landlord wanted a reply right away.

With a sigh, Marc negotiated the pebble to a telephone box. If Mathias agreed, he might be able to say yes to the deal. But there was one big problem about Mathias. He was a specialist on prehistoric man. As far as Marc was concerned, once you'd said that, you'd said it all. But was this the moment to be fussy about a man's academic speciality? In spite of the terrible gulf between them, they liked each other. It was odd, but that was what you had to hold on to, this strange affection, and not the peculiar choice Mathias had made to study hunter-gatherers and flint axeheads. Marc could still remember the phone number. Someone answered, saying that Mathias had moved, and gave him the new number. Doggedly, he dialled again. Yes, Mathias was in. Hearing his voice, Marc breathed again. If a guy of thirty-five is at home at twenty-past three on a Wednesday afternoon, it's a sure sign he's in grade A trouble. Good start. And when he agrees, without more ado, to meet you in a down-at-heel café in rue du Faubourg Saint-Jacques, that tells you he is likely to agree to anything.

All the same.

# III

ALL THE SAME. HE WASN'T THE KIND OF MAN YOU COULD PUSH
around. Mathias was obstinate and proud. As proud as Marc? Possibly
worse. He was the kind of hunter-gatherer who would chase his bison
until he was exhausted and then stay away from the tribe rather than
return home empty-handed. No. That sounded too much like an idiot,
and Mathias was more subtle than that. On the other hand, he was capable
of going two days without speaking, if one of his ideas came up against
reality. The ideas were probably too complex, or the desires too inflex-
ible. Marc (who could talk for France, to the weariness of his audience)
had more than once had to stop short when he came across this blond
giant in the corridor of the university, sitting silently on a bench, pressing
together his huge hands as if he was squeezing into pulp the contrari-
ness of fate, a great blue-eyed hunter-gatherer, away in pursuit of his
bison. Was he from Normandy perhaps, a descendant of the Vikings?
Marc realised that in the four years they had sat side by side, he had
never asked Mathias where he came from. But what the hell did it matter?
That could wait.

There was nothing to do in the café, and Marc sat waiting. With his
finger, he was doodling on the tabletop the outline of a statue. His hands
were long and skinny. He liked their precise engineering and the veins
standing out on them. As for everything else about his physique, he had
serious doubts. Why think of that? Because he was going to see the great
blond hunter again? Well, so what? Of course, Marc, being only of

middling height, and very thin, with a bony face and body, would not have made an ideal bison-hunter. He would have been sent up a tree, more likely, to shake down the fruit. A gatherer, in other words. Full of nervous dexterity. Well, what of it? Dexterity is useful. No money, though. He did still have his rings, four big silver rings, two with gold strips, conspicuous and complicated, part-African, part-Carolingian, on the fingers of his left hand. And yes, it was true that his wife had left him for a more broad-shouldered type. A dumbo, for sure. She would work it out one day. Marc was counting on that. But it would be too late.

He rubbed his drawing out with one swift stroke. His statue had gone awry. A fit of pique. He got them all the time, these fits of irritation, these impotent rages. It was easy to caricature Mathias. But what about himself? What else was he, apart from being one of those decadent medievalists, neat, dark, delicate but tough little creatures, the prototype of the researcher after useless information, a luxury product with dashed hopes, hitching his futile dreams to a few silver rings, to visions of the millennium, to ploughmen who had been dead for centuries, to a long-lost Romance language that nobody cared about any more, and to a woman who had abandoned him? He looked up. Across the street was a large garage. Marc did not like garages. They depressed him. Striding past it with long swinging steps, came the hunter-gatherer. Marc smiled. Still blond, his hair too thick to be properly combed, wearing his eternal sandals which Marc so much disliked, Mathias was keeping the rendezvous. He was still wearing no underclothes. Nobody knew how, but you could always tell. Sweater and trousers straight on to the body, Sandals and no socks.

Well, rustic or refined, tall or thin, there they were at a table in this dingy café. So no matter.


'You shaved off your beard,' said Marc. 'Aren't you doing pre-history any more?'

'Yeah, I am,' said Mathias.

'Where?'

'In my head.'

Marc nodded. The information had been accurate. Mathias was indeed down on his luck.

'What's up with your hands?'

Mathias looked down at his black nails.

'I've been working in an engineering shop. They kicked me out. They said I didn't have any feeling for machines. I managed to fuck up three in one week. Machines are complicated. Especially when they break down.'

'And now?'

'I'm selling tatty posters in the Châtelet Métro station.'

'Any money in that?'

'No. And you?'

'Nothing to say. I used to be a ghostwriter for a publisher.'

'Medieval stuff?'

'Eighty-page love stories. You have this guy, untrustworthy but good in bed, and this girl, radiant but innocent. In the end they fall madly in love and it's incredibly boring. The story doesn't say when they split up.'

'Of course not,' said Mathias. 'Did you walk out?'

'No, got sacked. I used to change whole sentences in the page proofs. Because I'm bitter and twisted, and because I was so fed up. They noticed. Are you married? Partner? Children?'

'No, nothing like that,' said Mathias.

The two men drew breath and looked at each other.

'How old are we now?' asked Mathias.

'Thirty-five-ish. We're meant to be grown-up by now.'

'Yeah, so I've heard. Are you still poking about in that medieval midden?'

Marc nodded.

'What a pain,' said Mathias. 'You were always a bit unreasonable about that.'

'Don't start, Mathias, it's not the moment. Where do you live?'

'In a room I've got to get out of in ten days. The posters don't pay enough to rent a bedsit. Let's say I'm going downhill.' Mathias squeezed his two powerful hands together.

'I can show you this house,' said Marc. 'If you'll come in with me on it, we might be able to forget the thirty thousand years between us.'

'And the midden too?'

'Who knows? What about it?'

Mathias, although he was uninterested in, indeed was hostile to anything that had occurred since 10,000 BC or so, had always – incomprehensibly – made an exception for his lanky medievalist friend, who always wore black with a silver belt. To tell the truth, he had always considered this weakness for his friend a lapse of taste on his part. But his affection for Marc, his appreciation of the other's versatile and sharp mind, had made him close his eyes to the distressing choice his friend had made to study that particularly degenerate phase of human history. Despite this appalling weakness of Marc's, Mathias tended to trust him, and had allowed himself to be dragged now and then into one of his quixotic enterprises. Even today, when it was clear that Don Quixote had been unhorsed and was reduced to trudging along like a pilgrim, in short, now that he was clearly down on his luck, just as Mathias was himself (and in fact that was rather pleasing), Marc had not lost his persuasive air of royal grace. There was a world-weary expression perhaps in the lines at the corner of the eyes, and some accretion of unhappiness, there had been shocks and traumas he would rather have done without, yes, there was all that. But he still retained his charm and the fragments of the dreams that Mathias had lost sight of in the underground corridors of the Châtelet Métro station.

True, Marc did not seem to have given up on the Middle Ages. But Mathias was ready to go along with him to this 'disgrace' that he was describing as they walked along. His hand, adorned with rings, waved arabesques as he explained the deal. What it seemed to be was a tumble-down house, with four floors if you counted the attic, and a bit of garden. Mathias wasn't put off. They would have to try to find enough money for the rent. Make a fire in the hearth. Find room for Marc's aged godfather. Why? He couldn't be abandoned, because it was either

that or a retirement home. OK. No problem. Mathias was not bothered. He could see Châtelet Métro station receding into the distance.
He followed Marc's lead, satisfied that his friend was in the same boat
as himself, satisfied that he was in the pathetic situation of an unemployed medievalist, satisfied with the showy ornaments his friend
dressed up in, and entirely satisfied with the wretch of a house, in which
they were certain to freeze to death because it was still only March. So
by the time they arrived at the rusty gate, through which you could see
the house across a patch of long grass, in one of those secret streets
that exist in Paris, he was incapable of viewing the dilapidation of the
site with any objectivity. He found the whole thing perfect. Turning to
Marc, he shook hands. It was a deal. But even with what he earned
selling posters, it still wasn't going to be enough. Marc, leaning on the
gate, agreed. Both men became serious. A long silence followed. They
were trying to think of names. Someone else as down and out as themselves. Then Mathias suggested a name: Lucien Devernois. Marc reacted
strongly.

'You're not serious? Devernois? Have you forgotten what he does?'

'Yes, I know,' sighed Mathias. 'He works on the history of the Great
War.'

'Come on, you can't be serious. We may not have much money, and
I know it's not the moment to be too fussy, OK. But still, there is a bit
of the past left to think about the future. And you're proposing we get
in a contemporary historian? Someone who works on the Great War?
D'you realise what you're saying?'

'Well, yes,' said Mathias. 'But he isn't a complete prat.'

'Maybe not. But still. It's not an option. There are limits.'

'Yeah, I know. Although if you push me, Middle Ages and contemporary history, it's all pretty much the same thing.'

'Oh, steady, watch what you're saying.'

'OK. But I think I heard that Devernois was seriously down on his
luck, although he may earn a bit on the side.'

Marc frowned.

'Down on his luck?'

'That's what I said. He left off teaching teenagers in a *lycée* up north. He's got a really dead-end job now, teaching part-time in a private school in Paris. Bored, disillusioned, writing, on his own.'

'So he really is down on his luck, like us. Why didn't you say so straightaway?'

Marc stood still for a few seconds. He thought fast.

'That changes everything,' he announced. 'Get going, Mathias. Great War or no Great War, let's turn a blind eye. Courage, men, France expects you to do your duty. You go find him and persuade him. I'll meet you both back here at seven with the landlord. We've got to sign the lease tonight. Go on, find a way, convince him. If all three of us are in such a bad way, we ought to be able to contrive a total disaster.'

Saluting, they went their separate ways, Marc at a run, Mathias at walking pace.

# IV

IT WAS THEIR FIRST EVENING IN THE DISGRACE IN RUE CHASLE. THE
Great War historian had turned up, shaken hands at speed, taken a look
at all four floors, and hadn't been seen since.

After the first moments of relief, now that the lease was signed, Marc
felt his worst fears reviving. The excitable modernist, who had turned
up with his pale cheeks, his long lock of hair falling in his eyes, his tightly
knotted tie, grey jacket, and a pair of shoes which had seen better days,
true, but which had been handmade in England, inspired in him a degree
of apprehension. Even setting aside his catastrophic choice of research
subject, Lucien was unpredictable: a mixture of stiffness and *laissez-aller*,
*bonhomie* and seriousness, good-natured irony and deliberate cynicism,
and he seemed to lurch from one extreme to the other, with short bursts
of fury and good humour. It was disconcerting. You couldn't anticipate
what was coming next. Sharing a house with someone who wore a tie
was a new experience. Marc looked over at Mathias, who was pacing
around the empty room with a preoccupied expression.

'Was it easy to persuade him?'

'Piece of cake. He stood up, twitched his tie, put his hand on my
shoulder and said, "The solidarity of the trenches. Theirs not to reason
why. I'm your man." A bit over the top. On the way, he asked me what
we were up to these days. I told him a bit about pre-history, selling
posters, the Middle Ages, ghostwriting romances, and machines. He
pulled a face – maybe it was the Middle Ages he didn't like. But he

recovered, muttered something about the melting-pot of the trenches, and that was it.'

'And now he's vanished.'

'He's left his rucksack. That's promising.'

Then the trenches expert had reappeared, carrying on his shoulder a packing case for firewood. Marc wouldn't have thought he had the strength. He might be OK after all.

So that was why, after a scratch supper, eaten off their knees, the three seriously unemployed historians found themselves huddled before a large fire. The fireplace was imposing and coated in soot. 'Fire,' Lucien Devernois announced with a smile, 'is our common starting-point. A modest example, but common to us all. Or if you prefer, it's our base. Apart from being out of a job, this is our only known point of contact. Never neglect points of contact.'

Lucien accompanied this with an expansive gesture. Marc and Mathias looked at him, without trying to work out what this meant, warming their hands over the flames.

'It's simple,' Lucien explained, getting launched. 'For the sturdy pre-historian among us, Mathias Delamarre, fire is essential. He thinks of groups of hairy men huddling around their life-giving fire at the cave mouth, because it keeps away wild animals: the invention of fire.'

'The invention of fire,' Mathias began, 'is a controversial . . .'

'Enough!' said Lucien. 'Please keep your expert opinion to yourself. I have no interest in who is right and wrong about the caves, but let us honour the importance of fire in prehistoric times. Moving on, we come to Marc Vandoosler, who racks his brains trying to calculate the medieval population and what does he count? "Hearths." Not so easy either, for the poor medievalists. Swiftly climbing the ladder of years, we get to me, and the firing line of the Great War: men under fire, the line of fire, reaching back to the dawn of mankind. Rather touching, isn't it.'

Lucien laughed, sniffed loudly and rekindled the blaze in the grate by pushing a log with his foot. Marc and Mathias smiled weakly. They were going to have to reckon with this impossible guy who was nevertheless indispensable, since he would be paying a third of the rent.

'Well,' said Marc, twisting his rings, 'when our disagreements get really serious and our chronological preferences too hard to face, all we have to do is make a fire, right?'

'It might help,' Lucien conceded.

'Sensible idea,' added Mathias.

So they stopped talking history, and warmed themselves by the fire. In fact they were more concerned about the weather that evening, and for the evenings to come. The wind had risen and heavy rain was leaking into the house. The three of them began to estimate the extent of the repairs needing to be done, and the work involved. For now, the rooms were all empty and they were sitting on packing cases. Tomorrow each would bring his own possessions. They would have to plaster the walls, rewire the electricity, fix the plumbing, prop up the ceilings. And Marc was going to collect his elderly godfather. He would explain that another time. Who was he? Just his old godfather, that's all. He was actually his uncle as well. And what did this uncle-godfather do? Nothing, he was retired. Retired from what? From his job, of course. What kind of job? Oh, Lucien was a pain with all his questions. He was a civil servant, if you must know. He would fill in the details another time.

# V

THE TREE HAD GROWN.

For more than a month, Sophia had been keeping watch from the second-floor window, observing the new neighbours. They interested her. Was there any harm in that? Three fairly young men, no women to be seen, and no children. Just three guys. She had immediately recognised the one who had been pressing his forehead against the rusty gates and had told her at once that her tree was a beech. She had been pleased to see him back in the street. He had brought with him two very different-looking fellows. A tall, fair-haired type, who wore sandals, and an excitable character in a grey suit. She was getting to know them rather well. Sophia wondered whether it was quite proper to be spying on them like this. Well, proper or not, it reassured and distracted her, and it was giving her an idea. So she went on doing it. They had been in perpetual motion for the whole month of April: transporting planks, buckets, sacks of stuff in wheelbarrows, or boxes on – what do you call those metal things with wheels? Trolleys, that was it. So, boxes on trolleys. Plenty of work going on, then. They had been criss-crossing the garden the whole time, and that was how Sophia had learnt their names, by leaving the window open. The thin one in black was Marc. The slow-moving, fair-haired one was Mathias, and the one always with a tie was Lucien. Even when he was making holes in the walls, he kept his tie on. Sophia touched her neckscarf. Well, each to his own mannerism.

Through the side window of a boxroom on the second floor, Sophia could also see what was going on inside the house next door. The newly repaired windows had no curtains and she did not think they would ever acquire any. Each resident seemed to have chosen a floor. The problem was that the tall, fair-haired one worked in his apartment half-naked, virtually naked, and sometimes completely naked, according to his fancy. As far as she could see, this bothered him not at all. It was embarrassing. He was good to look at, that wasn't the problem. But as a result, Sophia did not really feel at her ease perching in the boxroom. Apart from work on the house, which sometimes seemed to overwhelm them, but which they were pursuing with determination – they did a lot of reading and writing as well. Bookshelves had been filled with books. Sophia who had been born on the rocky shores of Delphi, and who had made her way in the world entirely by her voice, admired anyone who could spend time reading a book at a table with a reading lamp.

Then last week, there had been a new arrival. Another man, but much older. At first Sophia thought he was a visitor. But no, the elderly man had come to stay. For some time? Well, anyway there he was, in one of the attic rooms. It was pretty odd, all the same. He had a good face, she thought. He was far and away the most handsome of her neighbours. But the oldest too: sixty, seventy, maybe. To look at him you would suppose he would have a commanding voice, but on the contrary, he spoke so softly and mildly that to date Sophia had been unable to hear a single word of what he said. He held himself very erect and tall, very much the ex-commander of the fleet. Nor did he lend a hand with the repair work. He watched, and chatted. It was impossible to catch his name. For the moment, Sophia called him 'Alexander the Great' or 'the old bugger', depending on her mood.

The one you heard most often was the one with a tie, Lucien. His voice carried a long way and he seemed to take pleasure in giving a loud running commentary on what he was doing, giving all kinds of advice, only rarely followed by his companions. She had tried talking to Pierre about the neighbours, but he was no more interested in them than in the tree. As long as they didn't make too much noise in the disgrace next door, he was not going to concern himself with them. Yes, of course,

Pierre was preoccupied with his social work. Yes, of course, every day he had to deal with files on terrible cases, single mothers sleeping rough, young people chucked out by their families, homeless twelve-year-olds, old people wheezing away in slums, and he compiled reports on all that for the minister. And Pierre was the kind of person who was conscientious about his work. Even if Sophia hated the way he sometimes talked about 'his' cases, which he divided into categories and sub-categories, the way he did her fans. Which category would Pierre have put her in, when at twelve years old she was trying to sell embroidered handkerchiefs to tourists in Delphi? A 'social problem' for sure. So yes, one could understand how, with all that to think about, he couldn't give a damn about a tree or the four next-door neighbours. But still. Why would he never talk about them? Even for a minute?

# VI

MARC DID NOT EVEN LOOK UP WHEN HE HEARD LUCIEN FROM HIS third-floor eyrie shout an order of high alert, or some such warning. Marc was more or less learning to put up with the Great War historian, who had, for one thing, put in a huge amount of work on the house, and was, for another, given to impressively long periods of silent study. Indeed they were so intense that he was dead to the world for as long as he was grappling with the mudbath of the Great War. Lucien had made himself responsible for all the rewiring and replumbing, of which mysteries Marc knew absolutely nothing, and for which he would be eternally grateful to him. He had transformed the attic into a large double room, neither cold nor dilapidated, where the godfather was now happily settled. He paid a third of the rent and contributed a generous flow of donations, bringing some new refinement to the house every week. But he was also generous with speeches and occasionally with outbursts. He could deliver sarcastic military tirades, excesses of all kinds, and snap judgements. He was capable of ranting away for a whole hour at full stretch, over some tiny detail. Marc was learning to let Lucien's tirades go in and out of his consciousness like inoffensive monsters. Lucien wasn't even a militarist. He was trying, with determination and rigour, to penetrate the heart of the Great War, but not succeeding in locating it. Perhaps that was why he shouted so much. No, there must be some other reason. At any rate, this time Lucien came downstairs and burst into Marc's room without knocking.

'General alert!' he cried. 'Take cover! The neighbour's on her way.'

'Which neighbour?'

'The one on the Western Front. The one on the right, if you prefer. The rich woman who wears scarves. Not a word. When she rings the bell, nobody moves. Empty house. I'll tell Mathias.'

Before Marc could say anything, Lucien had run down to the first floor.

'Mathias,' he called, opening his door. 'General alert! Empty—'

Marc heard Lucien stop abruptly. He smiled and came downstairs after him.

'Oh for God's sake,' Lucien was saying. 'Do you have to be in the nude to put up some bookshelves! I mean, what is the point? Don't you ever get cold?'

'I'm not in the nude, I've got sandals on,' Mathias said calmly.

'Sandals, as if that made a difference! And if you must play at being prehistoric man, surely, whatever I may think of him, he wasn't daft enough to go around with no clothes on.'

Mathias shrugged.

'I know more about that than you do,' he said. 'And it's got nothing to do with prehistoric man.'

'What is it to do with, then?'

'It's just me. I don't like clothes, they make me feel imprisoned. I'm fine like this. What do you want me to say? It's not a problem for you, if I stay on this floor. You just need to knock before you come in. Anyway what's going on? Is there some emergency?'

The concept of an emergency did not figure in Mathias' mental make-up. Marc entered, smiling.

'"The serpent",' he remarked, '"on seeing a naked man, is frightened and escapes as fast as he can. But when it sees a man with clothes on, it attacks without fear." Thirteenth-century saying.'

'This isn't getting us anywhere,' said Lucien.

'What's going on?' Mathias asked again,

'Nothing. Lucien saw the neighbour from the Western Front advancing this way. Lucien has decided not to answer when she rings.'

'The bell still doesn't work,' observed Mathias.

'Pity it's not the neighbour from the Eastern Front,' said Lucien. 'She's pretty. I get the feeling one could negotiate a peace treaty with the Eastern Front.'

'How do you know?'

'I've conducted a few tactical reconnaissance missions. The east is more interesting and more accessible.'

'Well, this is the western one,' said Marc firmly. 'And I don't see why we shouldn't open the door to her. I like her fine, we chatted a bit one morning. In any case, it would do us no harm to be nice to the neighbours. Simply a matter of strategy.'

'Oh, well, of course,' said Lucien, 'if we are talking diplomacy.'

'Conviviality. Human relations, if you prefer.'

'She's knocking at the door now,' said Mathias. 'I'll go down and open it.'

'Mathias!' said Marc, taking hold of his arm.

'What's the matter. I thought you were in favour.'

Marc looked at him, gesturing silently.

'Oh shit,' said Mathias. 'I suppose I'd better put some clothes on.'

'I suppose you should.'

While the others went downstairs, he pulled on a sweater and a pair of trousers.

'I did tell him that sandals were *not* enough,' said Lucien.

'Now can you please hold your tongue, when we see her?' said Marc.

'It's not so easy to hold your tongue, and you know it.'

'True,' Marc admitted. 'But trust me. I know this neighbour, I'll open to her.'

'How do you know her?'

'I told you. We talked once. About a tree'.

'What tree?'

'A little beech tree.'

# VII

FEELING AWKWARD, SOPHIA SAT BOLT UPRIGHT ON THE CHAIR THEY
had offered her. After leaving Greece, her life had accustomed her either
to receive or to refuse entrance to journalists and fans, but not to go
knocking on doors. It must have been twenty years since she last went
to call on someone, like this, without notice. And now that she was sitting
in this room, with the three men around her, she wondered what they
must think of this tedious visit from a neighbour coming to call. People
don't do that these days. So she was tempted to begin by explaining
herself. Were they the kind of persons one could explain things to, as she
had come to believe from her second-floor look-out? Sometimes it's
different when you see people close to. There was Marc, half sitting, half
standing at the big wooden table, crossing his lanky legs: an attractive
pose, and an attractive face, looking at her without impatience. Opposite
her sat Mathias, with handsome features too, a little heavy in the jaw,
but with limpid blue eyes, straightforward and calm. Lucien, who was
busying himself with glasses and bottles, tossing his hair back from time
to time, had the face of a child and the collar and tie of a man. She felt
reassured. Why else had she come after all, except that she was already
frightened?

'Look,' she said, taking the glass which Lucien had offered her with a
smile. 'I'm so sorry to bother you, but I've come to ask a favour.'

Two faces waited for her to go on. It was time to explain, but how
was she going to broach such a ridiculous subject? Lucien wasn't listening.

He was coming and going, the complicated dish he was cooking requiring all his attention.

'It's a really silly thing. But I need to ask a favour,' Sophia said again.

'What sort of favour?' Marc asked gently, encouraging her.

'It's hard to ask, and I know you have been working very hard these last weeks. But I need someone to dig a hole in my garden.'

'Major offensive on the Western Front,' murmured Lucien.

'Of course,' Sophia was hurrying on, 'I would be prepared to pay, if we could agree. Should we say . . . three thousand francs, for the three of you?'

'Three thousand francs, for digging a hole?' Marc murmured.

'Attempt at subornation by enemy forces,' muttered Lucien under his breath.

Sophia was uncomfortable. And yet she thought she had come to the right place, and that she should press on.

'Yes, three thousand francs, for digging a hole. And for saying nothing about it.'

'But,' Marc started to say, '– Madame . . . ?'

'Relivaux, Sophia Relivaux. I'm your neighbour, from next door, on the right.'

'No,' Mathias said quietly, 'you're not.'

'Yes I am,' said Sophia. 'I'm your next-door neighbour.'

'Very true,' Mathias replied, still speaking softly. 'But you aren't Sophia Relivaux. You are the wife of Monsieur Relivaux. But you are Sophia Siméonidis.'

Marc and Lucien were staring at Mathias, astonished. Sophia smiled.

'Lyric soprano,' said Mathias. '"Manon Lescaut", "Madame Butterfly", "Aïda", Desdemona, "La Bohème", "Elektra" . . . and you haven't sung now for six years. Allow me to say how honoured I am to have you as a neighbour.'

With this, Mathias bowed his head as if in homage. Sophia looked at him and thought, yes, this was indeed the right house to have come to. She gave a happy sigh, as she looked round the large room, now with its tiled floor and plastered walls, every noise echoing since there was very little furniture. The three tall windows overlooking the garden were mullioned. It was a little like the refectory of a monastery. Through a low door, also arched, Lucien was appearing from time to time, holding a wooden spoon. In a monastery one says everything, especially in the refectory, in a low voice.

'Since he has told you, I don't need to introduce myself,' said Sophia.

'Well, we should introduce ourselves though,' said Marc, who was rather impressed. 'This is Mathias Delamarre, and . . .'

'That's alright,' Sophia cut him short. 'It's a bit embarrassing to say so, but I know who you are. You overhear a lot without meaning to between these two gardens.'

'Without meaning to?' asked Lucien.

'Well, sometimes on purpose, it's true. I have looked and listened, quite deliberately at times, I will admit.'

She stopped. She wondered whether Mathias would understand that she had seen him from her little window.

'I wasn't spying on you. You just interested me. I thought I might be able to call on your help. What would you say if, one morning, a tree was planted in your garden, and you had had nothing to do with it?'

'Frankly,' said Lucien, 'the state our garden is in, I doubt if we would notice.'

'That's not the point,' said Marc. 'You're talking about that little beech tree, aren't you?'

'That's right,' said Sophia. 'It just appeared one morning. Without a word from anyone. I don't know who planted it. It wasn't a present, so far as I can tell. And it wasn't my gardener, because I haven't got one at the moment.'

'What does your husband have to say about it?' asked Marc.

'He's not bothered about it. He's a busy man.'

'You mean he couldn't give a damn?' said Lucien.

'Worse than that. He doesn't want to hear me talk about it even. It irritates him.'

'That's odd,' said Marc.

Lucien and Mathias nodded their agreement.

'You think that's odd? Really?' asked Sophia.

'Yes, really,' said Marc.

'Me too,' said Sophia softly.

'Forgive my ignorance,' said Marc, 'but were you a very famous singer?'

'No. Not in the top class. I had some success, but I was never known as La Siméonidis. No, if you think this was some kind of eccentric fan-mail, as my husband suggested, you are mistaken. I have had admirers, but I didn't provoke any extravagant worshippers. Ask your friend Mathias, since he seems to know about it.'

Mathias waved his hand vaguely. 'You were more admired than you say, all the same,' he said quietly.

There was a silence. Lucien turned host and filled up the glasses.

'The fact is,' he said, pointing his spoon at Sophia, 'you are scared. You're not accusing your husband, you're not accusing anyone, you don't want even to think about it, but you are scared.'

'I am certainly worried,' Sophia said in a low voice.

'Because a tree being planted,' Lucien went on, 'means earth. Earth underneath it. Earth that nobody will disturb because it has a tree growing out of it. It's sealed-in earth. In other words, a grave. The problem is potentially interesting.'

Lucien was not one to mince words; he spoke as he found. In this case, he had hit home.

'Without going as far as that,' said Sophia, still quietly, 'let's say, I would rather set my mind at rest about it. I'd rather know, if there is anything beneath the tree.'

'Anything, or anyone,' said Lucien. 'Have you reason to suspect anyone? Your husband? Any dark doings? An importunate mistress?'

'Lucien, that will do,' said Marc. 'No-one's asking you to charge ahead like that. Madame Siméonidis came here to ask us about digging a hole, full stop. Let's stick with her request, if you don't mind. No need to stir up trouble without cause. For now it's just a matter of digging up the tree – is that right?'

'Yes,' said Sophia, 'for three thousand francs.'

'Why are you offering so much money? It's tempting, of course, because we haven't a bean.'

'I realised that,' said Sophia.

'But that's no reason to take that kind of money from you, just to dig a hole in your garden.'

'Well, that depends,' said Sophia. 'If, after the hole, there are . . . well, consequences, I might prefer to keep them quiet. And that would be worth a lot of money.'

'OK, we understand,' said Mathias. 'But is everyone agreed about the digging, consequences or no consequences?'

There was an awkward silence. The answer was not straightforward. The money was very attractive, given their circumstances. But on the other hand, becoming accomplices in something, just for money – and accomplices in what, exactly?

'You'll do it, of course,' said a gentle voice.

Everyone turned. Marc's godfather walked in, coolly poured himself a drink and greeted Madame Siméonidis. Sophia, on seeing him nearer to, decided that he wasn't exactly Alexander the Great. He was very thin and held himself erect, so he looked taller than he really was. But then there was his face. A weathered kind of beauty that could still make an impression. There was no hardness in it, but chiselled outlines, an arched nose, irregular lips, hooded eyes and a direct gaze, everything required to seduce someone at first sight. Sophia looked at it with a connoisseur's eye, mentally judging that face: intelligent, brilliant, gentle, perhaps treacherous. The older man ran his hand through his hair which was not grey, but black sprinkled with white and which he wore rather long so that it curled on his neck. He sat down. He had spoken. They would dig the hole. No-one thought to challenge him.

'I've been listening at doors,' he remarked. 'Madame has been watching from windows. In my case it's a reflex, and an old habit. It doesn't bother me at all.'

'Charming,' said Lucien.

'Madame is right on every point,' Marc's godfather went on. 'You will have to dig.'

Marc stood up, embarrassed.

'This is my uncle,' he said, as if that could excuse the indiscretion. 'My godfather. Armand Vandoosler. He lives here.'

'And he likes to put his oar in everywhere,' muttered Lucien.

'Drop it, Lucien,' said Marc. 'It was in the contract: no comment.'

Vandoosler senior waved this away with a smile.

'No need to get upset,' he said. 'Lucien isn't wrong. I do like to put my oar in, as he puts it. Especially when I'm right. He does the same thing himself, even when he's wrong.'

Marc, still standing, indicated with a look to his godfather that it might be a good idea if he absented himself, and that this conversation was none of his business.

'No,' said Vandoosler, looking at his nephew. 'I have my reasons for staying.'

He looked from Lucien to Mathias, to Sophia and back to Marc.

'It would be better if you told them the truth, Marc,' he said, smiling.

'This isn't the moment. You really are winding me up,' said Marc in a low voice.

'It never will be the moment for you,' said his uncle.

'Alright, tell them yourself, if you're so keen. It's your dirty linen, not mine.'

'Oh, for heaven's sake,' said Lucien, waving his wooden spoon again. 'Marc's uncle is an ex-policeman, that's all. That's not going to keep us awake at night.'

'And how do you know that?' said Marc, wheeling round to face Lucien.

'Oh, just a few little things I noticed when I was fixing the attics.'

'Well, I see that everybody here goes prying into everyone else's affairs,' said Vandoosler.

'You aren't a proper historian if you don't pry into people's affairs,' said Lucien with a shrug.

Marc was beside himself with irritation. Sophia was listening attentively and calmly, as was Mathias. They waited.

'Contemporary history is so dignified,' said Marc in acid tones. 'And what else did you manage to find out?'

'This and that. Your godfather has been in the drugs squad, the gambling squad . . .'

'. . . and seventeen years a *commissaire* in criminal justice,' the old man calmly finished the sentence. 'A position from which I was dismissed with dishonour. Chucked out without my service medal after twenty-eight years. With a reprimand, disgrace and public ignominy.'

'A fair summary,' said Lucien, nodding.

'Terrific,' said Marc through clenched teeth, glaring at Lucien. 'If you knew, why didn't you say anything?'

'Because to me it's wholly unimportant,' said Lucien.

'Great,' said Marc. 'Uncle, nobody asked you to do anything, not to come downstairs, or to listen at doors, and as for you, Lucien, nobody asked you to go peeping into papers and then open your big mouth. That could have waited, couldn't it?'

'No, as a matter of fact it couldn't,' said the older Vandoosler. 'Madame Siméonidis needs your help in a delicate matter, so it's best she should know that there's an ex-policeman in the attic next door. Better that she has the means to decide whether to withdraw her request or not. It's more honest this way.'

Marc looked defiantly at Mathias and Lucien.

'OK, if that's the way you want it,' he said, even more vehemently. 'Armand Vandoosler is an ex-*flic*, true enough. And he has been disgraced. But he's still a *flic* and he's still bent, believe me. And he still takes liberties with the law, and with life in general. And those liberties may or may not come back to haunt him.'

'As a rule they do,' Vandoosler confirmed.

'And that's not all,' Marc went on. 'You can please yourselves what you do about it. But I'm warning you, he's my godfather and my uncle. My mother's brother. So, it's not negotiable. That's how it is, full stop. Now, if that means you don't want to stay any more in this patched-up house . . .'

'"The disgrace",' said Sophia. 'That's what the neighbours call it.'

'OK, "the disgrace". Well, if you want to leave because my godfather was a policeman in his own special way, it's up to you. We'll manage somehow, me and him.'

'Why on earth is he getting so worked up?' said Mathias, looking mildly around with his clear blue eyes.

'I've no idea,' said Lucien. 'He's highly strung. They were like that in the Middle Ages, you know. My great-aunt used to work in the slaughter-house, but I don't go round boasting about it.'

Marc looked down, and folded his arms, suddenly calm again. He glanced at the opera singer from the Western Front. What would she say, now she knew about the disgraced policeman living next door, in the house that the neighbours called 'the disgrace'?

Sophia guessed what he was thinking. 'It doesn't bother me at all that he's here,' she said.

'For reliability,' said Vandoosler, 'a disgraced policeman is actually a good bet. He'll listen and try to find out answers, but he's obliged to keep his mouth shut. The ideal confidant in fact.'

'He may have had his faults,' said Marc in a quieter voice, 'but my godfather was a pretty good investigator. He might be able to help.'

'Don't worry,' said Vandoosler, looking at Sophia. 'Madame Siméonidis will make up her own mind. If there is a problem, that is. As for these three,' he said, pointing to the young men, 'they're not entirely half-witted. They may be able to help too.'

'Who said they were half-witted?' said Sophia.

'Well, it's sometimes best to make things clear,' said Vandoosler. 'My nephew Marc now . . . I know a thing or two about him. I looked after him in Paris when he was twelve, that is, almost grown up. He was already vague, pig-headed, on a high, off-balance, but too clever to sit still. I never was able to do much with him, except to impress on him a few sound principles about the disturbances one must constantly bring to bear on the world. And he picked that up. As for the others, I've only known them a week, and they look OK so far. They're a strange combination, each one with his great work he's writing. Funny lot. Anyway, I have never heard of a case like yours before. It's high time to do something about the tree.'

'But what could I do?' Sophia asked. 'The police would have laughed at me.'

'Very true,' said Vandoosler.

'And I didn't want to alarm my husband.'

'Quite right.'

'So I was waiting until . . . I knew these young people better.'

'But how can we help, without arousing your husband's suspicions?' asked Marc.

'What I was thinking,' said Sophia, 'was that you might pretend to be workmen. Checking on buried electricity cables or something. Anything that would explain digging a trench, one that runs under the tree, of course. I'd pay you extra for some overalls, and to hire a van and tools.'

'I'm on,' said Marc.

'Sounds do-able,' said Mathias.

'Well, if it's about digging trenches,' said Lucien, 'I'm all for it. I'll send a sick note to the school. It'll take a couple of days.'

'Can you face watching your husband's reaction when they turn up proposing to dig their trench?' asked Vandoosler.

'I'll do my best,' said Sophia.

'Won't he recognise them?'

'No, I'm sure he won't. He's taken absolutely no interest in them.'

'Perfect,' said Marc. 'It's Thursday today. We need a bit of time to organise the details. We'll be knocking at your door on Monday morning, first thing.'

'Thank you,' said Sophia. 'It's funny. Now we've arranged all this, I'm sure there's nothing under the tree.'

She opened her handbag. 'Here's the money,' she said. 'It's all there.'

'What, already?' said Marc.

Vandoosler senior smiled. Sophia Siméonidis was an unusual woman. She was timid and hesitant in manner, but she had brought the money with her. Was she so sure of persuading them? He found that interesting.

# VIII

ONCE SOPHIA HAD LEFT, NO-ONE KNEW QUITE WHAT TO DO, AS THEY all paced around the big room. Vandoosler senior preferred to take his meals upstairs. Before leaving the room, he looked at them. The three younger men were standing, oddly enough, each one in front of one of the tall windows, gazing into the dark garden. Standing like that, each framed in an archway, they looked like three statues with their backs to him. St Luke on the left, St Matthew in the middle, St Mark on the right. Each of them turned to stone in his niche. Strange figures and they made strange saints. Marc had crossed his hands behind his back and was standing stiffly, legs apart. Vandoosler had done a lot of stupid things in his life; but he loved his godson. Not that there had ever been a christening.

'Dinner time,' said Lucien. 'I've made some pâté.'

'What kind?' asked Mathias.

They had not moved, but were speaking to each other while still staring into the garden.

'Jugged hare. A good dry pâté. I think it will taste fine.'

'Hare? That's expensive,' said Mathias.

'Marc shoplifted it this morning and delivered it to me.'

'Terrific,' said Mathias ironically. 'Takes after the old man. Why did you pinch it, Marc?'

'Because Lucien wanted one and it cost too much.'

'Oh, of course, naturally,' said Mathias. 'Tell me something. How come your name is Vandoosler like his, if he is your mother's brother.'

'Because my mother wasn't married, dickhead.'

'Let's eat,' said Lucien. 'Why are you badgering him?'

'I'm not badgering him, I'm just asking him a question. And what did Vandoosler do to get thrown out?'

'He helped a murderer escape.'

'Oh, of course,' said Mathias again. 'And what sort of name is that anyway, Vandoosler?'

'Belgian. It should be written Van Doos-l-a-e-r-e. Too complicated. My grandfather came to France in 1915.'

'Aha,' said Lucien. 'Did he fight in the war? Did he leave any letters, or documents?'

'No idea.'

'You ought to do some digging,' Lucien remarked, without leaving his post by the window.

'Well, for the time being,' said Marc, 'we have to dig a hole. I don't know what we're getting ourselves into.'

'Big trouble,' said Mathias cheerfully. 'Just for a change.'

'Let's eat,' said Lucien. 'We can make believe we haven't a care in the world for now.'

# IX

VANDOOSLER WAS ON HIS WAY HOME FROM THE MARKET. HE WAS gradually taking over the shopping duties. He didn't mind. On the contrary, he liked strolling through the streets, looking at other people, listening in to conversations, joining in, sitting on benches and chatting about the price of fish. Old police habits, reflexes of a one-time seducer, and of a lifetime's wandering. He smiled. This new district was to his taste. So was the new lodging. He had left his old quarters without a backward glance, content to be able to make a new start. The idea of beginning afresh had always attracted him more than the notion of carrying on indefinitely.

Vandoosler stopped as rue Chasle came into sight, and reflected pleasurably on this new phase of his existence. How had he got there? By a succession of accidents. When he thought about it, his life seemed like a coherent whole, yet it had been made up of sudden impulses, inspired by the moment and melting away in the long run. Grand ideas, serious plans, yes, he had had those once. None of them had ever come to anything. Not one. He had always seen the firmest resolve melt at the first request, the most sincere commitments fade on the slightest of pretexts, the most passionate pronouncements fail before reality. That was the way it was. He was used to it now, and couldn't really feel regret. You just needed a little self-knowledge. His moves had often been sure-footed and even brilliant in the short run, but he knew he would never make a middle-distance runner. This rue Chasle, with its curiously provincial air, was just right. Another new beginning. But for how long this time? A passer-by stared at him. He was probably wondering what Vandoosler was doing, pausing on the pavement with his shopping bag. Vandoosler had no doubt that the passer-by would have been able to tell him exactly why he himself lived there, and even to predict his own future. Whereas he, Vandoosler, would have found it hard even to sum up his life so far. He viewed it as a great web of incidents, events, investigations, successful or not, opportunities seized, love affairs, a remarkable series of events, none of them lasting very long and leading in too many directions to make a single summary possible, and thank goodness for that. There had been some damage, to be sure. Inevitably. You have to put off the old to find the new.

Before going into the house, the ex-*commissaire* sat down on the low wall on the other side of the street. A ray of April sunshine is always worth stopping for. He avoided looking towards Sophia Siméonidis' house, where three municipal workers had been digging a trench since the day before. He looked over to the other neighbour. What was it that St Luke called it? The Eastern Front. What an obsessive he was. Why did he care so much about the Great War? Well, each to his own poison. Vandoosler had made some progress on the Eastern Front. He had gathered some scraps of information here and there. The neighbour on that side was called Juliette Gosselin, and she lived with her brother Georges, a strong, silent type. Well, that was the story. For Armand Vandoosler, nothing was ever taken at face value. Yesterday at any rate the neighbour in the east had been out gardening in the spring sunshine. He had exchanged a few words with her, just to see. He smiled. He was sixty-eight years old and needed to be circumspect. He had no wish to be rebuffed. But it cost nothing to fantasise. He had made a close study of this Juliette, who seemed pretty and energetic, about forty years old, and he had concluded that she would not be at all interested in an ex-*flic*. Even one who was considered good-looking, though he had never been able to see that himself. Too thin, too angular, not enough purity of line for his own taste. He would never have fallen for someone who looked the way he did. But other people had, rather often. That had been quite useful when he was in the police, not to mention in private life. But Armand Vandoosler did not like his thoughts to take him in this fateful direction. That was twice in a quarter of an hour. Probably because he was changing direction yet again, changing his home and the company he kept. Or maybe it was because at the fish shop he had seen those little twins.

He shifted to move his basket into the shade. Thereby closer to the Eastern Front. Why the devil did his thoughts have to take him back there again, to the old bruise? He had only to look out for the next-door neighbour and think about the fish he had bought for the three workmen on the other side. He felt the old bruise once more. But dammit, he wasn't the only one. True, he had been at fault. Especially towards Lucie and the twins, whom he had abandoned one fine day. The twins were three at the time. And yet he was fond of Lucie. He had even said he would stay with her always. And then in the end, no. He had watched them walk away from him on the station platform. Vandoosler sighed. He slowly moved his head back, pushing his hair out of his eyes. The little ones would be twenty-four now. Where were they? Oh God, what a mess, and what a fool he had been. Were they far away or near now? And Lucie? No point thinking about that. Never mind. Love affairs: there are plenty to choose from. It's not important. None are any better than the others, absolutely not. Vandoosler picked up the basket and walked over to the neighbouring garden, Juliette's. Still nobody around. What if he tried a bit harder? If his information was correct, she ran a little restaurant called *Le Tonneau*, a couple of streets further down. Vandoosler knew perfectly well how to cook the fish, but where was the harm in going to ask for a good recipe?

# X

THE THREE TRENCH DIGGERS WERE SO EXHAUSTED THAT THEY ATE THEIR fish without even noticing that it was sea bass.

'Nothing at all!' said Marc, helping himself to a drink. 'Absolutely nothing. Unbelievable. We're filling it in again now. We'll have finished by this evening.'

'What did you expect?' asked Mathias. 'A corpse? Did you really think that's what we would find?'

'Well, after all the build-up . . .'

'Well, don't build it up any more. We've already done too much imagining. There was nothing under the tree, full stop, end of story.'

'Are you sure?' asked Vandoosler, in a blank voice.

Marc raised his head. He recognised that tone. When the godfather sounded like that, it was because he had been thinking of the past.

'Absolutely,' said Mathias. 'Whoever planted the tree didn't dig very deep. A metre or so down, the layer of earth was undisturbed. It was a sort of platform, dating from the late eighteenth century, same as the house.'

Mathias brought from his pocket a fragment of clay pipe, blocked up with earth, and put it on the table. Late eighteenth century.

'There you are,' he said. 'For the archaeologists among us. Sophia Siméonidis can sleep in peace. And her husband didn't react at all when he was told workmen were going to dig up his garden. He can't be a man with a guilty secret.'

'Maybe not,' said Vandoosler. 'But at the end of the day, you haven't found the explanation for the planting of the tree.'

'Just so,' agreed Marc. 'No explanation at all.'

'Oh who cares about the tree?' said Lucien. 'It must have been some practical joker. We've got our three thousand francs and everyone's happy. We'll fill it in and tonight by nine o'clock we'll be in bed. I'm worn out.'

'No,' said Vandoosler. 'Tonight, we're going out.'

'*Commissaire*,' said Mathias, 'Lucien is right, we're dead on our feet. You go out if you like, for us it's kip.'

'You'll have to make an effort, St Matthew.'

'Stop calling me St Matthew.'

'Fair enough,' said Vandoosler, shrugging, 'but what does it matter? Matthew, Mathias, Lucien, Luke, same difference. It amuses me. I'm surrounded by evangelists in my old age. Where's number four? Nowhere. A car with three wheels, a chariot with three horses. I find that funny.'

'What's so funny?' asked Marc irritably. 'Is it heading for the ditch?'

'No,' said Vandoosler. 'Because it never goes where you expect it to, or where it ought to go. It's unpredictable. And that's funny, isn't it, St Matthew?'

'Oh, please yourself,' said Mathias, pressing his hands together. 'But that won't make me an angel.'

'Forgive me,' said Vandoosler, 'but an evangelist and an angel are not the same thing at all. However, let's forget it. Tonight there's a drinks party at the neighbour's. The Eastern Front. It seems she likes partying. I accepted on behalf of us all.'

'Drinks party?' said Lucien. 'No thanks. Plastic cups, vinegary white wine, nibbles on paper plates. No way. Even when we're down on our luck, or especially then, no way. Three-horse chariot or whatever. Either a grand reception or nothing at all. No compromise, no middle way. In the middle way I lose my bearings, totally.'

'It's not in her house,' said Vandoosler. 'She runs the restaurant down the road, *Le Tonneau*. She would like to offer you a drink. Nothing objectionable there. I think this lady, Juliette of the Eastern Front, is worth looking at, and the brother is in publishing. Who knows, that could come in useful. And what's more, Sophia Siméonidis and her husband will be there. They always come. It would interest me to take a look.'

'Sophia and our other neighbour are on friendly terms?'

'Yes, very.'

'Collusion between the Eastern and Western Fronts,' announced Lucien. 'We're being caught in a pincer movement. We're going to have to make a sortie. Oh well, plastic cups or not . . .'

'We'll make up our minds this evening,' said Marc, rather rattled by his godfather's changes of heart and peremptory commands. What was his game? A distraction? An investigation? The investigation was over – before it had begun.

'We told you, there was nothing under the tree,' he said. 'Forget the night out.'

'I don't see the connection,' said Vandoosler.

'I'm sorry, but you see it very well. You want to go on looking for clues. And it doesn't matter where, or who with, so long as you can go on sniffing around.'

'What's your problem?'

'Don't start inventing something that doesn't exist, just because you threw away something that did exist. We're off now, to fill in the hole.'

# XI

IN THE END, VANDOOSLER SAW THE EVANGELISTS ARRIVE AT *LE TONNEAU* at nine o'clock that evening. The trench had been filled in, their clothes had been changed, and they presented themselves with smiles and freshly combed hair. 'Volunteers reporting for duty,' Lucien whispered in the *commissaire*'s ear. Juliette had prepared a meal for twenty-five people and had closed the restaurant to customers. And in fact it became a good night out, since Juliette, as she circulated among the tables, had told Vandoosler that his three nephews were attractive, and he had passed the message on, with embellishments. This had immediately changed Lucien's view of his surroundings. Marc had been touched by the compliment and Mathias had no doubt appreciated it in silence.

Vandoosler had told Juliette that only one of the three was really his nephew, the one in black, gold and silver, but Juliette was not one for technical or domestic intricacies. She was the kind of woman who started to laugh before the end of the joke. This made her laugh a good deal, which appealed to Mathias. A very pretty laugh. She reminded him of his elder sister. Juliette was helping the waiter to serve the dinner and rarely sat down herself, by choice more than necessity. By contrast, Sophia was demureness itself. From time to time she looked at the three diggers and smiled. Her husband was sitting beside her. Vandoosler's gaze lingered on this man and Marc wondered what he hoped to discover there. Vandoosler often looked as if he was discovering something. Police tactics.

Mathias, for his part, was looking at Juliette. She was exchanging remarks quietly with Sophia, now and then. They looked as if they were enjoying themselves. For no particular reason, Lucien wanted to know if Juliette Gosselin had a man in her life, a boyfriend or some such. Since he was drinking rather a lot of a wine which had found favour in his sight, he thought of putting the question to her directly. And did so. It made Juliette laugh, as she explained that somehow or other she had ended up without anyone, but didn't really know why. She was a woman on her own, OK. And that made her laugh. That's the kind of attitude to have, said Marc to himself, envying her. He would have liked to know how she did it. Instead, he learned that the restaurant took its name from the wine-cask shape of the cellar, which had an arched stone ceiling, so that huge casks of wine could be stored there. The rooms were very fine: 1732, according to the date on the lintel. The cellar itself would be interesting to see. If the advance on the Eastern Front kept up progress, he might go and have a look.

The advance did make progress. Somehow or other, as sleep overtook other people, by three o'clock in the morning the only ones left, sitting round a table covered with glasses and ashtrays, were Juliette, Sophia and the inhabitants of the 'disgrace'. Mathias was next to Juliette, and Marc thought that he had managed this deliberately but discreetly. Oh no, the fool. He was sure that Juliette had excited feelings in his friend, even though she was five years older than the three evangelists – Vandoosler had found out her age and passed it on. She had fair skin, round arms, soft plump cheeks, long blonde hair, a clinging dress and, above all, that infectious laugh. But it had to be admitted she wasn't trying to seduce anyone. She seemed perfectly content with her single status, running her bistro, as she had said earlier. But Mathias was on the way to being smitten. Not seriously, but a bit, all the same. When you're down on your luck, it isn't very clever to fall for the first woman you run into in the neighbourhood, however charming she may be. It only complicates life, and this was not the moment. And it leads to other things. As Marc very well knew. But perhaps he was mistaken. Mathias had the right to be attracted to a woman without it leading to anything in particular.

Juliette, not noticing how still and attentively Mathias was sitting, was telling anecdotes: about the customer who ate his potato crisps with a fork, or the one who came in on Tuesdays for instance and looked at himself in a pocket mirror throughout his meal. At three in the morning, everyone is indulgent towards this kind of story, whether you're telling them or listening to them. So they allowed Vandoosler senior to tell them about a few criminal cases. He spoke slowly and persuasively. Lucien set aside his worries about rebuffing the advances from the Eastern and Western Fronts. Mathias went to fetch a glass of water and sat down again at random, without choosing a place, not even one from which he could study Juliette. That surprised Marc, who was not generally wrong about even the passing afflictions of his friends. So Mathias was not as easy to read as other people after all. Maybe he was operating in code. Juliette whispered something to Sophia. Sophia shook her head. Juliette appeared to insist. Nobody else heard what they were saying, but Mathias said:

'If Sophia Siméonidis doesn't want to sing, don't press her.'

Juliette looked surprised, and Sophia, on hearing this, changed her mind. A rare moment thus came about, for the benefit of four men sitting in a wine cask at four in the morning, Sophia Siméonidis sang, in private, accompanied on the piano by Juliette, who was quite talented, but who seemed chiefly to be used to playing for the singer. No doubt Sophia was in the habit of giving such secret recitals, after hours, far from the stage, for herself and her friend.

After such a rare moment, one doesn't know what to do. Tiredness seeped back into the muscles of the trench diggers. They stood up, and pulled on their jackets. The restaurant was closed and everyone walked home together. Only when they reached her house, did Juliette remark that one of the waiters had let her down two days before. He had left without warning. Juliette hesitated, before going on. She was thinking of advertising the job the next day but, as she seemed to have picked up a hint that . . .

'That we're down on our luck?' Marc completed her sentence.

'Yes,' said Juliette, her face clearing, after getting over the worst of the difficulties. 'So tonight, as I was playing the piano, I thought that after all a job is a job, and it might interest one of you. When you've been to university, a job as a waiter isn't exactly what you dream about, but to tide you over . . .'

'How do you know we've been to university?' asked Marc.

'It's very simple, when you haven't been there yourself,' said Juliette, laughing in the darkness.

Without knowing why, Marc felt put out. Easily identifiable, a marked man, and slightly cross.

'What about your piano-playing?' he asked.

'Ah, the piano's another matter,' Juliette replied. 'My grandfather was a farmer, but fond of music. He knew all there was to know about beetroot, flax, wheat, music, rye and potatoes. For fifteen years he pushed me to study music. It was a sort of obsession with him. When I came to Paris, I worked at cleaning people's houses, and there was no more music. Only years later did I take it up again, after he died and I inherited a lot of money from him. Grandfather had plenty of acres and plenty of ingrained ideas. He had set a condition before I could inherit: I had to take up the piano again. Of course,' added Juliette with a laugh, 'the solicitor said the condition couldn't be enforced. But I wanted to respect my grandfather's wishes. I bought this house and the restaurant and a piano. So there you are.'

'That's why you often have beetroot on the menu?' smiled Marc.

'Yes,' said Juliette. 'Beetroots in C major.'

Five minutes later, Mathias had been hired. He smiled, squeezing his hands together.

Later, going up stairs, Mathias asked Marc why he had not told the truth, pretending he couldn't take up the offer, because he had something else in mind.

'Because it's true,' said Marc.

'No, it isn't, you haven't got anything else lined up. Why didn't you take it?'

'Because it's a case of finders keepers.'

'What do you mean "finders" . . . Oh blast! where's Lucien?'

'Oh-oh, we've left him at the bottom.'

Lucien, who had drunk the equivalent of twenty plastic cups, had not been able to get past the first few stairs, and was asleep on the fifth. The others hoisted him up under an arm apiece.

Vandoosler, who was in perfect shape, had seen Sophia home, and now walked in.

'What a beautiful sight,' he remarked. 'The three evangelists all holding onto each other to attempt the impossible ascension.'

'Why the hell did we give him the third floor?' said Mathias, heaving Lucien up.

'We weren't to know he drinks like a fish. Anyway, there wasn't any choice, remember, if we observe chronology. On the ground floor, there is the unknown, primeval chaos, total confusion, i.e. the shared rooms. On the first floor, the first stirrings of conscious life, man in his nakedness stands erect and silent for the first time, that's you, Mathias. Moving up the ladder of time . . .'

'What the hell is he on about?' asked Vandoosler senior.

'He's preaching,' said Mathias. 'And why not? There's no curfew on public speaking.'

'Moving up the ladder of time, as I was saying, we jump over antiquity and land straight in the glorious second millennium, with the contrasts and the audacity of the Middle Ages, that's me on the second floor. Next the age of decadence and collapse, contemporary civilisation. This one,' said Marc, shaking Lucien by the arm. 'Up on the third floor, bringing the strata of history and the staircase proper to an end, with the shameful Great War. Even further up, we have the godfather who continues to disrupt the present day in his own special way.'

Marc stopped and sighed.

'You see, Mathias, even if it might be more practical to have Lucien on the first floor, we can't mess about with chronology and disturb the layers as set out by the staircase. The ladder of time is all we have left. We can't upset the staircase which is the only thing we have managed to keep in good order. The only thing, Mathias. We can't destroy it!'

'Quite right,' said Mathias gravely. 'That is not to be countenanced. We have to carry the Great War up to the third floor.'

'If I might interject at this point,' said Vandoosler senior in his mild voice. 'You're all as pissed as each other, and I would really like you to haul the Great War up to his correct layer of history so that I can reach the dishonourable stages of the present day where I lodge.'

To his great surprise, next morning at eleven-thirty, Lucien watched as Mathias got himself ready, after a fashion, to go to work. The final stages of the evening – and in particular Juliette's offer to employ Mathias as a waiter – had completely passed him by.

'Well,' said Mathias, 'you did embrace Sophia Siméonidis, twice, to thank her for singing. That was a bit familiar of you, Lucien.'

'No memory of that at all,' said Lucien. 'So now you've signed up for the Eastern Front, have you? And are you going off with a song in your heart and a flower in your rifle? Don't you know that everyone thinks it will all be over by Christmas, but in real life it takes longer?'

'You really were pissed last night,' said Mathias.

'Keep the home fires burning. Good luck, soldier!'

# XII

MATHIAS DUG IN ON THE EASTERN FRONT. WHEN LUCIEN WASN'T teaching, he and Marc crossed the line and ate their lunch at *Le Tonneau* to encourage him, and because they liked it there. On the first Thursday, Sophia Siméonidis ate lunch there too, as she had every Thursday for years.

Mathias operated steadily, carrying cups one by one, not trying to balance everything at once. After three days, he had worked out which was the customer who ate crisps with a fork. After a week, Juliette was giving him leftovers from the kitchen, and dinners in the disgrace had improved as a result. After nine days, Sophia invited the other two to share her Thursday lunch. The following Thursday, sixteen days later, she failed to appear.

Nobody saw her on the next day either. Juliette anxiously enquired of St Matthew if she might have a word with the ex-*commissaire*, after closing the restaurant. Mathias was rather put out that she called him St Matthew, but since the old man had used these ridiculous names the first time he had introduced his three fellow residents, she couldn't think of them in any other way. So after closing *Le Tonneau*, Juliette accompanied Mathias to the disgrace. He had explained to her the chronological division of the lodgings, so that she would not be shocked that the oldest resident lived at the top of the house.

Out of breath from climbing the four flights of stairs so quickly, Juliette sat down opposite Vandoosler senior, who listened attentively. She seemed to like the evangelists, but to value even more the advice of the former *commissaire*. Mathias, leaning against a roofbeam, thought that in reality she was rather attracted by the features of the elderly ex-policeman, and this somewhat annoyed him. The more attentive the old man became, the more handsome he looked.

Lucien, back from Reims where he had been giving a well-paid lecture on 'The Stalemate on the Western Front', asked for a summary of the facts. Sophia had not reappeared. Juliette had been to see Pierre Relivaux, who had said not to worry, she would be back. He seemed concerned, but quite confident. Which gave one to think that Sophia had explained where she was going before leaving. But Juliette couldn't understand why Sophia had not told *her*. It bothered her. Lucien shrugged. He didn't want to upset Juliette, but after all Sophia was under no obligation to tell her everything she was doing. Juliette however insisted. Never before had Sophia missed a Thursday lunch without telling her beforehand. She always had a special dish, veal casserole with mushrooms. Lucien pulled a face. As if the veal and mushrooms would matter, if there was some sudden emergency. For Juliette, of course, the veal with mushrooms did matter. And yet Juliette was an intelligent woman. But that was the way of things, wasn't it? Obsessed with one's own little preoccupations such as veal with mushrooms, one ends up saying silly things. She was hoping that the old *commissaire* could get more out of Pierre. Although she had understood that Vandoosler was not exactly above reproach.

'Still,' she said, 'once a policeman always a policeman.'

'Not necessarily,' said Marc. 'A *flic* who has been thrown out of the force might turn anti-*flic*, or monster.'

'Doesn't Sophia get fed up eating veal every Thursday?' asked Vandoosler.

'No, not at all,' replied Juliette. 'And she even has her own way of eating it. She lines up her little mushrooms, like notes on a stave, and eats her way through them bar by bar.'

'An orderly woman, then,' said Vandoosler. 'Not the sort to vanish without explanation.'

'If the husband isn't worried,' said Lucien, 'he must have good reasons, and he's not obliged to tell us about his private life, just because his wife has walked out and failed to eat her veal and mushrooms. Let it go. A woman has the right to go away for a bit if she wants to. I don't see why we should be chasing after her.'

'All the same,' said Marc. 'Juliette is thinking about something she's not telling us. It's not just the veal that's bothering you, is it, Juliette?'

'No, it's not,' she replied.

She appeared a pretty woman, as the glancing light from the attic windows fell on her. Having hurried up the stairs, she had taken no thought for her appearance. As she leaned forward, with clasped hands, her dress fell loosely open, and Marc noticed that Mathias had positioned himself in front of her, transfixed. It was worth it, he had to admit, for the glimpses of pale skin, rounded curves and bare shoulders.

'But if Sophia comes back tomorrow,' Juliette went on, 'I'd feel awful to have been gossiping about her with neighbours who hardly know her.'

'We may hardly know her, but we are her neighbours,' Lucien pointed out.

'And then there's the tree,' Vandoosler reminded them gently. 'The tree makes it more important to say something.'

'Tree? What tree?' asked Juliette.

'I'll tell you later,' said Vandoosler. 'Perhaps you could first just tell us what you know?'

It was hard to resist the old *flic* when he spoke in this tone of voice, and Juliette was no exception.

'Well,' Juliette began, 'she came over from Greece with her boyfriend. He was called Stelios. According to Sophia, he was a loyal, protective sort of man, but as far as I could see he was a fanatic, an attractive but temperamental guy, who wouldn't let anyone near her. He watched over Sophia, guarded her, kept her close. Until, that is, she met Pierre and walked out on her guardian angel. Evidently this caused the most awful drama, and Stelios tried to kill himself, or something like that. Yes, that's it, he tried to drown himself, but it didn't work. Then he ranted and raved and made threats, but finally he went off and she didn't hear from him again. That's all. Nothing really remarkable. Except the way Sophia talks about him. She never seems to feel safe. She thinks one day Stelios is going to come back, and that will mean big trouble. She says he's "very Greek", brought up on Greek tragedies and that's something that never goes away. Sophia says we forget that in the olden days the Greeks were really a big deal. And then, oh, about three months ago, or a bit more, she showed me a postcard she'd had, from Lyon. It just had a star drawn on it, not even very well drawn. I couldn't see what was wrong with it, but it upset her. I thought it meant a snowflake or Christmas, but she was convinced it meant Stelios, and that it wasn't good news. It seems that Stelios was forever drawing stars, because the Greeks had been good at astronomy and all that. But nothing happened, so she forgot about it. That's all. But now I'm wondering, well, whether she's had another card. Maybe she was right to feel afraid. Things we can't understand. The Greeks, after all, they were something special.'

'How long has she been married to Pierre?' asked Marc.

'Oh, a long time, fifteen or twenty years. Frankly the idea of someone wanting revenge twenty years on seems pretty far-fetched to me. Life's too short, to nurse a grudge so long, you know what I mean? If everyone who'd ever been jilted plotted their revenge for years, we'd all be at each other's throats, wouldn't we?'

'Well, you *can* go on thinking about someone for years, you know,' said Vandoosler.

'Killing someone right away, OK,' Juliette was going on, without hearing him, 'I know these things happen. A sudden rage. But getting murderous twenty years later, no, I can't see it. But Sophia does seem to believe in some sort of delayed reaction. Perhaps Greeks are like that, I don't know. But if I'm telling you all this, it's because Sophia took it very seriously. I think she's rather sorry she let her Greek go, and since Pierre's turned out to be a bit of a disappointment, maybe this is her way of remembering Stelios. She said she was afraid, but actually I think she rather likes thinking about Stelios, the long-time lover.'

'Pierre's a disappointment?' asked Mathias.

'Yes,' said Juliette. 'Pierre takes no notice of anything any more, that is, he doesn't take any notice of *her*. He just says yes and no, that's all.

He converses, as Sophia puts it, he reads the paper for hours on end, and doesn't look up when she goes past. Apparently that's how he is from first thing in the morning. I told her it was pretty normal, but she thinks it's sad.'

'Oh well,' said Lucien, 'if she's decided to run off with her Greek, what's that to us?'

'Well, for a start, there's the veal and mushrooms,' insisted Juliette obstinately. 'But anyway, I'd just like to know what's happening. I'd feel better about it if I knew.'

'It's not so much the lunch that bothers me,' said Marc. 'It's the tree. I don't know if we should just do nothing, when we have a wife who disappears without warning, a husband who doesn't give a damn, and a tree popping up in the garden. What do you think, *commissaire?*'

Armand Vandoosler raised his finely wrought profile. He was looking like a policeman now. He had a concentrated expression which seemed to draw his eyes in under his eyebrows; his nose appeared somehow more commanding. Marc recognised the look. The god-father had such an expressive face that you could tell the kind of thoughts he was having. When he looked serious, it was the twins and their mother, lost somewhere in the world; when it was medium-serious, it was police business; when it was sharp, it was some woman he was trying to seduce. At least that was the simple reading. Sometimes they all got mixed up together and then it was more complicated.

'I'm concerned, yes,' said Vandoosler. 'But I can't do much on my own. From what I saw of him the other night, Pierre Relivaux isn't going to bare his soul to the first disgraced policeman he meets. Certainly not. He's the kind of man who will only respond to officialdom. Still, we do need to know.'

'What?' asked Marc.

'Whether Sophia did give him a reason before going off, and if so what it was, and also whether there is anything under the tree.'

'Oh, not that again!' cried Lucien. 'There's nothing under the bloody tree. Just old clay pipes from the eighteenth century – or rather bits of them.'

'There *wasn't* anything under the tree,' Vandoosler said carefully. 'But what about now?'

Juliette was looking at them in puzzlement.

'What's all this about a tree?' she asked.

'A beech tree,' said Marc impatiently, 'close to the back wall in her garden. She asked us to dig under it.'

'The beech tree?' said Juliette. 'But Pierre told me himself he'd had it planted to hide the wall.'

'Well, well,' said Vandoosler. 'That's not what he told Sophia.'

'Why on earth would someone plant a tree in the middle of the night, without telling his wife? Getting her all worked up about nothing? That's idiotically perverse,' said Marc.

Vandoosler turned back to Juliette.

'Did Sophia say anything else? About Pierre? Any hint that she had a rival?'

'She doesn't know,' Juliette said. 'Pierre is sometimes away a lot on Saturdays or Sundays. Getting a breath of fresh air, he says. That sounds suspiciously like an excuse. So, as anyone would, she has wondered about it. That's one thing I don't have to worry about, I must say. It may not seem much of one, but it's a distinct plus.'

She laughed.

Mathias, still not moving, looked intently at her.

'We need to know,' announced Vandoosler. 'I'll try to fix a meeting with the husband, somehow get to see him. What about you, St Luke? Are you teaching tomorrow?'

'His name is Lucien,' muttered Marc.

'It's Saturday tomorrow,' said Lucien. 'A day off for saints, soldiers on leave, and some of the rest of the world.'

'You and Marc, follow Pierre Relivaux. He's both busy and prudent. If there is a mistress somewhere, he will have timetabled her in classic style: Saturdays and Sundays. Have you ever had to tail someone? Do you know what to do? No, of course you don't. Apart from following clues through history, you're good for nothing. But three historical detectives, who manage to work their way into the unfathomable past, ought to be able to stalk someone in the here and now. But perhaps you don't like the here and now?'

Lucien pulled a face.

'Think of Sophia,' said Vandoosler. 'Don't you care what happens to her, is that it?'

'Of course we do,' said Marc.

'OK then. St Luke and St Mark, you get on the trail of Pierre Relivaux all weekend. Don't let him out of your sight for a minute. St Matthew will be working, so he can stay in *Le Tonneau* with Juliette and keep his ears open. You never know. As for the tree . . .'

'What is there to do about that?' asked Marc. 'We've already played the card of being council workmen. But you don't seriously think . . .'

'Anything's possible,' said Vandoosler. 'With the tree, we'll have to tackle it head on. Leguennec will help. He's tough.'

'Who's Leguennec?' asked Juliette.

'Man I play cards with,' replied Vandoosler. 'We invented this crazy game called "Whaling". Great game. He knows a whole sector of the sea like the back of his hand, because he used to be a fisherman in his youth. A trawlerman, Irish Sea and so forth. Good guy.'

'What's the use of a card player who knows his way round the Irish Sea?' asked Marc.

'The card-playing fisherman joined the police.'

'Like you, is he?' asked Marc. 'A bit dodgy?'

'Not at all. And to prove it, he's still in the force. These days he's *inspecteur en chef* of the 13th *arrondissement*. He was one of the few people who stood up for me when I was chucked out. But I can't get in touch with him direct, that would put him in an awkward position. The name Vandoosler still raises hackles in the police. St Matthew will have to handle it.'

'On what pretext?' asked Mathias. 'What am I supposed to say to this Leguennec? That a lady we know didn't come home one day, and her husband doesn't seem worried? Far as I know, grown-up people have a right to go where they want, for heaven's sake, without the neighbours calling in the police.'

'A pretext? Easy. It seems to me, now I think about it, that a couple of weeks ago, three men came and dug up the lady's garden, claiming to be council workmen. They were impostors. There's your pretext: it'll do fine. You provide the other elements, and Leguennec will catch on. He'll be round.'

'Oh, thanks very much,' said Lucien. 'The *commissaire* encourages us to go dig up the tree, then the *commissaire* sets the police on to us. Terrific.'

'Use your brains, St Luke. I'm setting Leguennec on to you, that's different. Mathias doesn't need to give the names of the diggers.'

'Well, Leguennec will soon find them out, if he's any good.'

'I didn't say he was good, I said he was tough. Yes, he will find out the names, because I'll tell him myself, but only later. If necessary, that is. I'll tell you when to call him, St Matthew. And for now, I think Juliette is tired.'

'You're right,' she said, sitting up. 'I'm going home. But do we really need to call in the police?'

Juliette looked at Vandoosler. His words seemed to have reassured her. So she looked at him and smiled. Marc glanced at Mathias. The god-father's good looks were ancient, they had done good service, but they were still quite effective. How would Mathias' regular features be able to compete with the older man's faded but powerful beauty?

'I think it's time for bed,' said Vandoosler. 'Tomorrow morning, I'll pay a visit on Monsieur Relivaux. After that St Luke and St Mark will take over.'

'Mission logged,' said Lucien. And smiled.

# XIII

VANDOOSLER, CLIMBING ONTO A CHAIR, HAD PEERED OUT OF A
skylight to see whether anyone was getting up next door. On the Western
Front, as Lucien called it. What an oddball that one was. And yet he had
apparently written some reputable books about the Great War. How could
he get interested in all that stuff when there was plenty of excitement in
the corner of one's neighbour's garden? Well, maybe it was the same kind
of thing.

And perhaps he had better stop calling them St This and St That. It
got on their nerves, which was understandable. They weren't kids any
more. Yes, but it amused him. In fact he got a real kick out of it. And so
far in life, Vandoosler had never seriously considered giving up anything
that gave him pleasure. So he would see how they got on with the here
and now, the three time detectives. If you were into detection, what difference did it make whether you were researching the life of the hunter-
gatherers, the Cistercian monks, the lads in the trenches, or Sophia
Siméonidis? Anyway, for now he had to keep an eye on the Western Front,
to see when Relivaux woke up. There wouldn't be long to wait. He wasn't
the sort of person to sleep late in the morning. He was a determined and
disciplined man, of a slightly annoying kind.

By nine-thirty, Vandoosler decided from the stirrings next door that
Relivaux was ready. Ready to be called on by him, Armand Vandoosler.
He went downstairs, greeted the evangelists who had already gathered in
the common room and were sitting side by side eating their breakfast.

Perhaps it was the contrast between their talk and their action that amused him. He went next door and rang the bell.

Pierre Relivaux did not welcome the intrusion. Vandoosler had foreseen as much, and had opted for the direct approach: retired policeman, concerned about the missing woman, a few questions, perhaps we would do better to talk inside. Pierre Relivaux replied as Vandoosler had expected, that it was his business, and nobody else's.

'That's quite true,' said Vandoosler, installing himself in the kitchen without being invited to do so, 'but there's a slight problem. The police may come and see you, because they will take the view that it is their business. I thought the advice of a retired policeman might be useful.'

As expected, Relivaux frowned. 'The police? Why are they involved? My wife has a perfect right to go away, hasn't she?'

'Certainly she has. But there has been an awkward sequence of events. Do you remember the three workmen who came a couple of weeks ago to dig a trench in your garden?'

'Yes, of course. Sophia said they were checking old electricity cables. I didn't pay them much attention.'

'That's a pity,' said Vandoosler. 'Because they weren't municipal employees at all, nor were they from Électricité de France, or anything else official. There are no cables running through your garden. The men were impostors.'

'What on earth would anyone do a thing like that for?' Relivaux protested. 'What the hell is going on? And what does that have to do with the police, or with Sophia?'

'That's just it,' said Vandoosler, appearing to be genuinely sympathetic. 'Someone round here, a busybody, or at any rate someone who doesn't seem to like you, has found out they weren't genuine. I suppose he recognised one of the workmen and asked him. Anyway, he's told the police. I know about it, because I still have a few contacts down at the station.'

Vandoosler told lies with fluency and enjoyment, and it put him completely at ease.

'The police just laughed at him and didn't follow it up,' he went on. 'But they stopped laughing when this same busybody nosed around some more and discovered that your wife had "gone missing without telling anyone", as they are already saying in the neighbourhood. And furthermore that this mysterious trench was ordered by your own wife, who wanted it to go under that beech tree over there.'

Vandoosler pointed casually through the window to the tree.

'Sophia did that?' asked Relivaux.

'She did. According to this witness anyway. So the police now know that your wife was worried about a tree that appeared from nowhere. Also that she had someone dig underneath it. And that since then she has disappeared. For the police, that looks like a lot to happen in a couple of weeks. You have to look at it from their point of view. They're programmed to be suspicious of any little thing. So they'll certainly be round to ask you a few questions, you can count on it.'

'Who is this "witness"?'

'The information was anonymous. People are cowards.'

'And just what is your interest in all this? What if the police do come round to see me, what business is that of yours?'

Vandoosler was ready for this predictable question too. Relivaux was a conscientious, stiff kind of fellow, apparently without an ounce of originality. That was indeed why the former *commissaire* was prepared to bet he had a Saturday-and-Sunday mistress. Vandoosler looked at him: moderately bald, moderately fat, only moderately attractive, moderate in everything. For the moment, quite easy to manipulate.

'Let's say that if I were able to confirm your version of things, that would certainly calm their suspicions. They know me of old.'

'Why would you want to help me? What do you want from me? Money?'

Vandoosler smiled as he shook his head. Obviously Relivaux was moderately stupid too.

'Well,' Relivaux went on, 'it looks to me as if you people in that ramshackle disgrace you live in, forgive me if I'm mistaken, but you all seem to be . . .'

'Hard up,' Vandoosler finished the sentence. 'Quite right. I see you are better informed than you let on.'

'I'm used to dealing with down-and-outs,' said Relivaux. 'It's my job. Anyway, that's what Sophia has told me. So what's your motive?'

'Let's just say the police and I have had our little run-ins in the past. When they get a bee in their bonnet about you, it can go on and on. So I try when possible to help other people to avoid it. A small-scale revenge if you like. Anti-police protection service. And it keeps me busy. No charge.'

Vandoosler allowed Pierre to reflect on this specious and poorly argued motive. He seemed to swallow it.

'What do you want to know?' Relivaux asked.

'What *they* will want to know.'

'Which is?'

'Where has Sophia gone?'

Relivaux stood up, spread his arms wide in a gesture and turned round.

'She's gone away. She'll be back. There's nothing to get steamed up about.'

'They will want to know precisely why you're not getting steamed up about it.'

'Because I haven't put the kettle on. Because Sophia told me she was going away. She said something about meeting someone in Lyon, if you must know. It's not the other side of the world.'

'They might not believe you. Be more precise, Monsieur Relivaux. Your peace of mind could depend on it, and I believe you do care about that.'

'It's really of no particular interest. On Tuesday, Sophia got a post-card. She showed it to me. It just had a drawing of a star and a date to meet at a certain time in a hotel in Lyon. Take such and such a train tomorrow night. No signature. Instead of keeping calm, Sophia got into a state. She had got it into her head that the card was from an old boyfriend, a Greek called Stelios Kutsukis. Because of the star. I had a certain amount of trouble from him, on several occasions, before we got married. He was the mad-rhino kind of admirer.'

'I beg your pardon?'

'Oh, nothing. Anyway, one of Sophia's admirers.'

'A former lover.'

'Naturally, I tried to dissuade Sophia from going. If this card was from someone else, then God knows what she was letting herself in for. And if it was from Stelios, it wasn't much better. But no, there was no stopping her, she packed her bag and off she went. I admit I was expecting to see her back yesterday. And that's all I know.'

'And the tree?'

'What do you want me to say about the tree? Sophia made a huge fuss about it. I didn't imagine she would go to the length of digging underneath it. What on earth did she think was there? She's always making up fantasies. It can only be a gift from someone, what else? Perhaps you have heard that Sophia was quite well known until she gave up performing. She was an opera singer.'

'Yes, I know. But Juliette Gosselin said that you told her that *you* had planted the tree.'

'Yes, that's what I told her. One morning at the gate, Juliette asked me about the new tree. Sophia having made such a fuss about it, I didn't want to tell her that we had no idea where it came from, and then have that get all round the neighbourhood. As you guessed, I value my peace of mind. So I simply told her I had decided to plant a beech tree – to put a stop to the questions. That's what I should have told Sophia too. It would have saved a lot of trouble.'

'That's all very well and good,' said Vandoosler, 'but we only have your word for it. It would be helpful if you could produce the postcard. So that someone could get in touch with her.'

'Well, I'm sorry,' said Relivaux, 'but Sophia took it with her, because it had the instructions on it. That's logical, isn't it?'

'Ah. That's a pity, but it doesn't matter too much. The story sounds convincing.'

'Well, of course it does! Why would anyone think I'd been up to anything?'

'You know perfectly well what is the first thing the police think of when a wife disappears.'

'That's ridiculous.'

'Yes, it's ridiculous.'

'The police wouldn't dare go to those lengths,' said Relivaux putting his hand stiffly down on the table. 'I'm not just anybody.'

'No, indeed,' said Vandoosler gently. 'Nobody is.'

He got up slowly. 'If the *flics* do come and see me, I'll back up your story.'

'There's no need. Sophia will be back.'

'Let's hope so.'

'I'm not worried about her.'

'Well, so much the better. And thank you for being so frank.'

Vandoosler crossed the garden to go home. Relivaux watching him go, thought: 'What the hell is he up to, the busy body?'

# XIV

IT WASN'T UNTIL THE SUNDAY NIGHT THAT THE EVANGELISTS CAME UP with anything concrete. On Saturday, the only time Pierre Relivaux went out was to buy the newspapers. Marc had said to Lucien that he was sure Relivaux would say he was going to 'consult the national press', rather than 'read the papers', and that one day he would have to test this, just for the pleasure of it. Anyway, he had not stirred all day, having stayed at home with the national press. Perhaps he was worried about getting a visit from the police.

Then, maybe since nothing seemed to be happening, he appeared to regain confidence. Marc and Lucien had started tailing him when he left the house at about eleven on Sunday morning. He led them to a little house in the 15th *arrondissement* in south-west Paris.

'You were bang on target,' said Marc, summing up their day for Vandoosler. 'The girl lives in a fourth-floor flat. Nice enough girl, easy going, quiet sort, not fussy.'

'Let's just say she's nothing to write home about,' said Lucien. 'I have standards, you know, and Marc here will give anyone the benefit of the doubt . . .'

'You're on your own, with your standards,' said Marc.

'Quite so,' said Lucien. 'But that's not what we're discussing. Carry on with your report, lieutenant.'

'That's all. The girl has her flat paid for, all found. She doesn't go out to work, we asked the neighbours.'

'So Relivaux does have a mistress. You guessed right,' said Lucien to Vandoosler.

'It wasn't guesswork,' said Marc. 'The *commissaire* has a lot of experience.'

Godfather and godson exchanged glances.

'Mind your own business, St Mark,' said Vandoosler. 'Are you sure she was his mistress? Could she not have been a sister or a cousin?'

'We listened at the door,' Marc explained. 'Verdict: it's not his sister. Relivaux left there at about seven. I think he's a dangerous creep.'

'Don't jump to conclusions,' said Vandoosler.

'Don't underestimate the enemy,' said Lucien.

'Has the hunter-gatherer not come back yet?' asked Marc. 'Still up at *Le Tonneau*?'

'Yes,' said Vandoosler. 'And Sophia hasn't telephoned. If she wanted to keep the whole thing quiet but at the same time reassure her immediate friends, she would have told Juliette. But there's been nothing, not a peep. It's four days now. Tomorrow, St Matthew will call Leguennec. Tonight, I'll go over with him what he's to say. The tree, the trench, the mistress, the missing wife. Leguennec will go for it. He'll come and take a look.'


Mathias telephoned the police. He described the facts in a blank voice.

Leguennec went for it.

By mid-afternoon, two policemen were tackling the beech tree, under orders from Leguennec, who was holding Pierre Relivaux. He had not even questioned Sophia's husband formally, since he knew he was operating at the limits of legality. Leguennec was acting on impulse, meaning to make himself scarce very fast if nothing turned up. The two men digging under the tree were loyal to him. They wouldn't talk.

From the second-floor window, Marc, Mathias and Lucien crowded together to watch.

'It'll finish off the poor old beech,' remarked Lucien.

'Shut up,' said Marc. 'Don't you understand this is serious? Any minute now they could find Sophia underneath it. And you think that's funny?

For the last few days I haven't even been able to string together any sentences that make sense.'

'I had noticed,' said Lucien. 'You disappoint me.'

'Well kindly keep your thoughts to yourself. Look at Mathias. He's managing to control himself. He can keep his mouth shut.'

'That's how Mathias always is. One day, it's going to rebound on him. Hear me, Mathias?'

'I hear you. See if I care.'

'You never listen to anyone. You just hear them. That's a mistake.'

'Oh, shut up, Lucien,' cried Marc. 'I'm telling you, it's serious. I liked her very much, our Sophia Siméonidis. If they really find her there, it's going to make me sick to my stomach, and I'm moving out. Hush. One of the *flics* is looking at something. No, he's digging again.'

'Now then,' said Mathias. 'Your godfather's there, coming up behind Leguennec. What's he up to? Can't he keep out of the way for once?'

'No, it's impossible, he's got to be everywhere at once,' said Marc. 'That's what he's done all his life really. Anywhere he isn't, he thinks is crying out for him to be there. And because he's spent forty years going here, there and everywhere, he doesn't know where he is any more, and no-one else does either. In fact, my godfather is a combination of a thousand godfathers rolled into one. He talks like a normal person, he walks about, he goes shopping, but when you try to pin him down, you never know what will appear: a troublemaker, a top policeman, a traitor, a salesman, a creator, a saviour, a destroyer, a sailor, a pioneer, a tramp, an assassin, a protector, a slacker, a prince, a dilettante, a fanatic – whatever. Very practical in some ways. Except it's not you who gets to choose, it's him.'

'I understood,' said Lucien, 'that we were supposed not to be saying anything.'

'I'm on edge,' said Marc. 'I have a right to speak. This is my floor we're on.'

'While we're up here, was it you who threw together that stuff I read on your desk? About village trade in the eleventh century? Are those your ideas? Is there any evidence for them?'

'Nobody gave you leave to read that. If you don't want to come out of the trenches, nobody's forcing you.'

'No, I thought it was good. But what the hell is your godfather up to now?'


Vandoosler had come up silently behind the men who were working. He stood behind Leguennec, being a whole head taller than him. Leguennec was a Breton: short, stocky, with iron-grey hair and broad hands.

'Hello, Leguennec,' said Vandoosler softly.

The *inspecteur* turned round with a start. He stared at Vandoosler, quite overcome.

'Hey, don't you recognise your old boss?' said Vandoosler.

'Vandoosler . . .' said Leguennec slowly. 'So you're the one behind this.'

Vandoosler smiled. 'Of course,' he said. 'It's good to see you.'

'Same here,' said Leguennec. 'But . . .'

'I know. I won't let my name appear anywhere. At least not yet. It wouldn't be right. Don't worry, I'll be as discreet as you'll want to be, if you don't find anything.'

'Why did you call me in?'

'It looked as if it was your kind of problem. And anyway it's on your patch. And you were always nosy in the old days. You liked to go fishing, and even catching spider crabs.'

'Do you really think this woman has been killed?'

'I don't know. But I'm sure something's wrong here. Quite sure.'

'What do you know about it?'

'No more than you heard this morning in that telephone message. That was a friend of mine. By the way, don't bother looking for the workmen who dug the first trench: they were friends of mine as well. That will save you some time. Not a word to Relivaux. He thinks I'm trying to help him. He has a weekend mistress in the 15th. I can give you the address if you need it. Otherwise there's no reason to alert him, we let him stew and then come down on him if we have to.'

'Naturally,' said Leguennec.

'I'm off now. I don't want to cause trouble for you. And don't bother to contact me about the tree,' said Vandoosler pointing to the hole in the ground. 'I'll be able to see everything from next door, I live in the attic.'

He made a gesture towards the clouds in the sky and disappeared.


'They're filling it in again!' said Mathias. 'They didn't find anything.'

Marc gave a sigh of genuine relief.

'End of story,' said Lucien.

He rubbed his arms and legs which were stiff from the long vigil, squeezed between the hunter-gatherer and the medievalist. Marc closed the window.

'I'm going to tell Juliette,' said Mathias.

'Can't it wait?' asked Marc. 'You're working this evening anyway, aren't you?'

'No, it's Monday. We're closed on Mondays.'

'Oh, yes. Well, as you like.'

'I just thought,' said Mathias, 'that it would be an act of kindness to tell her that her friend is *not* buried under the tree. We've all worried enough about it. It's nicer to think she has just gone off somewhere, isn't it?'

'Yes, of course, do as you like.'

Mathias disappeared.

'What do you think?' Marc asked Lucien.

'I think Sophia got a card from this Stelios, that she went to see him, and being fed up with her husband, unhappy in Paris, and feeling home-sick for her native land, she's decided to run off with her Greek. Good idea. I wouldn't care to sleep with Relivaux. She'll send a message in a couple of months when the initial turmoil has calmed down. A postcard from Athens.'

'No, I was talking about Mathias. Mathias and Juliette, what do you think? Haven't you noticed?'

'No, nothing special.'

'Little things? Haven't you noticed little things?'

'Oh, little things. It happens all the time you know. Not worth getting worked up about. Does it bother you? Did you fancy her yourself?'

'No, no,' said Marc. 'I don't really think anything about it. I'm talking rubbish. Forget it.'

They heard the *commissaire* climbing the stairs. Without stopping, he called out that there was nothing to report.

'Cease fire,' said Lucien.

Before leaving the room, he looked at Marc who was standing at the window. The light was fading.

'You'd do better to get back to your villages and their trade,' he said. 'There's nothing to see. She's on some Greek island. She's playing games. Greek women like playing games.'

'Where did you get that information?'

'I just made it up.'

'You're probably right. She must have run away.'

'Would you like to share a bed with Relivaux?'

'Have a heart,' said Marc.

'Well, then, you'll see. She's run away.'

# XV

LUCIEN FILED THE WHOLE BUSINESS AWAY AT THE BACK OF HIS MIND. Everything he put there fairly soon ended up falling into inaccessible compartments of his memory. He opened his notes on his chapter about propaganda, which had suffered from the interruptions of the last fortnight. Marc and Mathias also went back to their books which no publisher had commissioned. They saw each other at mealtimes, and Mathias, who came back from his work late at night, would greet his friends soberly and pay a brief call on the *commissaire*.

Invariably, Vandoosler asked him the same question. 'Any news?'

And Mathias would shake his head and go back down to the first floor.

Vandoosler never went to bed before Mathias was back. He must have been the only one who remained on the alert, along with Juliette, who, especially on the Thursday, anxiously watched the door of the restaurant. But Sophia did not come back.

The next day, Friday, was a day of May sunshine. After all the rain that had fallen in the previous month, it seemed to act as a tonic on Juliette. At three o'clock, she closed the restaurant as usual, while Mathias was taking off his waiter's apron and, naked to the waist behind a table, was looking for his sweater. Juliette was not unaffected by this daily ritual. She was not the kind of woman to get bored, but since Mathias had been working in the restaurant, things had been better. She had little in common with the other waiter or the chef. It's true that she had nothing in common with Mathias either, but he was easy to talk to, about anything one liked, and that was very agreeable.

'Don't come back till Tuesday, Matty,' she said, taking a sudden decision. 'We're going to be closed for the weekend. I'm going back home to Normandy. All this kerfuffle with trees and trenches has upset me. I'm going to put on boots and go walking in the wet grass. I like wearing boots and the last days of May.'

'Good idea,' said Mathias, who couldn't imagine Juliette in rubber boots.

'Come too, if you like. I think it's going to be fine. You look the sort of man who likes the countryside.'

'Yes, I do,' said Mathias.

'You'd be welcome to bring St Mark and St Luke and the gothic policeman if you like. I'm not particularly anxious to be on my own. It's a big house and we wouldn't have to be in each other's way. But, as you like. Do you have a car?'

'We don't have a car, because of our little problem with money. But I know where I can borrow one. I've got this friend who works in a garage. Why did you call him "gothic"?'

'Oh, I just did. He's very fine-looking, isn't he? His lined face makes me think of those old churches with pillars going in all directions, that look as if they are falling apart but keep standing. He's rather dishy.'

'You know about churches?'

'I used to go to Mass when I was little, believe it or not. Sometimes my father would pack us off to the cathedral at Évreux and I would read the guidebook during the sermon. Sorry, but that's all I know about the gothic. Does it bother you that I compared the old man to Évreux Cathedral?'

'No, of course not,' said Mathias.

'I do know one or two other places besides Évreux. The little church in Caudebeuf is solid and very plain, goes back a long way, and it feels very restful. And that just about exhausts the subject of my acquaintance with churches.' Juliette smiled. 'After all that, I would really like to go walking. Or cycling.'

'Marc had to sell his bike. Do you have some down in the country?'

'Two. If it really tempts you, the house is at Verny-sur-Besle, a village not far from Bernay, just a small place. When you come along the main road, it's the big farmhouse to the left of the church. It's called Le Mesnil. There's a stream and some apple trees, nothing but apple trees. No beeches. Will you be able to remember all that?'

'Yes,' said Mathias.

'I'm off now,' said Juliette, winding down the shutters. 'No need to tell me if you're coming or not. There's no telephone anyway.'

She laughed, kissed Mathias on the cheek, and went off, with a wave of her hand. Mathias was left standing on the pavement. Cars went past, making exhaust fumes. He thought that he might be able to bathe in the stream, if it stayed sunny. Juliette had soft skin and it was nice to have advances made to one. He stirred himself, walking very slowly towards the house. The sun warmed the back of his neck. He was clearly tempted. Tempted to go and relax in this village of Verny-sur-Besle, and to cycle over to Caudebeuf, although he didn't really care much about old churches. But it ought to please Marc, at least. Because there was no question of going there alone. Being alone with Juliette, with her plump, agile body, pale-skinned and languorous, might lead to trouble. Mathias could see the risk and in some ways feared it. He felt so weighed down at the moment. The sensible thing would be to take the two others along, and the *commissaire* as well. The *commissaire* could go and visit Évreux in all its grandeur and appealing decadence. It would be easy to persuade him. The old man liked going places, seeing new things. Then he could persuade the other two. It was a good idea. It would do them all good, even if Marc preferred towns, and Lucien was sure to protest against going off to some godforsaken place in the country.

They were on the road by six o'clock. Lucien, who had brought some work with him, was grumbling in the back seat about Mathias' primitive rural tastes. Mathias smiled as he drove. They arrived in time for supper.

The sun stayed out all weekend. Mathias spent a lot of time skinny-dipping in the stream, though nobody else understood why he did not feel the cold. On Saturday, he got up very early and wandered round the garden, looking at the woodshed, the cellar, the old cider press, and went off to Caudebeuf to see whether he and the church had anything in common. Marc went off cycling for hours. Lucien spent most of the time sleeping in the grass on top of his papers. Armand Vandoosler told stories to Juliette, as he had done that first night at the *Le Tonneau*.

'Your evangelists are nice,' said Juliette.

'They're not really mine,' said Vandoosler. 'I just pretend they are.'

Juliette nodded. 'Do you have to call them St This and That?'

'No. It was just a silly fancy that came to me one night, when they were standing at the three windows. It was a game. I like playing games, I like telling lies too, and making things up. So I play my games, I gamble with them and that's how it comes out. Then I imagine they each have a little halo. Yes? It certainly annoys them. Now I've got into the habit.'

'So have I,' said Juliette.

# XVI

LUCIEN DIDN'T WANT TO ADMIT IT WHEN THEY RETURNED ON MONDAY
night, but the three days' holiday had been an excellent thing. His analysis
of the propaganda destined for the home front hadn't made much progress,
but everyone's peace of mind had. They had supper peaceably and nobody
got grouchy, not even him. Mathias had time to say a few words, and Marc
constructed some long sentences about little things. It was Marc who took
out the bag of rubbish every night to the main gate. He held the plastic
sack in his left hand, the one with the rings, to counterbalance the refuse.
He came back without the bag, looking preoccupied, and went out several
times over the next two hours walking as far as the gates.

'What's the matter?' Lucien asked him in the end. 'Are you inspecting
the grounds?'

'There's a girl sitting on the wall opposite Sophia's house. She has a
child sleeping on her lap. And she's been there more than two hours.'

'Leave her be,' said Lucien. 'She's probably waiting for someone. Don't
be like your godfather, nosy about everything. I've had enough.'

'Well, I'm worried about the child,' said Marc. 'I think it's getting cold.'

'Don't worry about it,' said Lucien.

But nobody left the big room. They made some more coffee. Then a
light rain began to fall.

'It's going to rain all night,' said Mathias. 'May 31. How dreary.'

Marc bit his lip. He went out again. 'She's still there,' he said, coming
back in. 'She's wrapped the kid up in her jacket.'

'What's she like?' asked Mathias.

'I didn't go and stare at her,' said Marc. 'I don't want to alarm her. She's not in rags if that's what you mean. But rags or not, we're surely not going to let a girl and her child wait for God knows what, are we, all night in the rain? OK? So come on, Lucien, lend me your tie. Hurry up.'

'My tie? What for? Are you going to lasso her?'

'No, stupid,' said Marc. 'Just so's not to frighten her. A tie is kind of reassuring. Come on,' he added, holding out his hand. 'It's raining.'

'Why don't I go myself?' asked Lucien. 'It would save me taking my tie off. Anyway it doesn't at all go with your black shirt.'

'You're not going because you're not the reassuring type,' said Marc, knotting the tie as fast as he could. 'If I do bring her back here, please don't stare at her as if she were your prey. Be natural.'

Marc went out and Lucien asked Mathias what he should do to look natural.

'Eat something,' said Mathias. 'Nobody can be frightened of someone who's eating.'

Mathias pulled over the breadboard and cut two slices, passing one to Lucien.

'I'm not hungry,' Lucien complained.

'Just eat.'

They had started to munch their thick slices of bread when Marc returned, gently ushering in a young woman who said nothing, who looked tired, and who was carrying a child about five years old. Marc wondered briefly why Mathias and Lucien were eating pieces of bread.

'Do please sit down,' he said rather formally, trying to be reassuring. He took her dripping wet coat from her.

Mathias left the room without a word, and returned with a duvet and a pillow with a clean pillow case. He signalled to the young woman to put the child on the divan in the corner by the fire. Gently, he put the quilt over the child, and stirred up the flames. Quite the big-hearted caveman, thought Lucien, pulling a face. But Mathias' wordless actions had touched him. He wouldn't have thought of them himself. Lucien was easily moved.

The young woman seemed less frightened now and far less cold. No doubt the fire blazing in the hearth helped: it always works its magic on fear as on cold, and Mathias had made a good blaze. But after that, he didn't know what to say. He squeezed his hands together as if to crush the silence.

'Which is it?' asked Marc. 'I mean the child, girl or boy?'

'Boy,' said the young woman. 'He's five.'

Marc and Lucien both nodded gravely.

The young woman undid the scarf from her head, shook out her hair, put the wet scarf on a chair and looked around her. Everyone was taking stock. But in no time the evangelists registered the fact that the face of the refugee was subtle enough to tempt a saint. Not a regular beauty at first sight, she must have been about thirty. A luminous face, with a childlike mouth, a clear jaw-line, thick dark hair cut in a bob. Marc wanted immediately to take that face in his hands. He loved people who were thin and almost too delicate. He couldn't work out whether the expression on her face was defiant, adventurous and darting, or whether it was fleeting, quivering, shadowy and timid.

The woman remained tense, glancing now and again at her son who was sleeping. She smiled a little. She didn't know where to begin. Names perhaps. Should we say our names? Marc introduced everyone, and added that his uncle was on the top floor – an unnecessary detail perhaps, but useful. The young woman seemed more reassured on hearing this. She even stood up and warmed herself by the fire. She was wearing narrow cotton trousers that clung to her slender hips and thighs, and a shirt that was too big for her. Quite the opposite of Juliette with her feminine off-the-shoulder dresses. But above the shirt was the beautiful little face.

'Don't tell us your name if you don't feel like it,' said Marc. 'It was just that it was raining, and with the little one, we thought, that is, we thought . . .'

'Thank you,' said the young woman. 'It was kind of you to think, I didn't know what to do. But I can tell you my name: Alexandra Haufman.'

'Are you German?' Lucien asked her abruptly.

'Half German,' she replied, looking surprised. 'My father's German, but my mother is Greek. I'm mostly called Lex.'

Lucien gave a little grunt of satisfaction.

'Greek?' said Marc. 'Your mother's Greek?'

'Yes,' said Alexandra. 'But what's so odd about that? Our family moves around a lot. I was born in France. We live in Lyon.'

There was no floor dedicated to antiquity, Greek or Roman, in the house of history. But inevitably everyone thought at once of Sophia Siméonidis. A young woman, half Greek, who had been sitting for hours opposite Sophia's house. A woman with very dark hair and dark eyes like Sophia. A woman with a deep musical voice like hers, with fine wrists, and long slender hands, like hers. Except that Alexandra had very short fingernails, possibly because they had been bitten.

'You were waiting for Sophia Siméonidis?' asked Marc.

'How did you guess?' asked Alexandra. 'Do you know her?'

'We're her neighbours,' Mathias pointed out.

'Of course, how silly of me. But Aunt Sophia has never mentioned you in her letters to my mother. She doesn't write all that often, it's true.'

'We're new to the neighbourhood,' Marc explained.

The young woman seemed to understand. She looked around.

'Ah, you must have moved into the empty house, the one they called "the disgrace" is that it?'

'Spot on,' said Marc.

'It doesn't look like a disgrace now. A bit bare perhaps. Almost like a monastery.'

'We've done a lot of work on it,' Marc said. 'But that's not very interesting. So you really are Sophia's niece?'

'Yes, that's right,' said Alexandra. 'She's my mother's sister. But you don't look pleased about it. Don't you like Aunt Sophia?'

'Yes, actually, we like her a lot,' said Marc.

'Oh good. I called her when I decided to come to Paris, and she said she would put me up with my little boy while I was looking for a new job.'

'You didn't have a job in Lyon?'

'Yes, but I walked out.'

'You didn't like it?'

'No, that wasn't it. It was a good job.'

'You didn't like Lyon?'

'No, I liked Lyon.'

'So,' Lucien interrupted. 'Why come to Paris?'

The young woman was silent for a moment, pursing her lips and trying to restrain herself. She folded her arms tightly.

'The situation had got a bit sad down there,' she said at last.

Mathias started cutting more slices of bread. After all, bread is always a good thing. He offered Alexandra a slice with jam on. She smiled, accepted and put out her hand. She had to look up to do so. Unquestionably, there were tears in her eyes. She managed with an effort to hold the tears in, not letting them spill down her cheeks. But her lips were trembling. It's one or the other.

'I don't understand,' Alexandra continued, eating her bread. 'Aunt Sophia had arranged it all two months ago. She had enrolled my son at the local school. Everything was ready. She was expecting me today, and she was supposed to come and meet me at the station to help me with the little one and the luggage. I waited for ages, then I thought maybe after ten years she hadn't recognised me, and perhaps we had missed each other on the platform. So I came to the house. But there's nobody here. I don't understand. I went on waiting. Perhaps they've gone to the cinema or something, but that would be odd. Aunt Sophia would surely not have forgotten.'

Alexandra wiped her eyes quickly and looked at Mathias. Mathias prepared another slice of bread and jam. She had not had anything to eat that evening.

'Where's your luggage?' asked Marc.

'I left it behind the wall there. No, don't go and fetch it. I'll call a taxi and go to a hotel, and I'll ring Aunt Sophia in the morning. There must be some misunderstanding.'

'I don't think that's the best solution,' said Marc.

He looked at the other two. Mathias was looking down at the bread-board. Lucien was walking round the room.

'Look,' said Marc. 'It's like this. Sophia has been missing for twelve days. She disappeared on Wednesday, May 19.'

The young woman stiffened and stared at the three of them. 'Missing?' she murmured. 'What on earth do you mean?'

The tears returned to those darting, timid, almond-shaped eyes. She had said she was sad. Maybe. But Marc was pretty sure there was more to it than that. She must have been counting on her aunt to help her to run away from Lyon, to run away from some disaster. He recognised the reflex. And she had travelled all this way, only to find that Sophia wasn't there.

Marc sat down beside her. He tried to find the right words to tell her how Sophia had disappeared, how there had been a message with a star on it, and how she was thought to have gone away with Stelios. Lucien came round behind him and slowly took back his tie without Marc seeming to notice. Alexandra said nothing as she listened to Marc's story. Lucien put his tie back on and tried to be helpful by remarking that Pierre Relivaux was not the greatest person in the world. Mathias lumbered round the room, putting more wood on the fire, adjusting the duvet over the child. He was a beautiful child with dark hair like his mother's, except that it was curly. And so were his eyelashes. But all children look beautiful when they are asleep. They would have to wait for the morning to see what he was really like. That is, if his mother consented to stay.

Alexandra pursed her lips and shook her head, looking hostile.

'No,' she said. 'Aunt Sophia would never have done that. She would have got in touch with me.'

'Same story,' thought Lucien. 'She's like Juliette. Why do people think they can't possibly be forgotten?'

'Something must have gone wrong. Something must have happened to her,' Alexandra said in a low voice.

'Nope,' said Lucien, passing round wine glasses. 'We went to some lengths. We even looked under the tree.'

'You cretin,' Marc hissed.

'Under the tree?' said Alexandra. 'You looked under a tree?'

'It's nothing,' said Marc. 'He's just talking nonsense.'

'I don't think so,' said Alexandra. 'What did he mean? She's my aunt, I've a right to know.'

Trying to keep his exasperation with Lucien out of his voice, Marc told her in clipped tones about the episode with the tree.

'And you all decided that Aunt Sophia had gone swanning off somewhere with Stelios?' said Alexandra.

'Yes. Well, pretty much,' said Marc. 'I believe the godfather, that is my uncle, doesn't really think so. And I'm still a bit bothered about the tree. But Sophia must have gone off somewhere, that's for sure.'

'But I tell you that's impossible,' said Alexandra, banging her fist on the table. 'Even if she was on Delos, my aunt would have called me to tell me what was going on. You could count on her. And anyway, she loved Pierre. Something must have happened to her. I'm sure of it! Don't you believe me? The police will believe me. I must go to the police.'

'Look, do that tomorrow,' said Marc, who was at his wits' end. 'Vandoosler will get *Inspecteur* Leguennec to come round and you can give him a statement, if you like. He will even start up the search again, if the godfather asks him to. I think my godfather can get Leguennec to do anything he wants. They're old friends who used to play cards on board ship in the Irish Sea. But you need to know that Pierre Relivaux was not all that attached to Sophia. When she disappeared, he didn't report it, and he still doesn't intend to. It's his right of course, to let his wife do what she wants. The police can't interfere.'

'Can't we call them now? I'll report her missing.'

'You're not her husband. And it's almost two o'clock in the morning,' said Marc. 'We'll have to wait.'

They heard Mathias, who had disappeared, slowly coming downstairs.

'Excuse me, Lucien,' he said, opening the door. 'I had to borrow your window to look out of, because mine isn't high enough.'

'If you will choose lowlife ages of history,' said Lucien, 'you can't complain about not being high up.'

'Relivaux is home,' said Mathias without paying any attention to

Lucien. 'He switched the lights on, went into the kitchen and now he's gone to bed.'

'I'm going round there, then,' said Alexandra, jumping up. Carefully she lifted the little boy, resting his dark-haired head on her shoulder, and with one hand picked up her scarf and jacket.

'No,' said Mathias, barring her way to the door.

Alexandra was not exactly frightened. But she looked as if she were. She didn't understand.

'I'm grateful to all three of you,' she said firmly. 'You were very kind, but since he's come home, I must go to my uncle's.'

'No,' said Mathias. 'I won't try to keep you here. If you prefer to go and spend the night somewhere else, I'll take you to a hotel. But you're not going to your uncle's house.'

He was blocking the door with his large frame. He looked at Marc and Lucien over Alexandra's shoulder, more to impose his will than to ask for their approval.

Obstinately, Alexandra turned to face Mathias.

'I'm sorry,' said Mathias. 'but Sophia has disappeared. I don't want to let you go in there.'

'Why?' said Alexandra. 'What are you hiding? Is Aunt Sophia in there? You don't want me to see her, is that it? You were lying?'

Mathias shook his head.

'No,' he said, deliberately. 'It's the truth. She is missing. Maybe she has gone away with Stelios. Or maybe, as you thought, something has happened to her. Personally, I think she's been murdered. And until we know who did it, I won't let you go next door to him. Not you and not the little boy either.'

Mathias remained standing in front of the door. He kept his eyes fixed on the young woman.

'He'd be more comfortable here than in a hotel, I think,' he said. 'Give him to me.'

Mathias held out his big arms and without a word, Alexandra passed the child over to him. Marc and Lucien said nothing, digesting the masterful way in which Mathias was taking control of the situation. He came away from the door, laid the child on the bed, and put the duvet back over him.

'He sleeps very soundly,' he said, smiling. 'What's his name?'

'Kyril,' said Alexandra.

She sounded defeated. Sophia murdered? What did this big guy know about it? And why was she letting all this happen?

'Are you sure, what you said just now? About Aunt Sophia?'

'No,' said Mathias. 'But I would rather be on the safe side.'

Lucien suddenly heaved a sigh. 'I think we should all bow to Mathias' age-old wisdom. His instincts go back to the Ice Age. He knows all about wild beasts and dangerous open spaces. Yes, I think you should listen to this man, and accept his protection. He may be primitive and have rather basic reactions, but I think he's right.'

'Yes, I agree,' said Marc, who was still feeling the shock of the suspicions Mathias had voiced. 'Would you like to stay until things get a bit clearer? There's a spare room here on the ground floor, where you could sleep. It won't be all that warm, and it's a bit . . . well, austere, as you said. It's funny, your Aunt Sophia calls this room the monks' refectory. We won't disturb you, we each have a floor upstairs. We only come down here to talk, shout, eat or make a fire to keep away wild beasts. You could tell your uncle that in the circumstances you didn't want to bother him. Here, whatever is going on, there's always somebody home. What do you think?'

Alexandra had learned enough in one evening to wear her out. She looked round at the faces of the three men, thought for a while, looked at Kyril fast asleep, and shivered.

'Alright,' she said. 'Thank you.'

'Lucien, go and fetch her case from outside,' said Marc. 'And Mathias, help me take the little one's bed into the other room.'

They shifted the divan and went up to the second floor to find another bed which Marc had kept from happier days, as well as a lamp and a rug which Lucien consented to lend.

'It's only because she looks so sad,' said Lucien, rolling up the rug.

Once the bedroom was more or less ready, Marc put the key on the inside of the door, so that Alexandra Haufman could lock herself in if she so wished. He did this tactfully and without a word. The discreet elegance of the impoverished aristocrat, thought Lucien. We should get him a ring with a seal, so that he can seal his letters with wax. He would like that, for sure.

# XVII

*INSPECTEUR* LEGUENNEC ARRIVED FIFTEEN MINUTES AFTER VANDOOSLER'S call the next morning. He had a short council of war with his former senior officer before asking to speak with the young woman. Marc left the main room and dragged his godfather out forcibly, so as to leave Alexandra in a *tête-a-tête* with the little *inspecteur en chef*.

Vandoosler strolled about in the garden with his godson.

'If she hadn't turned up, I think I might have let the whole thing drop. What do you think about that girl?'

'Not so loud,' said Marc. 'Little Kyril is playing in the garden. Well, she's not stupid and she's as beautiful as an angel. You noticed that, I dare say.'

'Naturally,' Vandoosler replied, rather irritated. 'That's pretty obvious. But what else?'

'Hard to tell in such a short time,' said Marc.

'You used to say five minutes was enough for you to make up your mind.'

'Well, not quite. When people have a sad story, it makes it harder. But if you want my opinion, in her case something dramatic must have happened. You can't see straight, it's as if you're going over a waterfall, you suddenly lose all your illusions. I know the feeling.'

'Did you ask her about it?'

'Not so loud, for God's sake, I told you. No, I didn't ask her about it. You don't ask about that kind of thing. I'm guessing, inventing and comparing. It's not that difficult.'

'Do you think some man's thrown her out?'

'Oh please, keep your big mouth shut.'

The godfather pursed his lips and kicked a stone.

'That was my stone,' said Marc tartly. 'I left it there last Thursday. You might ask before taking it over.'

Vandoosler kicked the pebble for a few minutes, then lost it in the long grass.

'Very clever,' said Marc. 'D'you think they grow on trees?'

'Go on,' said Vandoosler.

'OK, the waterfall. Add to that the aunt's disappearance. It's a lot to take. My impression is that the girl is straightforward. She's gentle, truthful, fragile, lots of delicate qualities to be careful not to break, like her neck. But she's touchy and susceptible. At the least thing, she sticks her lip out. Well, not exactly – let's say she's straightforward but has mixed feelings. Or perhaps straightforward thoughts in a mixed-up temperament. Oh hell, I don't know. Let's drop it. But where this business about her aunt is concerned, she won't let matters drop, you can be sure of that. Is she telling us the whole truth, though? I don't know. What is Leguennec going to do – or rather, what are you and he planning to do?'

'We're not going to keep it under wraps any longer. In any case, as you say, the girl is going to move heaven and earth to find Sophia. So we might as well go official. Open an investigation under some pretext. It's all been too vague, it's going to get away from us. We should try and make the first move. But it's impossible to check the story about the star on the card, and the rendezvous in Lyon. The husband doesn't remember the name of the hotel on the card. Or where the card was posted. He doesn't remember anything, Relivaux. Or else he's doing it on purpose, and the card never existed. Leguennec has run a check on the Lyon hotels. No-one of her name has registered.'

'Do you think the same as Mathias? That someone has killed Sophia?'

'Slow down, my boy. St Matthew is jumping to conclusions.'

'Mathias jumps to the right conclusion when he has to. Hunter-gatherers are like that sometimes. But why does it have to be a murder? It might have been an accident?'

'An accident? No, we'd have found a body long ago.'

'So you think it really is possible? Murder?'

'That's what Leguennec thinks. Sophia Siméonidis is extremely rich. Her husband on the other hand is at the mercy of a change of government and a return to a subordinate job. But we haven't found a body, Marc. No body, no murder.'

When Leguennec emerged, he and Vandoosler conferred again. He nodded and went off, a small determined figure.

'What's he going to do?' asked Marc.

'Open an official enquiry. Play cards with me. Try to reel in Relivaux – and it's no fun being reeled in by Leguennec, believe me. He has infinite patience. I've been on board a trawler with him, I know what he's like.'


Two days later, the news came as a bolt from the blue. Leguennec announced it that evening, though in measured tones. The fire services had been called out the night before to an intense fire in a deserted alleyway in Maisons-Alfort, in the southwest suburbs. The fire had already spread to some nearby houses, all empty and abandoned, by the time the firemen got there. It had not been put out until three in the morning. In the ashes were three burnt-out cars, and in one of them an unrecognisable body. Leguennec had been informed at seven o'clock, while he was shaving. He went to find Relivaux in his office at three that afternoon. Relivaux had positively identified a little piece of volcanic rock which Leguennec showed him. It was a fetish that Sophia had always had with her; it had been in her handbag or her pocket for the last twenty-eight years.

# XVIII

ALEXANDRA, DISBELIEVING, SITTING CROSS-LEGGED ON HER BED, HEAD in hands, was insisting on details and facts. It was seven in the evening. Leguennec had authorised Vandoosler and the others to stay in the room. It would be all over the papers in the morning. Lucien was watching to see whether the little boy had marked his carpet with his felt pens. He was concerned about that.

'Why did you go to Maisons-Alfort?' Alexandra was asking. 'What did you know?'

'Nothing at that stage,' Leguennec assured her. 'But I've got four missing persons in my zone. Pierre Relivaux didn't want to report his wife missing. He was sure she would come back. But because you had arrived, I had, let's say, persuaded him to make the report all the same. Sophia Siméonidis was on my list, and in my mind. I went to Maisons-Alfort because it's my job. I wasn't alone, I can tell you that. There were other *inspecteurs*, looking for missing teenagers and vanished husbands. But I was the only one looking for a woman. Women go missing far less often than men – did you know that? When a married man or a teenage boy disappears, we don't worry so much. But when it's a woman, there are reasons to fear the worst, you understand? But the body, forgive me, was unidentifiable. Even the teeth were gone, burnt to ashes.'

Vandoosler interrupted him: 'You can spare us the details, Leguennec.'

Leguennec, he of the jutting jaw, shook his bullet head. 'I'm trying, Vandoosler,' he said. 'But Mademoiselle Haufman wants facts.'

'Go on, *inspecteur*,' said Alexandra quietly. 'I need to know.'

The young woman's face was swollen with weeping, her black hair was ruffled and on end, from the times she had repeatedly run her wet hands through it. Marc wished he could dry it for her, comb it tenderly back into shape. But there was nothing he could do.

'The lab's working on it, and it'll take several days before we get any more results. But the burnt body was small, indicating a woman. The wreck of the car has been gone through with a toothcomb, but there was nothing, not a shred of clothing, no belongings, nothing. The fire must have been started with many cans of gasoline, and quantities of it had been thrown not only all over the body and car but on the ground around it and the façade of the nearby house, which fortunately was empty. Nobody lives in the alley. It's down for demolition and there are only a few abandoned cars there. Tramps sometimes use them to shelter in at night.'

'So the place had been chosen deliberately, is that what you're saying?'

'Yes. Because by the time the alarm was raised, the fire had already done what it was meant to.'

*Inspecteur* Leguennec kept twisting with his fingertips the plastic bag containing the black stone, and Alexandra could not take her eyes off this exasperating movement.

'And then?' she asked.

'Beside the feet, we found two lumps of melted gold, which suggested a ring or a chain. So it was someone well-enough off to have some gold jewellery. And finally on what was left of the front passenger seat, we found a little black stone that had survived the fire, a chunk of basalt, probably all that remained from a handbag placed on the seat by a woman driver. Nothing else. Keys ought to have survived too. But oddly enough, there is no sign of any keys. I placed all my hopes on the stone. You understand? My other missing persons are all men, and big tall ones. So the first person I called on was Pierre Relivaux. I asked him if his wife took her keys with her when she went away, as most people would. And no, she didn't. Sophia used to hide her keys in the garden, like a child, according to Relivaux.'

'Of course,' said Alexandra with a fleeting smile. 'My grandmother was scared stiff of losing her keys. She taught us all to hide our keys like squirrels. We never carry them about.'

'Ah,' said Leguennec. 'That makes things clearer. Then I showed Relivaux the piece of basalt, without telling him what we had found at Maisons-Alfort. He recognised it at once.'

Alexandra held out her hand for the plastic bag.

'Aunt Sophia picked it up on a beach in Greece, the day after her first big success on stage,' she said softly. 'She never went anywhere without it. In fact that used to annoy Pierre. The rest of us would laugh at her about it, and now this little stone . . . One day they went off to the Dordogne, and had to go back when they were already a hundred kilometres out of Paris because Sophia had forgotten her stone. It's true, she put it in her handbag or in her pocket. On stage, whatever kind of costume she had, she insisted they sew in a little pocket for it. She never went on stage to sing without it.'

Vandoosler sighed. How tiresome Greeks could be sometimes.

'When you've finished your enquiries,' Alexandra was saying in an undertone, 'and, you know, if you don't need it, I'd like to have it. Unless, that is, Uncle Pierre . . .'

She gave the plastic bag back to *Inspecteur en chef* Leguennec who nodded.

'We'll hold on to it for now, of course. But Relivaux didn't say he wanted it.'

'So what are the police concluding?' asked Vandoosler.

Alexandra liked to hear the voice of the old policeman, the uncle or godfather of the one with the rings, if she had got it right. She was a little distrustful of the ex-*commissaire*, but his voice had a very calming and encouraging effect, even when he wasn't saying anything in particular.

'Shall we go into the other room?' said Marc. 'We could have a drink perhaps.'

They moved as one in silence and Mathias put on his jacket. It was time for him to go to work in *Le Tonneau*.

'Juliette hasn't closed the restaurant?' asked Marc.

'No. But I'm going to have to do all the work. She can hardly stand upright. When Leguennec asked her to identify the stone, she asked for explanations.'

With a distressed expression, Leguennec spread his short arms.

'People will ask for explanations,' he said. 'It's normal, and then they wish they hadn't, and that is normal too.'

'See you this evening then, St Matthew,' said Vandoosler. 'So what do you conclude, Leguennec?'

'That two weeks after disappearing, Madame Siméonidis has been found. As you won't need me to tell you, the state of the body, which is burnt to cinders, makes it impossible to say when she died. She could have been killed two weeks ago, and hidden in the abandoned car, or she could have been murdered last night. In that case, what was she doing in between times, and why? Or she might have gone into the alleyway herself, to wait for someone, and was taken by surprise. The state the alley is in now, it's impossible to draw any conclusions. There's soot and rubbish everywhere. Frankly, the investigation is going to be difficult. All our lines of approach are weak. The angle "how did it happen?" is stymied. The angle "who has an alibi?" is no use, because we've got a timescale of two weeks. As for physical clues, it's hopeless. The only line of questioning we have left is "why?" with all that that entails. Possible inheritors, enemies, lovers, blackmailers, all the usual suspects.'

Alexandra pushed away her empty cup and went out of the 'refectory'. Her son was on the first floor, where Mathias had settled him at a small desk, to do some drawing. She came downstairs with him and took a jacket from the bedroom.

'I'm going out,' she told the four men sitting round the table. 'I don't know when I'll be back. Don't wait up for me.'

'With your little boy?' said Marc.

'Yes. If I'm late back, Kyril will sleep in the back of the car. Don't worry. I just need to get away.'

'Car? What car?' asked Marc.

'Aunt Sophia's car. The red one. Pierre gave me the keys and said I could use it when I wanted to. He has his own.'

'You've been over to see Relivaux again?' said Marc. 'On your own?'

'My uncle would have been surprised, don't you think, if I hadn't even been to see him for two days. Mathias can say what he likes, but Pierre was just fine with me. I don't want the police harassing him. He's got enough on his plate without that.'

Alexandra was at the end of her tether, clearly. Marc wondered if he had not been too hasty after all, to take her in. Perhaps they should send her to stay with Relivaux? No, it really was not the right moment. And Mathias would bar the door again, like a rock. He looked at the young woman, holding her son firmly by the hand, with an expression on her face that was hard to fathom. The waterfall of disillusions, he had almost forgotten the waterfall. And where would she go now in the car? She had said she knew nobody in Paris. Marc ran his hand through Kyril's curly hair. The kid's hair was absolutely irresistible. That did not stop his mother being a complete pain when she was worked up.

'I want to have supper with St Mark,' said Kyril. 'And St Luke. I don't want to go in the car again.' Marc looked at Alexandra and gestured that it would be no trouble to look after the little boy for the evening, he was not going out.

'Very well,' said Alexandra. She kissed her son, told him they were really called Marc and Lucien, and walked out stiffly, with arms folded, after a nod to *Inspecteur* Leguennec. Marc suggested to Kyril that he finish his drawing before supper.

'If she thinks she's going to Maisons-Alfort,' said Leguennec, 'she's wasting her time. The street's cordoned off.'

'Why would she go there?' Marc asked, suddenly irritated, forgetting that a few minutes earlier he had been wishing Alexandra would go elsewhere. 'She's just going to go somewhere for the sake of it, that's all.'

Leguennec shrugged and spread his hands without replying.

'Will you have her followed?' asked Vandoosler.

'Not tonight. She won't get up to anything significant tonight.'

Marc stood up, glancing from Leguennec to Vandoosler and back.

'Follow her? What the hell do you mean?'

'Her mother will inherit, and Alexandra stands to gain,' Leguennec said.

'So what?' cried Marc. 'She's not the only one, I dare say! Oh, for God's sake, take a look at yourselves. The original hard-boiled cops! Never giving an inch! Always thinking the worst! This girl goes off, absolutely shattered with grief, she's just going to drive round the streets, and you're already thinking of having her followed. Because you think, aha, there's no way she's going to pull the wool over our eyes, we weren't born yesterday. Well, that's bullshit! Anyone can play that game. You know what I think of people who like to "control the situation"?'

'Yes, we do know,' said Vandoosler. 'You can't stand them.'

'You bet I can't stand them. There are times in this world when it's better to behave as if you *were* born yesterday. Cynical, case-hardened, or what? I don't think they come much worse than you, uncle.'

'Meet my nephew, St Mark,' Vandoosler said to Leguennec, smiling. 'The least little thing and he'll rewrite the gospel for you.'

Marc shrugged, finished his glass of beer and banged it down on the table.

'I'll let you have the last word, uncle, since you'll take it anyway.'

He left the room and went upstairs. Lucien followed him quietly and caught him by the shoulder as they reached the landing. Unusually for him, Lucien spoke in a normal voice.

'Calm down, soldier,' he said. 'We'll win through in the end.'

# XIX

MARC LOOKED AT HIS WATCH AS LEGUENNEC CAME DOWN FROM Vandoosler's attic. It was ten past midnight. They had been playing cards. Unable to sleep, he heard Alexandra come in at about three in the morning. He had left all the doors open, so as to be able to look out for Kyril if he woke up. Marc told himself it would not be proper to go down and listen. Nevertheless, he did go down and cocked his ear from the seventh stair. The young woman was moving about quietly, so as not to disturb anyone. Marc heard her fill a glass with water. It was as he had thought. You go shooting off, confidently into the unknown, you take a few firm, if contradictory decisions, but in fact you are just going nowhere, and you end up coming back home.

Marc sat on the seventh stair. His thoughts were in a whirl, clashing or diverging. Like the plates that move along on top of the hot heaving magma underneath, the molten mantle of the earth. It's a scary thought, those plates sliding in all directions over the earth, unable to stay put. Tectonic plates, they're called. Well, he was having tectonic thoughts. The thoughts were sliding about inside his head and sometimes, inevitably, they clashed. With the usual sodding consequences. When tectonic plates move apart, there's an earthquake, and when they meet, there's an earthquake. What was Alexandra Haufman up to? How would Leguennec's interrogation sessions go? Why had Sophia been burnt to death in Maisons-Alfort? Had Alexandra been in love with Kyril's father? Should he wear some rings on his right hand, why on earth do you need a piece of basalt in order to sing well? Ah yes, basalt. When the plates move apart, basalt comes erupting up, and when the plates clash it's something else. What was it? Andesite. That was it, andesite. And why was there that difference? No idea, he had forgotten the answer. He heard Alexandra preparing to go to bed. And as he sat there at three in the morning, on his stair, he was waiting for the tectonic activity to subside. Why had he shouted at his godfather? Would Juliette make an *île flottante* pudding for them tomorrow, as she usually did on Fridays? Was Relivaux going to own up about his mistress? Who was going to inherit Sophia's money? Were his ideas about village trade a bit too far-fetched, and why did Mathias go about in a state of undress?

Marc rubbed his eyes. There comes a time when your thoughts are in such a godalmighty tangle that you can't get a needle through them. All you can do then is drop everything and try to go to sleep. Retire in good order, as Lucien would put it, away from the firing line. And was Lucien in a state of eruption? Could you say that? No, Lucien was more a case of chronic low-level volcanic activity. What about Mathias? Not tectonic at all, Mathias, he was like water, but a vast stretch of water, an ocean. The ocean cools down the lava flow. But on the ocean bed, things aren't as calm as all that, there's a lot of bad stuff down there: rifts, trenches, and even some revolting forms of animal life.

Alexandra had gone to bed. There were no more sounds from downstairs, no lights showing. Marc was drowsy but he didn't feel cold. A light came on on the landing, and he heard the godfather coming softly down the stairs until he reached his level.

'You really should go to sleep, Marc,' whispered Vandoosler.

And the old man went on down with his pocket torch. He was going to take a leak outside, presumably. A simple, straightforward and healthy act. The older Vandoosler had never shown any interest in tectonic plates and yet Marc had often talked to him about them. Marc didn't want to be sitting on the stairs when the old man came back up. He ran upstairs, opened his window to get some fresh air, and lay down. Why was the old man carrying a plastic bag, if he was just going to take a leak outdoors?

# XX

THE NEXT DAY, MARC AND LUCIEN TOOK ALEXANDRA TO DINNER AT Juliette's restaurant. The questioning sessions had begun and they were turning out to be slow, long-winded and unproductive.

Relivaux had been called in that morning, for the second time. Vandoosler passed on to all the information he'd gleaned from *Inspecteur* Leguennec. Yes, Pierre had a mistress in Paris, but he didn't see what business that was of theirs, or how they knew about her already. No, Sophia had not known about it. Yes, he stood to inherit one-third of her estate. Yes, it was an enormous sum of money, but he would have preferred Sophia to be alive. If they didn't believe him, they could go and take a running jump. No, Sophia didn't have any personal enemies. A lover? That would surprise him.

Next came the turn of Alexandra Haufman. She had had to tell them everything over again, four times. Her mother would inherit a third of the estate. But her mother would certainly not refuse Alexandra anything, would she? So Alexandra would have a direct interest in all this money coming into the family, wouldn't she? Yes, agreed, but so what? Why had she come to Paris? Who could confirm Sophia's invitation to her? Where had she been last night? Nowhere. And you expect us to believe that?

Alexandra had been questioned for three hours.

In the late afternoon, it was Juliette's turn.

'Juliette doesn't look too happy,' Marc observed to Mathias between courses.

'Leguennec upset her,' Mathias replied. 'He didn't believe an opera singer could be friends with someone who runs a café.'

'Do you suppose he's irritating everyone on purpose?'

'Maybe. At any rate if he wanted to wound her, he managed that.'

Marc looked at Juliette who was tidying away glasses in silence. 'I'm going to have a word with her,' he said.

'No point,' said Mathias. 'I've already tried.'

'Well, maybe I'm not going to say the same things,' said Marc, catching Mathias' eye for a moment.

He got up and began making his way through the tables to the counter.

'Don't worry,' he murmured to Mathias as he went past, 'I've nothing clever to say to her. But I've got a big favour to ask her.'

'You do what you like,' said Mathias.

Marc put his elbows on the counter and gestured to Juliette to come over. 'Did Leguennec upset you?' he asked her.

'It's not serious, I'm used to it. Did Mathias tell you?'

'Just a word or two – that's a lot for Mathias, you know. What did Leguennec want to know?'

'It's not hard to guess. How come a famous singer finds time to talk to someone whose parents were provincial shopkeepers? So what? Sophia's grandparents looked after goats, like everyone else back in Greece.'

Juliette stopped fussing about behind the counter.

'To tell the truth,' she said with a smile, 'it's my own fault. Because he was putting on his act of the policeman who doesn't believe you, I started justifying myself like a child. I said that Sophia had these grand friends in circles I would never move in, but they weren't the kind of people you could have a nice quiet conversation with. But he went on looking as if he didn't believe a word.'

'It's just their policy.'

'Perhaps it is, but it works. Because instead of thinking, I started saying really stupid things. I showed him my books, to prove I can read. To show him that all these years of being on my own, I've read and read, thousands of pages. So he looked at the bookshelves and he did begin to accept that I might have been a friend of Sophia's. What a stupid bastard!'

'Sophia said she hardly ever read anything,' said Marc.

'That's right. And I didn't know anything about opera. So we exchanged ideas and discussed things up in my study. Sophia was sorry she had missed the boat with reading. I told her that sometimes you read because you've missed some other boat. It sounds silly, I know, but there were some evenings when Sophia would sing while I played the piano and others when I would read while she smoked her cigarettes.' Juliette sighed. 'The worst thing was that Leguennec went straight off and asked my brother, to see whether by chance all those books belonged to him! As if. Georges only likes doing crosswords. He's in publishing, but he never reads a word, he looks after distribution. Mind you, he's pretty good at crosswords. Anyway, there it is: if you keep a café, you don't have the right to be the friend of Sophia Siméonidis, unless you can prove to them that you've torn yourself away from your Normandy farm and brushed all the mud off your boots.'

'Don't get worked up,' said Marc. 'Leguennec's getting up everyone's nose. Can I have a glass of something?'

'I'll bring it to your table.'

'No, on the counter please.'

'What's the matter, Marc? Are you upset too?'

'Not exactly. I want to ask you a favour. You know the little house in your garden?'

'Yes, the one you saw. It's nineteenth-century, must have been built for the servants, I suppose.'

'What's it like inside? Is it in good condition? Could someone live in it?'

'Why, d'you want to get away from the others?'

'Tell me, Juliette, is it habitable?'

'Yes, it's properly maintained, it's furnished. It's got everything you need, electricity, water and so forth.'

'Why did you kit it out?'

Juliette bit her lip.

'Just in case, Marc, just in case. I may not be on my own for ever. You never know. And since my brother lives with me, a little place where one can be on one's own if necessary . . . Does that seem silly? Are you laughing?'

'Not at all,' said Marc. 'Have you got anyone in mind for it at the moment?'

'No, you know I haven't,' said Juliette with a shrug. 'So what is it you want?'

'I'd like you to offer it to someone else. Tactfully. If you don't mind. For a small rent.'

'To you, or Mathias? Or Lucien? The old policeman? Aren't you getting on with each other?'

'No, no, it's not that, we're fine. It's Alexandra. She says she can't go on staying with us. She says she and her son are in our way, that she can't settle in and I think, most of all, she wants a bit of peace and quiet. She's started looking for places in the small ads, so I thought . . .'

'You don't want her to go too far away, is that it?'

Marc fiddled with his glass. 'Mathias says we ought to keep an eye on her. Just until this business has been sorted out. If she could use your cabin, she could be on her own with her son, and at the same time she'd be quite close.'

'That's what I mean, close to you.'

'No, Juliette, you're wrong. Mathias really thinks it would be best if she's not left alone.'

'Well, it's all the same to me,' Juliette cut him off briskly. 'I don't mind at all if she moves in with the child. If it's to help you, yes, that's fine. Anyway she's Sophia's niece. It's the least I could do.'

'You're very kind, Juliette.'

Marc kissed her on the forehead.

'But she doesn't know?' asked Juliette.

'No, of course not.'

'So how do you know she'll want to stay near you? Have you thought of that? How are you going to get her to accept?'

Marc looked gloomy. 'Can I leave it to you? Don't say it was my idea. You'll find some good reason.'

'You're asking me to do your dirty work?'

'I'm counting on you. Don't let her go away somewhere else.'

Marc went back to the table where Lucien and Alexandra were stirring their coffee.

'He kept on asking where I went last night,' Alexandra was saying. 'What's the point of trying to explain to him that I didn't even take in the names of the villages. He didn't believe me, and I don't care.'

'Was your father's father German too?' Lucien interrupted.

'Yes, but what has that got to do with anything?'

'Was he in the Great War? Did he leave any papers or letters or anything?'

'Lucien, for God's sake, can't you control yourself?' asked Marc. 'If you must talk, can't you find some other subject? Try and you'll see, you might find something else to talk about.'

'OK,' said Lucien. 'Are you going driving again tonight?' he asked after a pause.

'No,' said Alexandra smiling. 'Leguennec confiscated my car this morning. Pity, because the wind is getting up. I love the wind. It would be a nice night for driving.'

'I don't get it,' said Lucien. 'Driving round for no reason and going nowhere. Frankly I don't see the point. Could you keep going all night like that?'

'All night, I don't know. I've only been doing it for eleven months every now and then. Up to now, I've always given up at about three in the morning.'

'Given up?'

'Yes. So I come back. Then a week later I start again, I think it's going to help. But it doesn't.'

Alexandra shrugged, and pushed her hair back behind her ears. Marc would have liked to do it for her.

# XXI

GOODNESS KNOWS HOW JULIETTE MANAGED IT, BUT THE FOLLOWING day, Alexandra moved into the garden house. Marc and Mathias helped to carry her luggage. With the help of this distraction, Alexandra relaxed a bit. Marc, who was knowledgeable about that kind of thing and could easily spot the signs, had been watching the shadows of some secret sorrow reflected in her face. He was glad to see them fade, even if he knew that the respite might only be temporary. During the respite, Alexandra proposed that they say 'tu' to each other and that they call her Lex.

Lucien, rolling up his floor rug, to take it back upstairs, muttered that the line-up of forces on the battleground was getting more and more complex. The Western Front had tragically lost one of its major players, leaving only a doubtful husband behind, while the Eastern Front, already reinforced by Mathias in *Le Tonneau*, was now being augmented by a new ally, accompanied by a child. The new ally had originally been marked out to occupy the Western Front, had temporarily stopped in no-man's-land and was now deserting it for the eastern trenches.

'Has the Great War really turned your brain?' Marc asked, 'or are you carrying on like this because you're sorry Alexandra is leaving?'

'I'm not carrying on, as you put it,' said Lucien. 'I'm rolling up my rug and I'm commenting on the present state of affairs. Lex – she said to call her Lex – wanted to get out of here, and yet she's staying very nearby. Very near her Uncle Pierre, very near the epicentre of the drama. What's she after? Unless that is,' he said, straightening up, with the rug under his arm, 'the whole Operation Eastern Base was dreamed up by you.'

'Why would I do that?' said Marc, defensively.

'To keep an eye on her or to keep her within reach, take your pick. Personally I'd opt for the second. Anyway, congratulations. It seems to have worked.'

'Lucien, you are really getting on my nerves.'

'Why? You want her, that's perfectly obvious. Well, look out, you're going to get hurt again. You're forgetting that we're still up shit creek, and when that's the case, you might slip. You have to go slowly, step by step. Certainly not go haring ahead like a madman. Not that I disapprove of a poor guy in the trenches having a bit of a distraction. Not at all. But Lex is too pretty, she's too touching, and she's too intelligent to be written off as a mere distraction. You're not just going to have a bit of fun, you're running the risk of being in love. That way madness lies, Marc, madness.'

'What do you mean madness, you no-brain soldier?'

'Because, you no-brain worshipper of courtly love, you suspect, just as I do, that Lex and her little boy have been chucked out or abandoned. Or something like that. So like an idiot knight on a white horse, you imagine that there's a vacant place in her affections and that you can move in. Big mistake, let me tell you.'

'Look, idiot of the trenches, I know more about empty hearts than you do. And I can tell you that the emptiness takes up much more space than when it's occupied.'

'You show remarkable lucidity for someone who stays behind the front line,' said Lucien. 'You're not entirely stupid, Marc.'

'Does that surprise you?'

'Not at all. I've done a bit of snooping.'

'I'm not installing Alexandra in the garden house next door because I want to pounce on her. Even if she does attract me. And who wouldn't be attracted?'

'Mathias for one,' said Lucien, raising his finger in the air. 'Mathias is attracted by the beautiful and brave Juliette.'

'And you?'

'As I told you, I move slowly and I observe. That's all. For the moment.'

'I don't believe you.'

'Maybe you're right. It's true that I'm not totally without feelings, or the urge to help. For instance, I suggested to Alexandra that she could keep my rug for the cabin if she wanted to. Answer: she couldn't care less.'

'Naturally. She's got other things to think about than your rug, even without problems of the heart. And if you really want to know why I'd rather she stays close to here, it's because I don't like the turn of mind of *Inspecteur en chef* Leguennec, nor of my godfather, if it comes to that. They go fishing together, those two. Lex has been called in again for more questioning, the day after tomorrow. So I think we should be around, just in case.'

'Oh, you really are the knight in shining armour, Marc. Even if you don't have a horse. And what if Leguennec's not entirely wrong? Have you thought of that?'

'Of course I have.'

'And?'

'And it bothers me. There are some things I'd like to have cleared up.'

'And you think that's going to happen?'

Marc shrugged. 'Why not? I asked her to come over here once she's settled in. With the rather ignoble thought at the back of my mind that I might ask her some questions myself about the things that bother me. What d'you think?'

'That's bold and possibly painful, but the offensive could be an interesting one. Can I sit in on it?'

'On one condition: that you stuff a flower in your rifle and say nothing.'

'If it sets your mind at rest,' said Lucien.

# XXII

ALEXANDRA ASKED FOR THREE LUMPS OF SUGAR IN HER BOWL OF TEA. Mathias, Lucien and Marc listened to her as she told them how out of the blue Juliette had said she was looking for a tenant for the garden house, that Kyril's room was lovely, that the house itself was beautiful and full of light, that she could breathe easily in it, that there were plenty of books to read if she couldn't sleep, that they could see the flowers from the windows and that Kyril liked flowers. Juliette had taken Kyril off to the restaurant to make some pastry. The day after tomorrow, Monday, he would go to his new school. And she would go to the police station. Alexandra frowned. What did Leguennec want with her now? She had told him everything she knew.

Marc thought this was the moment to launch the bold and painful manœuvre, but it didn't seem such a good idea any more. He got up and sat on the table to give himself confidence. He had never been very good at sitting normally on a chair.

'I think I know what he wants from you,' he began, rather weakly. 'I could put some questions to you, if you like, to give you a bit of practice.'

Alexandra raised her head with a start. 'You want to question me too now, do you? So that's what you all think, is it? You don't trust me? You think I'm hiding something? Because of Aunt Sophia's money?' She had stood up. Marc took hold of her hand to stop her. The contact gave him a frisson in the pit of his stomach. Yes, he had certainly been lying to Lucien when he had said he didn't want to pounce on her.

'No, no, that's not it at all,' he said. 'Why don't you sit down and drink your tea. I could ask you in a friendly way the kind of thing Leguennec will ask brutally. Why not?'

'I don't believe you,' said Alexandra. 'But I don't care, if you want to know. Go ahead and ask your questions, I'm not afraid of you or the others, or of Leguennec, I'm not afraid of anyone except myself. Go ahead, Marc. Settle your troubled mind.'

'I'm going to cut some slices of bread,' said Mathias.

Alexandra, her face showing strain, was leaning back on her chair and tipping it up.

'Never mind,' said Marc. 'Don't let's bother.'

'That's my brave soldier,' muttered Lucien.

'No, go right ahead,' said Alexandra. 'I'm ready for your questions.'

'Courage, soldier,' whispered Lucien, walking behind Marc.

'OK, then,' said Marc in a dull voice. 'OK. Leguennec will certainly ask you why you arrived here at just this moment, setting the investigation in motion again, and leading two days later to the discovery of your aunt's body. If you hadn't turned up, the case would have sat in the files, and everyone would have thought your Aunt Sophia was on some Greek island. And without a body, there's no death, and without a death, there's no inheritance.'

'So what? I already told you. I came because Aunt Sophia suggested it to me. I needed to leave home. It wasn't a secret from anyone.'

'Apart from your mother.'

The three men all turned round towards the door where, once again, Vandoosler was standing, having come silently downstairs.

'We didn't invite you down,' said Marc.

'No,' said Vandoosler. 'You don't often invite me down these days, but it doesn't stop me intruding, you will observe.'

'Oh, go away,' said Marc. 'What I'm doing is difficult enough as it is.'

'Because you're setting about it in a stupid way. You want to forestall Leguennec? To undo the knots before he gets there, and free the young lady? Well, if that's your plan, at least do it properly. May I?' he said to Alexandra, sitting down beside her.

'I don't seem to have any choice,' said Alexandra. 'If I have to, I'd prefer to be questioned by a real *flic*, even if he's bent, as you keep telling me, than by three pretend *flics* whose motives are more doubtful. Except for Mathias' decision to cut some bread, which is a good idea. Go ahead, I'm listening.'

'Leguennec telephoned your mother. She knew you were coming to Paris. She knew the reason. Heartbreak, we call it, a sort of shorthand. Too small a word for what it stands for.'

'You know all about broken hearts, do you?' said Alexandra, who was still frowning.

'Oh yes,' said Vandoosler slowly. 'Because I have caused some in my time. One rather serious one in particular. Yes, I do know about heartbreak.'

Vandoosler ran his hands through his black and white hair. There was a silence. Marc had rarely heard his uncle speak so simply and seriously. Vandoosler, his face calm, was quietly drumming his fingers on the table. Alexandra was watching him.

'Let's move on,' he said. 'Yes, I know the score on that one.'

Alexandra bowed her head. Vandoosler asked whether tea was compulsory, or whether one was allowed to drink something else.

'That is to say,' he went on, pouring himself a drink, 'that I believe you when you say you ran away. I knew it was true from the start. Leguennec checked up, and your mother confirmed it. Since you had been on your own with Kyril for a year, you had been wanting to go to Paris. But what your mother did not know was that Sophia had agreed to put you up. You had told her you would go to friends.'

'My mother has always been a bit jealous of her sister,' Alexandra said. 'I didn't want her to think I was leaving her for Sophia, I didn't want to risk hurting her. Us Greeks, you know, we imagine all kinds of things, and we like to. Or so my grandmother used to say.'

'A generous motive,' Vandoosler replied. 'OK. Let's go on to what Leguennec might be imagining. Alexandra Haufman, unhinged by distress, desperate for revenge . . .'

'Revenge?' whispered Alexandra. 'What revenge?'

'Don't interrupt me, please. A policeman's strength lies either in a long monologue that crushes the opposition, or in a rapid response that kills it dead. You should never deprive a policeman of these well-rehearsed pleasures. Or he might turn nasty. When you see Leguennec the day after tomorrow, don't interrupt him. So, as I was saying, desperate for revenge, disillusioned, embittered, determined to find a way of getting on top, short of cash, envious of your aunt's fortunate style of life, looking for a way to avenge your mother who has never succeeded, in spite of a few pathetic attempts at singing, now lost to memory, you plan to eliminate your aunt, and get your hands on a big share of the inheritance, through your mother.'

'Brilliant,' said Alexandra, through clenched teeth. 'Didn't I tell you already that I was very fond of Aunt Sophia?'

'That's both childish and naïve as a defence, young lady. A police inspector doesn't listen to that kind of talk, if he has pinpointed both the motive and the means. Especially since you haven't seen your aunt for ten years. That doesn't quite fit the picture of an affectionate niece. OK, let's go on. You had a car in Lyon. Why did you come by train? And why, the day before you left, did you take the car to the garage and ask the garage owner to put it up for sale, saying that you thought it was too old to take all the way to Paris?'

'How do you know that?'

'Your mother told me that you had sold your car. I telephoned all the garages in your district until I found the right one.'

'But what's wrong with that?' cried Marc suddenly. 'What are you on about? Leave her alone, for heaven's sake!'

'Look, Marc,' sighed Vandoosler, looking up. 'You wanted to help her rehearse for Leguennec? That's what I'm doing. You want to play the policeman, and you can't even take the first set of questions. I know what she really will be up against on Monday. So shut up and listen. And you, St Matthew, can you tell me why you are slicing the bread as if you were expecting twenty people to dinner.'

'To make me feel comfortable,' said Mathias. 'Anyway Lucien eats the slices. Lucien likes bread.'

Vandoosler sighed again and turned back to Alexandra, whose tears were welling up as her anxiety grew. She wiped her eyes with a tea towel.

'You've already done all that?' she asked. 'You've made all those phone calls, asked all those questions. Is it such a crime to sell your car? It *was* clapped out. I didn't want to risk driving it all the way to Paris with Kyril. And anyway it brought back memories. I got rid of it. Is that a crime?'

'Let me pursue the same line of reasoning,' said Vandoosler. 'The week before that, let's say on the Wednesday, you leave Kyril with your mother, and you drive to Paris in your car, which isn't, by the way, as clapped out as all that, according to the man at the garage.'

Lucien, who was as usual pacing round the table, took the tea towel out of Alexandra's hands and replaced it with a handkerchief.

'It wasn't very clean,' he whispered.

'. . . not as clapped out as all that,' repeated Vandoosler.

'I told you, the car brought back memories!' said Alexandra. 'If you can understand why people run away, you can surely understand why they might want to sell their fucking car!'

'Yes, indeed. But if these memories were so painful, why didn't you get rid of the car sooner?'

'Because . . . because you think twice about dumping the fucking memories!' cried Alexandra.

'A word of advice, Alexandra. Don't say "fucking" twice to a policeman. With me, it doesn't matter. But on Monday don't do it. Leguennec won't react, but he won't like it. Don't say "fucking" to him. Anyway you should never say it to a Breton, the Breton gets to say it to you. That's the rule.'

'So why did you call in Leguennec in the first place?' asked Marc. 'If he isn't going to believe a blind word anyone says, and if he doesn't like people saying "fucking" to him?'

'Because Leguennec is a good officer; because he's a friend; because it was on his patch; because he will pick up all the possible clues for us; and because at the end of the day I'll be able to do what I want with the clues. I'm talking about me, Armand Vandoosler.'

'So you say,' cried Marc.

'Stop shouting, St Mark, it won't get you to heaven, and stop interrupting me. I'll continue. Alexandra, you gave up your job three weeks ago, because of your plan to leave Lyon. You sent a postcard to your aunt with a star on it, and a rendezvous in Lyon. The whole family knows about the old affair with Stelios and they all know what a star would mean to Sophia. You get to Paris in the evening, you intercept your aunt and you tell her some story about Stelios being in Lyon, you take her off in your car, and you kill her. Right? You dump the body somewhere, in Fontainebleau forest, for instance, or Marly forest, whatever, in some remote spot, so that she won't be found too quickly – because that will make it harder to date the time of death and alibis will be hard to disprove. And you go back to Lyon the next morning. Days pass, nothing in the papers. That's fine, it's what you wanted. But then you start to get anxious. The spot is too remote. No body, no inheritance. It's time to come back again. You sell the car, you take care to explain that you would never take it to Paris, and you come up by train. You make sure somebody notices you, by sitting stupidly in the rain with the little boy, without even going to the nearest café for shelter. You certainly don't want anyone to think that Sophia disappeared voluntarily. So you make a fuss, and the police enquiries start up again. You borrow your aunt's car on Wednesday night, you go off to fetch the corpse, taking great care to leave no traces in the boot of the car – and that's a painful task, you need plastic bags, protective material, various grisly details – and you transfer it to an abandoned old car in some street in a low-class district. You set it on fire, so as to destroy all trace of the handling, the transport and the plastic bags. You know that Sophia's little good-luck stone will survive the fire. It had already survived the volcano that spewed it up. So, the job is done, the corpse is satisfactorily identified. You don't officially borrow the car your uncle offers you until the next day. And then the story is that you just want to drive round in the night, without any special purpose. Or perhaps you wanted to cover up for the night when you *were* driving with a very precise purpose, just in case somebody saw you. And one more thing. Don't look for your aunt's car. It went off to the forensic lab to be examined yesterday morning.'

'Yes, I know, you don't have to tell me,' Alexandra interrupted.

'They'll examine the boot, the seats and so on,' Vandoosler went on. 'You must have heard of the kind of thing. You'll get it back when they've finished with it. There we are, that's all,' he said, patting the young woman's shoulder.

Alexandra sat quite still, with the vacant look of one who is surveying a scene of total disaster. Marc was wondering whether he should kick his bloody godfather out of the house once and for all, take him by the shoulders of his impeccable grey jacket, punch him in his beautiful face, and push him out of the window.

Vandoosler looked up and met his eyes, 'I know what you're thinking, Marc. It would make you feel better, I'm sure. But save your breath and leave me alone. I can be useful, whatever happens, and whatever they pin on her.'

Marc remembered the murderer whom Vandoosler had allowed to get away, against all the rules of justice. He was trying not to panic, but the scenario that his godfather had outlined was perfectly plausible. Very plausible even. He suddenly heard once more Kyril's little voice saying that he wanted to have supper with them because he'd had enough of the car. Had Alexandra taken him with her the previous night? The night she had gone to fetch the body? No, surely not, it was too awful to contemplate. The child must have been thinking of some other journey. Alexandra had been driving round at night for eleven months.

Marc looked at the others. Mathias was crumbling a piece of bread. Lucien was dusting a shelf with the dirty tea towel. And he was waiting for Alexandra to react, to explain, to start shouting.

'It makes a lot of sense,' she said at last.

'Yes, it makes sense,' Vandoosler agreed.

'You're crazy, say something else!' Marc beseeched Alexandra.

'She's not crazy at all,' said Vandoosler. 'She's very intelligent.'

'But what about the others?' said Marc. 'She's not the only one who would inherit Sophia's money. There's her mother . . .'

Alexandra clenched the handkerchief in her fist.

'Her mother's out of it,' said Vandoosler. 'She hasn't budged from Lyon. She's been to her office every day, Saturdays included. She works part time and fetches Kyril from school every afternoon. Cast-iron and checked.'

'Thank you,' breathed Alexandra.

'Well, what about Relivaux?' asked Marc. 'He must surely be the one who stands to get the most, isn't he? And, what's more, he has a mistress.'

'Relivaux's not looking too good, that's true. Quite a few night-time disappearances since his wife vanished. But he didn't do anything to try and find her, remember. No body, no inheritance.'

'Oh, come on. He knew she'd be found sooner or later.'

'It's possible,' conceded Vandoosler. 'Leguennec isn't letting him off the hook, don't worry.'

'And what about the rest of the family?' asked Marc. 'Lex. Who else is there in the family?'

'Ask your uncle. He seems to know everything before anyone else does.'

'Eat some bread,' Mathias said to Marc. 'It'll relax your jaw.'

'D'you think so?'

Mathias nodded and passed him a slice, which Marc munched idiotically, as he listened to Vandoosler communicating more information.

'The third inheritor is Sophia's father, who lives in Dourdan,' Vandoosler said. 'Siméonidis *père* is one of his daughter's greatest fans. He never missed any of her concerts. In fact he met his second wife at the Paris Opera. The second wife had come along to see her son, who just had a walk-on part, and she was very proud of him. And she was also very proud to have met, simply by the accident of being next to him in the stalls, the father of the *prima donna*. She probably thought he could help her son, but things went further, they got married and they live in his house in Dourdan. Two points: Siméonidis isn't rich, and he can still drive. But the bottom line is this: he's passionately devoted to his daughter. He was absolutely prostrated to hear of her death, he has collected everything there is to know about her, press cuttings, photos, the lot. Apparently it takes up a whole room in his house. So – true or false?'

'Well, it's what the family say,' Alexandra murmured. 'He's a nice old man, a bit bossy, maybe, but he married a stupid woman second time round. She's younger than him, and she seems to be able to do what she likes, except where Sophia is concerned. Anything to do with Sophia is sacred, and she's not allowed to poke her nose in.'

'This woman's son is a bit odd.'

'Aha,' said Marc.

'Don't get too excited,' said Vandoosler. 'Just odd in the sense that he's a bit slow, a bit gormless, doesn't settle to anything, a bit of a voyeur, I'd say, and living off his mother's money at the age of forty. He's pretty useless: now and again he gets some little business going, but it doesn't last – in short, he's pathetic rather than sinister. Sophia got him a few more walk-on parts, but even when he didn't have to say anything, he was no good, and he soon got tired of it.'

Alexandra was wiping the table absently with the handkerchief Lucien had given her. Lucien was looking concerned about the handkerchief. Mathias got up to go and work at *Le Tonneau*. He said he would give Kyril something to eat in the kitchen there, then take a few minutes off to bring him back to the garden house. Alexandra smiled at him.

Mathias went upstairs to get changed. Juliette had insisted that he be properly dressed under his waiter's uniform. This was tough for Mathias. He felt as if he were bursting under three layers of clothes. But he understood Juliette's point of view. She had also requested that he stop getting changed half in the kitchen, half in the restaurant when the customers had left, 'in case someone saw him'. Mathias failed to see what was so embarrassing about that, but he didn't want to upset her. So now he got changed in his bedroom, which meant he had to leave the house fully dressed, underpants, socks, shoes, black trousers, shirt, bow tie, waistcoat, jacket and he felt really uncomfortable. But he liked the work. It was the kind of job that doesn't stop you thinking while you're doing it. And sometimes, if they weren't too busy, Juliette let him go home early. He would not have minded staying all night with her, but since he said very little, she was unlikely to guess that. So she let him go home. As he buttoned up his hateful waistcoat, Mathias thought about Alexandra and the number of slices of bread he had had to cut to keep the situation under control. Vandoosler senior certainly didn't beat about the bush. All the same it was amazing how many slices of bread Lucien could eat.

Once Mathias had gone, everyone fell silent. It was often like that living with Mathias, Marc reflected. When he was there, he hardly said anything and nobody took any notice of him. But when he left, it was as if the stone bridge they had all been standing on had suddenly disappeared and they had to find their balance again. He shivered and gave himself a shake.

'You're sleepy, soldier,' said Lucien.

'No, I'm just moving about while sitting still. It's a question of tectonic plates, but you wouldn't understand.'

Vandoosler stood up and with a touch of his hand got Alexandra to look at him.

'Yes, your version makes plenty of sense,' Alexandra repeated. 'Sophia's father couldn't possibly have killed her, because he loved her. His stepson couldn't have done it, because he's too useless. His mother couldn't, because she's too silly. My mother couldn't have, because she's my mother. Anyway she never left Lyon. So that leaves me. And I've been running about all over the place, I've told my mother lies, I sold my car, I haven't seen Aunt Sophia for ten years, I'm bitter and twisted, I got the police to start up their enquiries when I got here, I haven't got a job, I went out driving at night with no proper reason. I'm sunk. Well, I was already in deep trouble anyway.'

'So are we,' said Marc. 'But there's a difference between being in deep trouble and being sunk. You might be floundering if you're in trouble, but you're under water if you're sunk. Not at all the same thing.'

'Don't play word games,' said Vandoosler. 'She doesn't need that at this point.'

'A little word game from time to time doesn't hurt anyone,' objected Marc.

'What I told Alexandra is more useful to her just now. All the mistakes she made tonight, panicking, crying, getting angry, interrupting me, saying "fucking" twice, shouting, looking defeated and confused, she won't make them on Monday. Tomorrow she's going to lie in, read a book, take the child out to the park or down to the Seine. Leguennec will probably have her followed. That's likely to be arranged. She mustn't give any sign of noticing that. On Monday, she will take the child to school, and then go to the police station. She knows what they're going to say. She will tell the truth as she sees it, without being aggressive, and that will be the best thing to slow down the investigation.'

'She'll tell the truth, but Leguennec won't believe her.'

'I didn't say "the truth", I said "the truth as she sees it".'

'Do you think she's guilty then?' Marc exploded again.

Vandoosler raised his hands and dropped them back onto his knees. 'Marc, it may take a little time to make "the truth" and "the truth as she sees it" mean exactly the same thing. Time is what we need right now. And I'm trying to gain a little time. Leguennec's a good detective, but he tends to want to catch his whale right away. He's a harpooner, and yes, they're necessary. But I prefer to stalk the whale, let it dive, let out a bit of rope, watch where it comes up, try again and so on. Take my time.'

'But what do you expect from more time?' Alexandra asked.

'Reactions. After a murder, nothing stands still. I'm waiting for reactions, even little ones. They will happen. One just has to be on the look-out for them.'

'And you're going to sit up in your attic waiting for reactions?' said Marc. 'Without going anywhere, without looking for clues, without budging? You think reactions are going to fall on your head like pigeon shit? Do you know how often I've been hit by pigeon shit in the twenty-three years I've lived in Paris? Just once, that's all. And there are millions and millions of pigeons flying around every day. So what on earth do you expect? That something is going to turn up on your doorstep?'

'Just so,' said Vandoosler, 'because this . . .'

'This is the front line,' said Lucien.

Vandoosler stood up and nodded. 'He catches on fast, your Great War friend.'

There was a heavy silence. Vandoosler felt in his pockets, and found two five-franc pieces. He chose the brighter and disappeared into the cellar where they kept the tools. They heard the sound of an electric drill. Then he came back, holding the coin which now had a hole through it, and nailed it to the upright wooden beam on the left of of the fireplace.

'Have you finished this circus act?' Marc said.

'Since we're talking whaling, I'm nailing this coin to the mainmast. It will go to whoever catches the murderer.'

'Do you have to?' said Marc. 'Sophia is dead, and you're playing games. You want to be Captain Ahab. It's pathetic.'

'It's not pathetic, it's symbolic. There's a difference. Bread and symbols, not circuses. That's basic.'

'And you're the captain of the ship, of course?'

Vandoosler shook his head. 'I don't know the answer. It's not a race. I want to catch the murderer and I want everyone to work at it.'

'You've been more indulgent towards murderers in the past,' said Marc.

Vandoosler turned round sharply. 'This one,' he said, 'will get no indulgence from me. This one is a bastard.'

'You know that already?'

'Oh yes. This one is a killer. A real killer, you understand? Good night everyone.'

# XXIII

ON MONDAY, AT ABOUT MIDDAY, MARC HEARD A CAR DRAW UP AT THE gate. Dropping his pencil, he rushed to the window. Vandoosler was getting out of a taxi with Alexandra. The old man accompanied her to the garden house next door and came back humming to himself. So that was what he had been doing: he had gone to pick her up from the police station. Marc clenched his teeth. The subtle omnipotence of his godfather was beginning to infuriate him. A vein was throbbing in his temple. He couldn't help these attacks of blind fury. The tectonic plates were shifting. How on earth did Mathias manage to remain so foursquare and laconic, even though nothing was working out for him either? Marc felt as if he was wasting away with exasperation. He had practically chewed his way through a pencil that morning spitting splinters of wood onto the paper. Perhaps he should try wearing sandals? No, that was ridiculous. Not only would he have cold feet, but he would lose the last shreds of originality he possessed, which lay in his sophisticated clothes. No, sandals were definitely out.

Marc tightened his silver belt and smoothed his tight black trousers. Alexandra hadn't even come over to see them the night before.

But then why should she? Now that she had her own little house, she had her independence and freedom. She was the kind of girl who liked to feel free, and one had to watch out. Still, she had spent Sunday doing exactly what Vandoosler had told her to. She had gone to the park with Kyril. Mathias had seen them playing ball and had joined in for a while.

The June sunshine was warm. The idea had not even occurred to Marc. Mathias knew how to perform quiet comforting acts which Marc would never have dreamed of, they were so simple. Marc had gone back to his study of village trade in the eleventh and twelfth centuries, though his enthusiasm for it had waned. The problem of the surplus of rural production was so treacherous that you had to lie flat on top of it, if you weren't to plunge up to your waist in its quicksands. Bloody complicated. He might have done better to go and play ball; at least you can see what you're throwing and what you're catching. As for the godfather, he had spent the whole day perched on his chair, watching the neighbourhood from his skylight, the silly old bugger. Playing at being the watcher on high or the captain of the ship might make him look important to those who didn't know him, but that kind of showing off was not going to impress Marc.

He heard Vandoosler climbing the stairs, but didn't move, determined not to let his uncle have the satisfaction of hearing him asking for news. But Marc's resolve weakened quickly, as it generally did over little things, and twenty minutes later, he was opening the attic door.

The godfather was standing on a chair, peering out through the skylight.

'You look really stupid like that,' said Marc. 'What are you waiting for? Reactions? Pigeon shit? Moby Dick?'

'I'm not doing anyone any harm that I can see,' said Vandoosler, getting down from the chair. 'Why are you so worked up?'

'You're making out you're important, indispensable. You're Mr Big. That's what gets on my nerves.'

'Yes, I agree, it's annoying. But you're used to it and it doesn't usually bother you. Now, because I'm doing something for Lex, that rankles. You're forgetting that if I am keeping my eye on her, it's to avoid worse things happening for everyone. Do you want to be the one who does it? You don't have the experience. And since you get worked up and don't listen to anything I say, you're unlikely to acquire it. In any case, you don't have any pull with Leguennec. So if you want to help her, you're going to have to put up with my interference. And you may even have to do what I tell you, because I can't be everywhere at once. You and the other evangelists could be useful.'

'What for?'

'Wait, now is too soon.'

'You're waiting for the pigeon shit to start falling?'

'Call it that if you like.'

'Are you sure it will happen?'

'Pretty sure. Alexandra played her cards well at the session this morning. Leguennec has been slowed down. But he's got hold of something that's not to her advantage. Do you want to know what it is, or don't you care to be involved in what I'm up to?'

Marc sat down.

'They examined Sophia's car and in the boot they found two hairs. They are certainly Sophia's.'

Vandoosler rubbed his hands together and chuckled.

'And you think that's funny?' cried Marc, in despair.

'Hold your horses, young Vandoosler, how many times do I have to tell you?' He laughed again and poured himself a drink. 'Do you want some?'

'No thanks. But that's serious, finding hairs. And you're laughing. It's disgusting. You're cynical and sick. Unless . . . unless you think they won't lead anywhere. After all, if it was Sophia's car, it's not surprising that they found some of her hairs inside.'

'In the boot?'

'Why not? They could come from a coat or something?'

'Sophia Siméonidis wasn't like you. She wouldn't have chucked her coat in the boot. No, I was thinking of something else. Don't worry. A police investigation doesn't depend on one little clue. I have plenty up my sleeve. And if you would just take the trouble to settle down and stop worrying about my getting too friendly with Alexandra, and remember that I brought you up, and not as badly as all that, in spite of your dopey habits and my own, and if you would just give me a little credit, and keep your fists in your pockets, I have a small favour to ask of you.'

Marc thought for a moment. The business of the hair was really worrying him. The old man looked as if he knew more than he was saying. Anyway there was no point putting the question, he was not about to throw his uncle, read godfather, out of the house. And that, as Vandoosler would say himself, was the bottom line.

'OK, go ahead,' Marc sighed.

'This afternoon, I have to go out. They are going to question Relivaux's mistress and they're seeing him again too. I'm going to hang around. And I need a watchman here for the pigeon shit, if it happens. You could replace me as look-out.'

'What do I have to do?'

'Just stay up here. Don't go away, not even down to the shops. You never know. Stay at the window.'

'But what am I supposed to be looking out for, for heaven's sake?'

'I don't know. That's why you have to be on the look-out. Even for something very ordinary. OK?'

'OK. But I still don't see where this is getting us. Anyway, if you do go out, bring back some bread and half a dozen eggs. Lucien is teaching until six. I was supposed to do the shopping.'

'Is there anything there for lunch?'

'There's a bit of cold meat from the other day. Not very tempting. Shall we go to *Le Tonneau*?'

'It's shut on Mondays. Anyway, I told you, we can't leave the house unoccupied, remember?'

'Not even to get something to eat?'

'No. We'll eat the cold meat. Then you can go back up to the window and wait. Please do *not* take a book with you. Stay at the window and keep your eyes open.'

'I'm going to be bored out of my skull,' said Marc.

'No, you won't, you'll see, there's plenty to look at out there.'


From one-thirty on, Marc was grumpily at his post at the second-floor window. It was raining. There weren't many people in their little street as a rule, and even fewer when it was raining. And it was hard to see who was going past under umbrellas. As Marc had predicted, absolutely nothing happened. Two ladies went up the street one way, a man went the other. Then Juliette's brother ventured out at about half-past two, under a large black umbrella. They certainly didn't often see plump Georges. He worked on and off, when the publishers sent him to make a delivery in the provinces. He would be away a week then home for a few days. So you might meet him out for a walk or having a beer somewhere. He was a pleasant enough chap, with fair skin like his sister, but you didn't get much out of him. He would pass the time of day, but didn't make conversation. He never came to the restaurant. Marc had not dared to ask Juliette about him, but she did not seem over-proud of her over-weight brother, still living with his sister when he was nearly forty. She didn't talk about him much. It was rather as if she was protecting him. He was never seen in the company of a woman, so Lucien had hinted that he was perhaps Juliette's lover. But that was absurd. The physical resemblance was plain to see, although she was the good-looking version, and he wasn't. Disappointed, but bowing to the evidence, Lucien had changed tack and said he had seen Georges going into a special shop in the red-light district. Marc shrugged. Lucien liked making up stories, delicate or indelicate.

At about three o'clock, he saw Juliette come running in, protecting her head with a cardboard box, then Mathias, following her more slowly, made his way home. On Mondays, he often went to help Juliette get in the week's supplies. He was dripping wet, but of course that didn't bother him. Then another woman came past. Then another man a quarter of an hour later. Everyone was hurrying because of the rain. Mathias knocked at the door to ask for a pen. He hadn't even dried his hair.

'What are you doing there?' he asked.

'I'm on duty,' Marc replied wearily. 'The *commissaire* has told me to be the look-out. So I'm looking out.'

'Ah. What for?'

'That's what I don't know. Needless to say, nothing whatsoever has happened yet. They found two of Sophia's hairs in the boot of the car that Lex borrowed.'

'Ah. Not good.'

'You said it. But the godfather just laughs. Oh look, here comes the postman.'

'D'you want me to take over?'

'No thanks. I'm getting used to it. I'm the only one here who's not working. So it does me good to have a mission, even if it's a pointless one.'

Mathias pocketed a pen, and Marc stayed at his post. Ladies went by with umbrellas. Schoolchildren started to come home. Alexandra went past with little Kyril. Without giving a glance at their house. And why should she?

Pierre Relivaux parked his car shortly before six. They must have given his car a going-over as well. He slammed the garden gate. Being interrogated by detectives does not improve anyone's temper. He must have been alarmed that the business of his mistress in the 15th *arrondissement* would reach the ears of his superiors at the ministry. Nobody knew yet when the burial could take place of the pathetic remains of Sophia. The police were still holding on to them. But Marc did not expect Relivaux to collapse at the funeral. He looked concerned, but not devastated by his wife's death. At any rate, if he was the murderer, he was certainly not play-acting, which was a strategy like any other, Marc supposed. At about six-thirty, Lucien came back. Goodbye peace and quiet. Then Vandoosler, soaked to the skin. Marc stretched his limbs, now stiff from sitting still. It reminded him of the time they had watched the police digging under the tree. Nobody mentioned the tree any more. And yet, it had all started with that. Marc couldn't forget it. That tree.

Well, that was a waste of an afternoon. No excitement, not even any minor incident, or the slightest pigeon shit. Nothing.

Marc went downstairs to report to the godfather who was lighting a fire to dry himself by.

'Nothing to report. I've got a crick in my neck from keeping watch for five hours. What about you? How is the questioning going?'

'Leguennec is starting to clam up on me. We may be friends, but he's got his pride. He doesn't know which way to turn next, so he doesn't want me to be an eyewitness. And because of my record, he only trusts me up to a point. And he's further up in the hierarchy these days. He's getting fed up at finding me under his feet all the time. He thinks I'm laughing at him. Especially since I did laugh when they found the hairs.'

'And why was that, by the way?'

'Tactics, my boy, tactics. Poor old Leguennec. He thought he was on to something and now he has half a dozen potential culprits, any of whom would fit the bill. I'm going to have to invite him round to play cards to get him to loosen up.'

'Half a dozen? What do you mean? Were there some more candidates?'

'Well, I pointed out to Leguennec that young Alexandra might have got off to a bad start, but that was no reason to risk putting his foot in it. Don't forget that I'm trying to buy some time. That's the whole point. So I suggested plenty of other plausible suspects. This afternoon, Relivaux, who is putting up a good defence, made a favourable impression on him. So I had to add my two pennyworth. Relivaux insists that he never went near his wife's car. That he gave Alexandra the keys. I had to tell Leguennec that Relivaux had kept the spares at home. In fact, I brought them in for him. What do you think of that, eh?'

The fire had started to blaze up in the fireplace and Marc had always liked that brief moment when the flames jump up wildly, before the kindling collapses and ordinary burning takes over, which is captivating too, but for other reasons. Lucien arrived and warmed himself. It was June, but their hands still felt cold in the upper rooms at night. Except for Mathias, of course, who had just come in stripped to the waist to start cooking the supper. Mathias had a muscular but practically hair-less torso.

'Well, fantastic,' said Marc suspiciously. 'How did you get hold of the keys?'

Vandoosler sighed.

'Oh. I get it. You broke in while he was away. You're going to get us into big trouble.'

'You pinched a hare the other day,' replied Vandoosler. 'Old habits die hard. I wanted to see inside his house. I had a good look round. Letters, receipts, keys. He's a methodical fellow, Relivaux. Nothing compromising lying about.'

'How did you find the keys?'

'Easy. They were hidden behind the volume C, for *Clef*, of the Larousse Encyclopedia. The fact that he hid the keys doesn't necessarily mean he's guilty, though. He's probably scared and it might have seemed simpler to say he didn't have a spare.'

'Why not just throw them away?'

'In times of stress, it might be useful to have a car to which in theory you don't have a key. As for his own car, it's been given a thorough going over. Nothing to report.'

'And the mistress?'

'She didn't stand up for long to Leguennec. St Luke was wrong about her. She's not happy just to be Relivaux's ladylove, she's using him. He's subsidising her and her real boyfriend, who doesn't seem to mind pushing off when Relivaux turns up for the weekend. Not being the world's most perceptive character, Relivaux doesn't suspect a thing, according to the girl. Occasionally the two men have bumped into each other, but he thinks the boyfriend is her brother. According to her, he was happy with things as they stood, and I can't see what she would have to gain by marrying him, since that would rob her of her freedom. And I can't see what Relivaux would get out of it either. Sophia Siméonidis was a much more prestigious wife for him to show off in the social circles he aspired to. I did probe a bit harder though. I suggested that Elizabeth – that's the girl – might be lying all along the line, and was really hoping to benefit from the advantages of hooking Relivaux, once he had got rid of his wife and inherited her money. She might have succeeded in marrying him, since she's strung him along for six years, she's quite pretty and a lot younger than he is.'

'And the other suspects?'

'Naturally, I lined up Sophia's stepmother and her son. They have alibis for each other on the night of the Maisons-Alfort fire, but it's entirely possible that one of them went there. It isn't far from Dourdan. Nearer than Lyon, for sure.'

'That still doesn't give us half a dozen,' objected Marc. 'Who else have you suggested to Leguennec?'

'Well, there's St Luke, St Matthew and you. That will give him plenty to think about.'

Marc leapt up from his seat, while Lucien smiled. 'For Christ's sake! Are you crazy?'

'Do you want to help Alexandra, yes or no?'

'For crying out loud! It won't help Alexandra one bit. And what earthly reason would Leguennec have to suspect us?'

'No problem,' Lucien intervened. 'Three unoccupied men in their mid-thirties in a chaotic house. See? Not very respectable neighbours, are they? One of them takes the lady out, then brutally rapes her and sets fire to the car to cover his tracks.'

'What about the postcard, then?' shouted Marc. 'The postcard with the star and the appointment? Did we send that too?'

'It does complicate things a bit,' Lucien conceded. 'Let's imagine that the lady had talked a bit about Stelios, and about the card she received three months ago. To explain her fears and to persuade us to dig under the tree. Don't forget that, we did dig up her garden.'

'As if I could forget that damned tree.'

'Well,' Lucien went on, 'to lure the lady out of her house, one of us used the same rather crude trick, met her at the Gare de Lyon, took her somewhere else and so forth.'

'But Sophia didn't say anything to any of us about Stelios!'

'Maybe not, but see if the police care. They would only have our word for it, and that wouldn't carry much weight if we were already looking bad.'

'Oh, that's just perfect.' Marc was trembling with anger. 'Perfect. My godfather has such brilliant ideas. OK – what about him? With his record, and his fantastic adventures in the police force, and with women, he might fit the bill. So what do you think, *Monsieur le Commissaire*?'

Vandoosler shook his head.

'No, think about it. Old men of sixty-eight don't suddenly start going about raping people. If they were like that, they'd have a bit of form already. Any policeman will tell you that. But men in their thirties, living on their own, and a bit peculiar with it, well, who can tell what they might get up to?'

Lucien burst out laughing. 'Priceless!' he said. 'You really are priceless, *commissaire*. Your hints to Leguennec are just hilarious.'

'I don't see the joke,' said Marc.

'That's because you are pure in heart,' said Lucien, patting him on the shoulder. 'You don't want to have a stain on your escutcheon. But your image is not what's at stake here. It's just a matter of creating a diversion. Leguennec can't prove anything against us. But by the time he runs a check on us, where we're from, what we've done, etcetera, etcetera, we'll have bought another day, and he'll have had two of his men tied up for hours for nothing. That's at least one we can put across the enemy.'

'I still think it's stupid.'

'No, I bet Mathias finds it funny – don't you Mathias?'

Mathias gave a brief smile. 'If you want to know, I couldn't care less,' he said.

'We could have the police on our backs, thinking we might have raped Sophia, and you couldn't care less?' asked Marc.

'So what? I know I'll never rape a woman. What anyone else might think is of no consequence, because I know the truth.'

Marc sighed.

'The hunter-gatherer is wise,' suggested Lucien. 'And what's more, since he's been working in *Le Tonneau*, he has started to learn to cook. Since I am neither wise nor pure, I propose we have something to eat.'

'Eating, that's all you think about, that and the Great War,' said Marc.

'Let's eat,' said Vandoosler.

He came up behind Marc and squeezed his shoulder. It was the same kind of touch his uncle had used ever since he was a small boy when they had had a row, a gesture that meant 'Calm down, young Vandoosler, I'm on your side, don't get so worked up, you're too jumpy, calm down.' As he felt this quick squeeze, Marc felt his anger subside. Alexandra had not been charged with anything, at least, and that was what the old man had been working on for the last four days. Marc glanced at him. Expressionless, Vandoosler was sitting at the table. Love him or hate him, it was hard to decide. But he was his uncle, and Marc, despite all his protests, trusted him at heart. Well, for some things, anyway.

# XXIV

NEVERTHELESS, WHEN VANDOOSLER CAME INTO HIS BEDROOM, WITH Leguennec at his heels at eight o'clock the next morning, Marc started up in panic.

'I'm just off,' Vandoosler said. 'I have to go with Leguennec. Just do the same as yesterday, it'll be fine.'

Vandoosler disappeared. Marc remained in bed, rubbing his eyes, with the feeling that he had narrowly escaped being charged with something. His godfather had not been asked to wake him in the morning. The old man was losing it. No, that wasn't it. It must be that he was anxious to accompany Leguennec and was asking Marc to keep watch during his absence. The godfather obviously hadn't told Leguennec all that he was up to. Marc got out of bed, took a shower and went down to the ground floor. Mathias, who had been up since some godforsaken hour, was already putting logs in the woodbox. He was the kind of guy who got up at dawn when nobody had asked him to. Marc, still feeling dazed, made himself some strong coffee.

'Do you know why Leguennec came round?' he asked.

'Because we don't have a phone,' Mathias told him. 'He has to come over if he wants to talk to your uncle.'

'I see. But why so early? Did he say anything to you?'

'Not a thing,' said Mathias. 'He looked like a Breton worrying about a gale warning, but I expect he often looks like that, even when there isn't one. He just nodded to me and went straight upstairs. I think I heard him grumbling about houses with four floors and no phone. But that's all.'

'We're going to have to wait,' said Marc. 'And I'm going to have to sit at the window again. It's not a lot of fun. I've no idea what he's hoping for. I just see men, women, umbrellas, the postman, our neighbour Georges and that's about it.'

'And Alexandra,' said Mathias.

'What do you think of her?' said Marc hesitantly.

'Adorable.'

Both satisfied and jealous, Marc put his coffee cup and a couple of pieces of bread on a tray, took it all upstairs and pulled up a high stool to the window. At least he wouldn't have to stand up all day.

This morning it was not raining. It was a perfect June day. With luck, he was in time to see Lex take the little boy to school. Yes, just in time. She went past, looking a bit sleepy, holding Kyril by the hand: he seemed to be telling her all sorts of things. As before, she did not glance up at their house. And why should she, Marc asked himself once more. Anyway, it was better that way. If she had seen him perched on his stool, eating his breakfast, it would hardly have been to his advantage. Marc couldn't see Relivaux's car. He must have left very early. An honest fellow going to work, or a murderer? The godfather had said that the murderer in this case was a real killer. A killer like that would not be as colourless as Relivaux, and a lot more dangerous. The idea was much more scary. Marc didn't think Pierre was made of that kind of stuff; he didn't feel at all frightened of him. Mathias, now, he would make a perfect killer: tall, solid, unflappable, a man of the woods, with silent and sometimes weird ideas, a secret opera-goer – yes, Mathias would make a perfect suspect.

Time passed with thoughts like this, and it was suddenly half-past nine. Mathias came in to give him back his pen. Marc told him that he could imagine him as a killer and Mathias shrugged.

'How's the look-out going?'

'Zero,' said Marc. 'The old man's lost the plot and I'm going along with his crazy ideas. It must run in the family.'

'If you're going to stay there all day, I'll bring you some lunch before I go off to the restaurant.'

Mathias closed the door quietly and Marc heard him go to his desk on the floor below. He shifted on the stool. He would have to bring a cushion in future. For a moment, he imagined himself imprisoned there for years, looking out of the window, sitting in a specially comfortable armchair for a pointless vigil, with Mathias his only visitor, bringing him food on a tray. Relivaux's cleaning lady arrived at ten o'clock, letting herself in with her own keys. Marc picked up the thread of his convoluted thoughts. Kyril had olive skin, curly hair and round limbs. Perhaps the boy's father was fat and ugly, why not? Dammit. Why did he keep thinking about him? He shook his head and looked out again at the Western Front. The little beech tree looked rather healthy. It seemed glad it was June at last. Marc somehow could not manage to put the tree out of his thoughts, but he seemed to be the only one to feel concerned. Still, he had seen Mathias stop at the Relivaux gate the other day and glance in. It had looked as if he was observing the tree. Or rather the foot of the tree. Why was Mathias so secretive about everything he did? Mathias knew masses of obscure stuff about Sophia's career. He already knew who she was, when she had come round that first time. He knew a lot of things and he never talked about them. Marc promised himself that when Vandoosler let him leave his post, he would go and take a look at the tree. As Sophia had done.

He saw another woman go past the house. He noted: '10.20 a.m. A lady went past looking busy with her shopping basket.' He had decided to note everything down, so as not to get too bored. He looked down at the paper and added: 'in fact it wasn't a basket, it was a string bag.' A string bag: what an old-fashioned sort of thing that was, something you saw in the country, or being carried by old ladies. When did people first start carrying string bags? The idea of looking that up cheered him a bit. Five minutes later, he was writing again: '10.25: a thin man is ringing Relivaux's doorbell.' Marc started. Yes, it was true: a skinny-looking man was ringing the bell at the Relivaux house, and it was not the postman or the meter reader or anyone local.

He got up, opened the window and leaned out. That was a lot of effort for a small reward. But Vandoosler was attaching such importance to this surveillance job. Marc felt that he had gradually become persuaded in spite of himself of the significance of his mission, and was starting to take every little thing for a key event. So he had pinched a pair of opera glasses from Mathias' room – evidence that Mathias must have been serious about opera. He focused the little glasses and took a good look. Yes, a man. Tall, thin, balding, with a teacher's briefcase, a respectable, light-coloured coat. The cleaning lady opened the door and from her gestures, Marc understood that she was saying *Monsieur* was not at home, that the visitor would have to come back some other time. The thin man seemed to be insisting. The cleaning lady repeated her negative gestures, and accepted a card which the man had taken from his pocket and on which he had scribbled something. She shut the door. Right. A visitor for Pierre Relivaux. Should he go and see the cleaner? Ask to see the card? Marc wrote a few notes on his piece of paper. When he looked up again, he saw that the man had not gone away. He was standing by the gate looking undecided, disappointed, and as if he was trying to make up his mind. What if he had been asking for Sophia? In the end, he went off, swinging his briefcase. Marc leapt up, rushed downstairs and ran into the street, catching the man up in a few minutes. Since he had spent so long at his window, he was not going to let the first likely customer escape, even if it led nowhere.

'I'm a neighbour,' Marc said. 'I saw you ring the bell. Can I help?'

Out of breath from running, Marc was still clutching his pen. The man looked at him with some interest and even, Marc sensed, hope.

'Thank you,' he said. 'I wanted to see Pierre Relivaux, but he wasn't there.'

'Try again this evening,' Marc said. 'He'll be back at about six or seven.'

'Apparently not. His cleaner said he was away for a few days and she didn't know where he was going, or when he'd be back. Maybe Friday, maybe Saturday. She couldn't say for sure. It's very inconvenient, because I've travelled from Geneva.'

'If you like,' said Marc, who was anxious not to let his first minor incident fizzle out, 'I could try to ask around. I'm sure I could find out where he's gone.'

The man hesitated. He looked as if he was wondering why Marc was so concerned with his affairs.

'Have you got a phonecard?' Marc asked.

The man nodded and followed him, without making any serious object-ion, towards the phone box on the corner.

'We don't have a phone,' Marc explained.

'Ah,' said the man.

Keeping an eye on his companion, Marc asked directory enquiries for the number of the police station in the 13th *arrondissement*. It was a piece of luck that he had brought his pen. He wrote the number on his hand and called Leguennec.

'Can I please speak to *Commissaire* Vandoosler, he's my uncle, it's urgent.'

Marc thought that the word 'urgent' was a key word that worked like magic if you wanted the police to help you. A few minutes later, Vandoosler was on the line.

'What's going on? Have you discovered something?'

Marc realised at that moment that he had discovered nothing at all.

'No, I don't think so. But ask your Breton policeman where Relivaux has gone, and how long he'll be away. He must have had to inform the police that he was leaving.'

Marc waited a few moments. He had left the door of the phone box open so that the man could hear what he was saying, and he wasn't looking surprised. So he knew about Sophia Siméonidis' death.

'Still there?' said Vandoosler. 'He went on official business to Toulon this morning. We checked with his ministry, it's genuine. It's not clear when he'll be back, it depends on how his negotiations there go. He could be back tomorrow, or it could be Monday. The police can contact him if necessary, via the ministry, but you can't.'

'Thanks,' said Marc. 'What about you?'

'They're working on the father of Relivaux's lady friend, you remember, Elizabeth? Her father has been in jail for ten years for multiple stabbing of the supposed lover of his wife. Leguennec is wondering if violence runs in the family. He's called Elizabeth in, and is questioning her now to see whether she takes after her father or her mother.'

'Perfect,' said Marc. 'Tell your Breton friend that there's a gale warning for Finistère. That'll distract him if he likes storms.'

'He knows already. He said "All the boats in harbour are tied up. But they're waiting for another eighteen that are still at sea".'

'Right,' said Marc. 'See you later.'

He hung up and returned to the thin man. 'I've found out where he is. Come with me.'

Marc was determined to get the man into the house, and find out what he wanted with Pierre Relivaux. It was probably something to do with his work, but you never knew. For Marc, Geneva conjured up images of boring administration.

The man followed him, still with a slightly hopeful expression, which Marc found intriguing. He sat him down in the refectory and after fetching some cups and putting the coffee on, took the sweeping brush and knocked hard on the ceiling. Since they had started using this way of calling Mathias, they were careful always to bang on the same place so as not to make marks all over the ceiling. The broom left little dents in the plaster and Lucien said they ought to tie a rag on top of it with string, which they still had not done.

While he was doing this, the man had put his briefcase on a chair and was looking at the five-franc coin nailed to the post. It was probably because of the coin that Marc broached the subject straightaway.

'We're looking for whoever murdered Sophia Siméonidis,' he said, as if that explained the coin.

'So am I,' said the man.

Marc poured out the coffee and they sat down together. So he did know, and he was looking too. He didn't look upset, so Sophia could not have been a close friend. There must be some other reason. Mathias came in and sat down on the bench, with a nod.

'Mathias Delamarre,' Marc introduced him. 'And I am Marc Vandoosler.'

The man was obliged to follow suit. 'My name is Christophe Dompierre. I live in Geneva.'

And he offered them a card.

'It was good of you to find out about Relivaux for me,' Dompierre went on. 'So when will he be back?'

'He's in Toulon, but the ministry can't say for certain when he will be home. Some time between tomorrow and Monday. It depends on the job. And we can't reach him.'

The man shook his head, and bit his lip. 'That's a nuisance,' he said. 'And you're enquiring into Madame Siméonidis' death?' he asked. 'You're surely not . . . in the police?'

'No, not at all. But she was our neighbour and we took a great interest in her. We are hoping for a result.' Marc realised that he was speaking rather formally, and the way Mathias was looking confirmed it.

'M. Dompierre is doing some looking too,' he explained.

'What for?' asked Mathias.

Dompierre looked at Mathias, whose calm features and limpid blue eyes must have inspired confidence, since he took off his coat and settled more comfortably in his chair. When someone takes a decision, there's a fraction of a second when their face tells you that they are going to. Marc was very good at spotting that fraction of a second, and thought it was easier than getting a pebble up onto the pavement. Dompierre had just made his decision.

'You might be able to do me a favour,' he said. 'Can you let me know as soon as M. Relivaux gets home. Would that be a nuisance?'

'No, by no means,' Marc replied. 'But what do you want with him? He claims to know nothing about his wife's murder. The police are keeping an eye on him, but for the time being, there's nothing serious against him. Do you know something we don't?'

'No, no. I was hoping that *he* knows something. Whether his wife had received any visits, that kind of thing.'

'I don't quite follow,' said Marc.

'That's because I'm still in the dark myself. I just don't know. And it's been that way for fifteen years. The death of Madame Siméonidis has given me some hope I might find what I'm looking for. Something the police didn't want to know about at the time.'

'At the time of what?'

Dompierre shifted on his chair. 'I can't tell you that yet,' he said. 'I'm not sure of anything. I don't want to make a mistake, because it would have grave consequences. And I really don't want the police interfering, is that understood? Absolutely no police. If I find what I'm after, the missing link, I'll go to them myself. Or rather, I'll write to them. I don't want to see them. They caused enough havoc for me and for my mother, fifteen years ago. They wouldn't listen to us when it all started. It's true that we had very little to go on. Just a desperate little sliver of belief, a feeling. That doesn't mean much to the police.' Dompierre gestured in the air. 'You probably think I'm being emotional,' he said, 'and in any case I'm talking about things that don't concern you. But I still cling to this desperate belief, and so did my mother, who is dead now. That's two of us who believed it. And I just don't want to let some dumb policeman come along and dismiss it out of hand. Not again.'

He stopped speaking and looked at them both in turn.

'You seem to be alright,' he said after examining them carefully. 'You don't look as if you would dismiss it out of hand. But I would still rather wait a bit before I ask you to help me. I went to see Madame Siméonidis' father at the weekend, in Dourdan. He showed me all his personal archives, and I think I might have found one or two little pointers. I left him my contact number in case he finds any more documents, but he didn't seem to be listening at all. He is absolutely devastated. And the killer is still at large. I'm looking for a name. Tell me, have you been her neighbours for long?'

'Only since March 20,' said Marc.

'Oh, that's not long. She won't have confided in you. She went missing about May 20, didn't she? Did anyone come to see her before that? Somebody unexpected? I don't mean an old friend or acquaintance. No, someone she thought she would never see again, or even someone she didn't know at all?'

Marc and Mathias shook their heads. They had not known Sophia for very long, but perhaps one could ask the other neighbours.

'Well, someone very unexpected did come to see her,' said Marc, frowning. 'Not someone, exactly, some*thing*.'

Dompierre lit a cigarette and Mathias noticed that his thin hands were trembling. Mathias had decided he would like this man. He was too thin, and far from handsome, but he was principled, he was following his hunch, his own private conviction. That was how Mathias was, when Marc teased him about hunting the bison. This fragile-looking man would not abandon his bow and arrow, that was certain.

'It was a tree, actually,' said Marc. 'A beech sapling. I don't know if that would mean anything to you, because I don't know what it is you're looking for. But I keep thinking about that tree, although everyone else has stopped caring. Shall I tell you about it?'

Dompierre nodded as Mathias brought him an ashtray. He listened to the story attentively.

'Yes. Well,' he said. 'I wasn't expecting that. And right now, I can't see what it has to do with anything.'

'Neither can I,' said Marc. 'I suppose it doesn't mean anything. And yet I keep thinking about it. All the time. I don't know why.'

'I'll think about it too,' said Dompierre. 'Can you let me know please, when Relivaux reappears. He may have been visited by this person without realising how important it was. I'll leave you my address. I'm staying at a little hotel in the 19th *arrondissement*, Hôtel du Danube, rue de la Prévoyance. I used to live near there as a child. Don't hesitate to call me, even at night, because I could be recalled to Geneva at any minute. I'm here on official European business. I'll give you the hotel address and phone number. I'm in room 32.'

Marc gave him back his card and Dompierre wrote his address. Marc got up and slipped the card under the five-franc piece on the fireplace. Dompierre watched him. For the first time, he smiled and for a moment looked almost charming.

'This is the *Pequod*, is it?'

'No,' said Marc, smiling in turn. 'It's a research deck. We do research on all periods, all mankind, all continents. From 500,000 BC to 1918. From Africa to Asia and from Europe to the Antarctic.'

'"And hence", Dompierre said, quoting, '"not only at substantiated times, upon well known separate feeding grounds could Ahab hope to encounter his prey; but in crossing the widest expanses of water between those grounds he could, by his art, so place and time himself on his way, as even then not to be wholly without prospect of a meeting."'

'Do you know *Moby Dick* by heart?' asked Marc, greatly impressed.

'No. Just that sentence, because I have often had occasion to use it.'

Dompierre shook hands with them warmly. He looked back once more at his card, wedged on the fireplace, as if checking that he had forgotten nothing, picked up his briefcase and left. Each standing at a window, Marc and Mathias watched him walk away towards the gate.

'Intriguing,' said Marc.

'Very,' said Mathias.

Once one was standing in one of the big window bays, it was difficult to move away. The June sunshine lay serenely over the untended garden. The grass was growing at top speed. Marc and Mathias stayed looking out of their windows for a long while. Marc was the first to speak.

'You'll be late for your lunchtime shift,' he said. 'Juliette will be wondering what you're up to.'

Mathias gave a start, went upstairs to put on his waiter's uniform, and Marc saw him leave at a run, buttoned up in his black waistcoat. It was the first time Marc had seen him run. He ran well. A very good hunter.

# XXV

ALEXANDRA WAS DOING NOTHING. WELL, NOTHING USEFUL OR PROFI-
table. She was sitting at a table, her head in her hands. She was thinking
about tears, the tears that nobody sees, that nobody knows about, the
tears shed in vain and unheeded. But which flow all the same. Alexandra
pushed hard on her temples and gritted her teeth. It didn't help, of course.
She sat up. 'Greeks are free, Greeks are proud,' her grandmother used to
say. She said a lot of things like that, Grandmother Andromache.

Guillaume had said he wanted to spend a thousand years with her.
Well, it had lasted just about five. 'Greeks take a man at his word,' her
grandmother used to say. Maybe so, Alexandra thought, but in that case,
the Greeks are stupid. Because afterwards she had had to walk away,
trying to hold her head high and her back straight, leaving behind familiar
places, sounds, names, and a face. To walk away with Kyril along churned-
up paths, trying not to fall headfirst into the bitter ditch of lost illusions.
Alexandra stretched her arms. She had had enough of this. She looked
at the clock. Time to go and fetch Kyril. Juliette had suggested a special
rate for Kyril to have his lunch after school at *Le Tonneau*. It had been
a stroke of luck to find people like this: Juliette, the evangelists. Here
she was, in this little house near them all, and it was restful. Perhaps
because they all seemed to have plenty of troubles of their own. Talking
of troubles, Pierre had promised her he would try to find her a job. If
she believed Pierre, she would be believing in someone's word again.
Alexandra quickly pulled on her boots and put on her jacket. Too much

crying left you with a headache. Combing her hair with her fingers, she set off for the school.

There were few customers in *Le Tonneau* at this time of day, and Mathias gave them the table in the window. Alexandra was not hungry and asked him only to give some food to Kyril. While the little boy ate, she went up to the bar and gave Mathias a big smile. He found her brave, and would have preferred to see her eat. To keep her courage up.

Juliette gave her a little dish of olives and Alexandra nibbled them, thinking of her old grandmother who had an almost religious respect for black olives. She had really adored Andromache and all the damned sayings she came out with at every turn. Alexandra rubbed her eyes. She was drifting away, dreaming. She had to pull herself together, and say something. 'The Greeks are proud.'

'Tell me, Mathias,' she asked, 'this morning while I was dressing Kyril, I saw Monsieur Vandoosler going off with Leguennec. Has anything happened? Do you know?'

Mathias looked at her. She was still smiling, but she had wobbled a little while back. The best thing to do was talk to her.

'Vandoosler didn't say anything when he went out,' he said. 'But Marc and I met a weird guy, name of Christophe Dompierre, from Geneva, very odd character. He had a story about something that happened fifteen years ago, that he wanted to sort out all by himself, and somehow connected with Sophia's murder. It was some ancient bee in his bonnet. But he absolutely insisted that we weren't to say a word to Leguennec, so we promised. I've no idea what he's on about, but I wouldn't want to give him away.'

'Dompierre? The name doesn't mean anything to me,' said Alexandra. 'What was he hoping to find?'

'He wanted to see Relivaux, ask him some questions, find out if he had had any unexpected visitors lately. It wasn't clear. But he's definitely waiting to see Relivaux, he's determined to do that.'

'He's going to wait for him? But Pierre's away for a few days. Didn't you tell him? You didn't know? We can't let this guy hang about in the street all day, even if he is crazy.'

'Marc told him. Don't worry, we know how to reach him. He's taken a room in rue de la Prévoyance – nice name, isn't it? Danube Métro station. I've seen the real Danube. Well this won't mean anything to you, but it's a quiet part of town, where he was brought up apparently. Odd chap, very single-minded. He even went to see your grandfather in Dourdan. We only have to let him know when Relivaux gets back, that's all.'

Mathias came round to the front of the bar, and took Kyril a yoghurt and a slice of tart, and patted his head.

'He's got a good appetite, your little boy,' said Juliette. 'It's nice to see.'

'What about you, Juliette?' asked Mathias, coming back to the bar. 'Does that ring any bells with you? An unexpected visitor? Sophia didn't say anything?'

Juliette thought for a while, but shook her head.

'No, nothing at all. Apart from the famous postcard with the star, nothing happened. Well, nothing that disturbed her. You could always tell with Sophia and I think she would have said something to me.'

'Not necessarily,' said Mathias.

'Well, no, perhaps you're right. Not necessarily.'

'People are coming in, I'd better see to them.'

Juliette and Alexandra stayed at the bar, chatting, but Mathias arrived with the orders and Juliette disappeared into the kitchen. There was too much noise now. It was impossible to talk peacefully at the bar.

Vandoosler called in. He was looking for Marc, who was no longer at his post. Mathias said that he was probably hungry, which would be normal at one o'clock. Vandoosler grumbled and went out again before Alexandra could ask him anything. He found his nephew at the gate to their house.

'Deserting your post, I see?'

'Oh, please don't talk like Lucien,' said Marc. 'I just went to get a sandwich because I was feeling weak. Come on, I've been working the whole bloody morning for you.'

'For her, St Mark.'

'Meaning?'

'You know perfectly well who I mean – Alexandra. We're still getting nowhere. Leguennec is interested in Elizabeth's father's criminal record, but he can't forget the two hairs in the car. Alexandra had better keep very quiet. If she steps out of line at all, he'll nab her.'

'Is it really that bad?'

Vandoosler nodded.

'Your Breton's an idiot.'

'My dear Marc,' said Vandoosler, 'if everyone who got in our way was an idiot, it would be too easy. I suppose you didn't get a sandwich for me?'

'You didn't say you'd be back. Shit, you only had to telephone.'

'We don't have a phone.'

'Oh no, of course.'

'And don't say "shit" to me, it gets on my nerves. I've still got police reflexes.'

'Yeah, it shows. Shall we go in? You can share my sandwich, and I'll tell you all about Monsieur Dompierre. The pigeon arrived this morning.'

'See, I told you it would.'

'Excuse me, I had to go out and catch it. I cheated. If I hadn't run downstairs, I would have lost it. But I don't know whether this is any use at all. Maybe just a sparrow. Whatever you think, I'm giving notice, I'm resigning from this look-out business. I've decided to go to Dourdan tomorrow.'

Vandoosler seemed greatly interested by the story of Christophe Dompierre, but he couldn't say why. Marc thought perhaps he didn't want to say why. Several times, his uncle read the card wedged on the fireplace under the coin.

'And you don't remember the quotation from *Moby Dick*?' he asked.

'No, I told you. It was a rather grand sentence, technical and lyrical, with "widest expanses" in it, but it didn't have anything to do with what he was talking about. It was philosophical, a quest for the unattainable, that kind of thing.'

'Still,' said Vandoosler. 'I would have liked it if you could have identified it.'

'You don't think I'm going to read the whole book to find it for you, do you?'

'That would be too much to hope for. Your idea of going to Dourdan is all very well, but you're going without any idea what to look for. From what I know of him, I'd be surprised if Siméonidis has anything to say to you. And Dompierre certainly won't have told him about the "few little pointers" he found.'

'I want to see what the second wife and stepson are like. Can you take my place this afternoon? I need to think and stretch my legs.'

'Off with you, then, Marc, I need to sit down. I'll borrow your window.'

Vandoosler spent the rest of the day watching the street. It kept him entertained, but what Marc had told him of Dompierre was worrying him. He found it surprising that Marc had chased after the man. Marc was good at impulsive actions. Despite his underground lines of conduct, which were firm and even a bit too pure, recognisable by those who knew him well, Marc fired off in all directions when he attempted to analyse things, yet his many deviations, in terms both of logic and temperament, could sometimes lead to valuable results. Marc was torn between the twin perils of angelism and impatience. One could count on Mathias as well, not so much for detective work as for registering things. Vandoosler thought of his St Matthew as a kind of dolmen, a great standing stone, sacred, but unconsciously absorbing all kinds of perceptible events, its particles of mica open to the winds. Well, anyway, a complicated man to describe. Because he was also capable of brusque movements, of racing off, of taking risks at judiciously chosen moments. As for Lucien, he was an idealist, liable to be tempted by every manner of excess, from the top of the scale to the bottom. In the cacophony of his agitation, collisions and impacts were always possible, striking unexpected sparks.

And Alexandra?

Vandoosler lit a cigarette and returned to the window. Marc was drawn to her, that was all too likely, but he was still very entangled in his feelings about the wife who had left him. Vandoosler found it hard to follow what was going on with his nephew, because he himself had never kept for more than a few months promises meant to last fifty years. Why did he make so many promises, anyway? The face of the young woman with her Greek ancestry touched him. From what he had seen of her so far, Alexandra was an interesting combination of vulnerability and boldness, authentic but repressed feelings, and moments of wild but sometimes silent bravado. It was the kind of mixture of enthusiasm and sweetness that he had known and loved long ago in another person. Whom he had abandoned in half an hour. He could still clearly see her walking back down the platform with the twins, until they were just three little dots in the distance. Where were those three little dots now? Vandoosler sat up and gripped the balcony rail. He had neglected for ten minutes to watch the street. He threw away his cigarette and reviewed once more the string of plausible arguments incriminating Alexandra that Leguennec had drawn up. He still needed to play for time, and for something else to crop up to slow down the investigation by the Breton *inspecteur*. Dompierre might just do.

Marc came in late, followed shortly thereafter by Lucien, whose turn it was to do the shopping, and who had the day before asked Marc to get hold of two kilos of langoustines, if they looked fresh and if it looked easy to steal them.

'It wasn't easy,' Marc said, putting the big bag of langoustines on the table. 'Not at all easy. In fact what I did was pinch the bag belonging to the man ahead of me in the queue.'

'Very ingenious,' remarked Lucien. 'You really do deliver, don't you?'

'Next time, try to have a craving for something simpler,' said Marc.

'That's always been my problem,' said Lucien.

'You wouldn't have made a very effective soldier, then, if you don't mind me saying.'

Lucien stopped short in his preparations for supper, and looked at his watch. 'Shit!' he exclaimed. 'The Great War!'

'What about the Great War? Have you been called up? Does your country need you?'

Lucien put down the kitchen knife, with distress written all over his face.

'It's June 8,' he said. 'This is a disaster. I can't cook the langoustines.

I'm supposed to be at a commemorative dinner tonight, I can't not go.'

'Commemorative? Some mistake surely? It's World War Two you commemorate at this time of year, and anyway it's May 8 not June 8. You've mixed it up.'

'No, no,' said Lucien. 'Yes, of course, the 1939–45 dinner was supposed to be on May 8. But they wanted to ask two veterans of the First War, so as to give it a more historical dimension, see? But one of them was ill. So they put the veterans' night off for a month, so it's tonight. I can't miss it, it's really so important: one of the veterans is ninety-five but he's absolutely all there. I must meet him. It's a choice between History and the langoustines.'

'Guess it'll have to be History then,' said Marc.

'Of course. I'm off to get changed.'

Lucien gave a final glance full of genuine regret at the kitchen table and went upstairs. Then he left the house at a run, asking Marc to save him a few langoustines for when he got home later that night.

'You'll be too drunk to appreciate this gourmet stuff,' said Marc. But Lucien was out of earshot and running towards 1914–18.

# XXVI

MATHIAS WAS ROUSED FROM SLEEP BY A SERIES OF SHOUTS. JUMPING out of bed, he went to the window. Lucien was standing in the street calling his name and Marc's. He had climbed up onto a big rubbish bin, it wasn't clear why; perhaps he thought his voice would carry better from there, but he looked very precarious. Mathias picked up the broom handle and knocked on the ceiling to wake Marc. Hearing no response, he decided to do without his help and reached Lucien just as the latter was tottering from his perch.

'You're completely pissed,' said Mathias. 'What is it with you, yelling at the top of your voice in the street, at two in the morning?'

'Lost my keys,' said Lucien indistinctly. 'Took them out of my pocket to open the gate and dropped them. Really, I promise you. Just slipped out of my hands. Passing the Eastern Front. Couldn't find them in the dark.'

'You're the one who's lost. Come on in, we'll find them in the morning.'

'Noooo, I want my keys!' Lucien wailed, with the childish petulance and insistence of someone who is seriously drunk.

He escaped Mathias' grip and started fumbling around uncertainly, nose to the ground, in front of Juliette's gate.

Mathias saw Marc, who had woken up in turn and was coming up the path. 'What took you so long?' said Mathias.

'I'm not a caveman,' said Marc. 'I don't jump at the first sound of a wild beast. But do get a move on. Lucien's going to wake the whole neighbourhood, he'll wake Kyril. And Mathias, do you realise you're walking about stark naked? Not that I've anything against it, I'm just telling you.'

'So what?' said Mathias. 'This idiot got me out of bed in the middle of the night.'

'You'll catch your death.'

In fact Mathias felt a warm glow in the small of his back. He couldn't understand why Marc felt the cold so much.

'It's OK,' he said, 'I'm feeling quite warm.'

'Well, I'm not,' said Marc. 'Come on, you take one arm and I'll take the other, and we'll get him indoors.'

'No, no!' cried Lucien. 'I need my keys.'

Mathias sighed and went a few yards along the cobbled street. Perhaps the idiot had dropped them long before he got home. No, there they were, between two cobblestones. Lucien's keys were easy to spot. They were attached to an old lead soldier with red trousers and blue cape. This kind of thing left him cold, but Mathias could see why Lucien was attached to them.

'Found them,' he said. 'OK, now we can go in.'

'There's no need to hold on to me,' said Lucien.

'Just get going,' said Marc, not letting him go. 'We've still got to get you up to the third floor. There's no end to this.'

'Military stupidity and the immensity of the sea are the two things which convey the idea of infinity,' said Mathias.

Lucien stopped short in the middle of the garden. 'Where did you hear that?' he said.

'From a trench newspaper called *Making Progress*,' he said. 'It was in one of your books.'

'I didn't know you read my stuff,' said Lucien.

'It's a good idea to know who you're living with,' said Mathias. 'And meanwhile, let's get cracking. I really am starting to feel cold now.'

'Ah,' said Marc. 'What did I tell you?'

# XXVII

NEXT MORNING AT BREAKFAST, MARC WAS AMAZED TO SEE LUCIEN tucking into the leftover langoustines with his morning coffee.

'You've completely recovered, I see,' he said.

'Not entirely,' said Lucien, pulling a face. 'My head's shot to bits.'

'That should please you,' said Mathias. 'War wound.'

'Ha ha, very funny,' said Lucien. 'These langoustines are excellent, Marc. You must have chosen a good fish shop. Next time take a salmon.'

'What did your veteran have to say?' asked Mathias.

'He was great. I've got a date to see him, week Wednesday. But I can't remember much else about the evening.'

'Shut up,' said Marc, 'I'm listening to the news.'

'Why, what do you expect to hear?'

'About the storm in Brittany. I want to hear what's become of it.'

Marc was fascinated by storms, though he knew that was not very original. At least it gave him something in common with Alexandra. That was better than nothing. She had said she liked the wind. He put on the table his little transistor radio, covered with spots of white paint.

'When we're grown up, we'll get a TV set,' said Lucien.

'Oh, can't you shut up!'

Marc turned up the volume. Lucien was making an appalling din with his langoustine shells.

The morning news bulletin was being read. The French Prime Minister was meeting the German Chancellor. The Bourse was in a gloomy mood.

The storms over Brittany were abating and moving towards Paris, but in less severe form. What a pity, Marc thought. *Agence France Presse* reported the discovery of the body of a man, in the car park of his hotel in Paris. The murdered man was named as Christophe Dompierre, aged forty-three, unmarried, no family, a delegate to the European conference. Was this a political crime? No other details had been released to the press.

Marc grabbed the radio and stared wild-eyed at Mathias.

'What's the matter?' said Lucien.

'Did you hear, it's the man who was here yesterday!' Marc shouted. 'Political crime? No way!'

'You didn't tell me his name,' said Lucien.

Marc was running upstairs four steps at a time. Vandoosler, who had been up some time, was standing at his table reading.

'Someone's killed Dompierre!' Marc said, panting.

Vandoosler turned round slowly. 'Sit down,' he said. 'Tell me about it.'

'I don't know any more than that,' cried Marc, still out of breath. 'It was on the radio. He's been killed, that's all they said. Murdered! They found him in the hotel car park.'

'Oh! the damn fool!' said Vandoosler, banging his fist on the table. 'That's what you get if you try to be the lone ranger. Somebody caught up with the poor fellow. Oh, the damn fool!'

Marc was shaking his head in sorrow. He felt his hands trembling.

'Maybe he was stupid,' he said. 'But he was on to something, we can be sure of that now. You'll have to tell your Leguennec, because the police will never make the link with Sophia Siméonidis if we don't tell them. They'll go looking for some motive in Geneva or whatever.'

'Yes, better tell Leguennec. And we'll get a real bollocking from him, for not having told him yesterday. He'll say that might have avoided this murder, and he could be right.'

Marc groaned. 'But we promised Dompierre not to tell a soul. What else could we have done?'

'I know, I know,' said Vandoosler. 'So let's get our story straight. You didn't go chasing after Dompierre, he came knocking at your door, because you were Relivaux's neighbour. And the only people who knew about his visit were you three. I didn't know anything about it, you didn't tell me. It was only this morning you told me all this. OK?'

'Oh great!' cried Marc. 'You just run along and tell him that. We three will be in the shit and have to be questioned by Leguennec and you'll be in the clear!'

'Come on, young Vandoosler, use your head! As if I care whether I'm in the clear or not. Getting told off by Leguennec leaves me completely cold. All that matters is if he goes on keeping me in his confidence, d'you understand? That's the only way we'll get the information we need.'

Marc nodded. Yes, he did understand. He had a lump in his throat though. 'It leaves me completely cold.' That expression reminded him of something. Yes. Last night, when they were bringing Lucien indoors, Mathias had felt warm, yet he, Marc, with his pyjamas and a sweater, had felt cold. The hunter-gatherer was really extraordinary. But what did that matter now? First Sophia, and now Dompierre had been killed. Who else had Dompierre given his hotel address to? To everyone. To the people in Dourdan, and perhaps other people, and in any case, he might have been followed. Should they tell Leguennec everything. But what about Lucien? Lucien who had been out late last night?

'I'm off,' said Vandoosler. 'I'll tell Leguennec and we'll certainly go to the crime scene. I'll stick close to him and report back what they know afterwards. Pull yourself together, Marc. Was it you making all that racket last night?'

'Yes. Lucien had lost his lead soldier keyring in the street.'

145

# XXVIII

LEGUENNEC WAS DRIVING AT TOP SPEED, ABSOLUTELY FURIOUS, WITH Vandoosler at his side, and his siren sounding so as to be able to shoot red lights and make plain his anger.

'I'm really sorry,' Vandoosler was saying. 'My nephew didn't realise Dompierre's visit might be important, and he didn't bother to tell me about it.'

'Is your nephew a half-wit or what?'

Vandoosler stiffened. He could argue with Marc for hours himself, but he didn't like other people speaking ill of him.

'Can't you switch off that racket?' he asked. 'I can't hear a thing with that blasted noise. Dompierre's dead now, five minutes isn't going to make any difference.'

Without speaking, Leguennec turned off the siren.

'Anyway, he isn't a half-wit,' said Vandoosler crossly. 'And if you were as good at detecting as he is at medieval history, you'd have been promoted out of this district. So listen. Marc did mean to tell you about this yesterday. But he's looking for a job and he had some important interviews. In fact, you're lucky he did open the door to this peculiar character with his odd story, otherwise the police would be looking in Geneva for clues. And the link with this case would never have come out. You ought to be grateful to him. OK, Dompierre got himself killed. But Marc wouldn't have been able to tell you any more about him yesterday than I've told you today, and you certainly wouldn't have put Dompierre under police protection, would you? So nothing would have changed. Slow down! We're there.'

'When we see the *inspecteur* of the 19th *arrondissement*,' said Leguennec grumpily, but less angrily, 'you're one of my colleagues, OK? And you leave things to me? Understood?'

Leguennec flashed his police card to get through the barrier set up across the entrance to the hotel car park, which was simply a dingy little inner courtyard reserved for the hotel's customers. Vernant, the *inspecteur* from the local station, had been told Leguennec was on his way. He was not unhappy to hand the case over, because it was looking decidedly difficult. No woman, inheritance, or political scandal seemed to be involved. Nothing to go on. Leguennec shook hands, introduced his colleague inaudibly and listened to what Vernant, a young man with fair hair, had so far picked up.

'The owner of the Danube called us this morning just before eight. He found the body when he was bringing in the dustbins from the street. It gave him a horrible shock and he's still getting over it. Dompierre had been in the hotel for two nights and had come from Geneva.'

'By way of Dourdan,' Leguennec interrupted. 'OK, go on.'

'He hadn't taken any phone calls or had any mail, except a letter without a stamp put through the hotel letterbox yesterday afternoon. The boss picked it up at five o'clock and put it in Dompierre's pigeon-hole, room 32. Needless to say, we haven't found the letter on him, or in his room. It's pretty obvious that this was the message that lured him out of doors. Presumably it was about a meeting. And the murderer took back his letter. The courtyard is the perfect site for a murder. Apart from the back of the hotel, the other two walls have no windows, and it just gives on to a rat-infested alleyway. What's more, the hotel guests have a key that opens the back door into the yard, because the front door shuts at eleven. It would be easy enough to get Dompierre to come down the service stairs late at night and come out through the back door for a rendezvous between two cars. According to what you tell us, he was after some information and probably didn't suspect anything. He got a savage blow on the head and two stab wounds in the stomach.'

The doctor attending to the body looked up. 'Three,' he said. 'Whoever it was was taking no chances. Poor chap must have died within minutes.'

Vernant pointed to some broken glass spread out on a plastic sheet.

'Dompierre was hit over the head with a small bottle of water,' he said. 'No prints of course.' He shook his head. 'What's it coming to when the dimmest hoodlum knows enough to wear gloves?'

'What was the time of death?' Vandoosler asked quietly.

The police doctor stood up and dusted down his trousers. 'I'd say about eleven-ish last night. I can be more precise after the post-mortem, because the owner knows when Dompierre had dinner. I'll let you know my first conclusions later tonight. It can't have been later than about two o'clock.'

'What kind of knife?' asked Leguennec.

'Probably just an ordinary kitchen knife, quite a big one. The usual sort of weapon.'

Leguennec turned to Vernant.

'And the hotel owner didn't notice anything special about the envelope?'

'No, he says the name was written in biro, and in capitals. Just an ordinary white envelope. Everything's ordinary, nothing remarkable at all.'

'Why did Dompierre choose this downmarket hotel? He didn't seem short of money.'

'The owner says Dompierre used to live in the area when he was a child,' said Vernant. 'He liked coming back here.'

The body had been taken away. Nothing was left except the chalk outline indicating where it had lain.

'Was the back door still open this morning?' Leguennec asked.

'No, it had been shut, probably by an early departing guest who left at about seven-thirty, according to the owner. Dompierre still had his room key in his pocket.'

'And the guest didn't notice anything?'

'No. Even though his car was parked close to the body. But the driver's door was on the other side from the corpse. So his car, which was a big Renault, was between him and it. He must just have driven off forwards, out of the courtyard, without noticing anything.'

'OK,' Leguennec concluded. 'I'll come along with you for the formalities, Vernant. You don't mind passing this case over to me?'

'Not at all,' said Vernant. 'For the moment, the Siméonidis link looks the most promising. So be my guest. If you draw a blank, you can send it back to us.'

Leguennec dropped Vandoosler off at the Métro on the way to the police station.

'I'll be over your way presently,' he said. 'I need to check some alibis. But first I need to contact the ministry to see where Relivaux is. In Toulon, or wherever.'

'Would you like a game of cards tonight,' suggested Vandoosler, 'with your old shipmate?'

'That depends. I'll be along some time anyway. Why haven't you got round to putting in a phone?'

'No money,' said Vandoosler.

It was almost midday. Anxiously, Vandoosler looked for a phone box before taking the Métro. If he waited until he had crossed Paris, it might be too late to find out the answer to his question. He didn't trust Leguennec. He called the number at *Le Tonneau* and got Juliette.

'Hello, it's me, Vandoosler,' he said. 'Is St Matthew there?'

'Have they found anything?' asked Juliette. 'Do they know who did it?'

'If you think they can do that in a couple of hours, my dear. No, it's going to be complicated and perhaps impossible.'

'OK,' sighed Juliette. 'Here's Mathias.'

'St Matthew? Can you keep your voice down when you answer me. Is Alexandra eating there today?'

'It's Wednesday, so Kyril's off school, but she's here with him. She's got into the habit of coming. Juliette makes up nice little dishes for Kyril. Today he's got courgette purée. Yum.'

Under Juliette's maternal influence, Mathias was starting to appreciate good cooking, that was clear. Perhaps, Vandoosler thought passingly, this new interest was distracting him from a rather more attractive prospect, Juliette herself and her fair white shoulders. In his place, Vandoosler would have thrown himself at Juliette rather than at a plate of courgette purée. But Mathias was a complex individual, who calculated his actions and never ventured into open country without long reflection. Each to his own way with women. Vandoosler forced from his mind the idea of Juliette's white shoulders, which gave him a thrill, especially when she leaned across to pick up a glass. It was definitely not the moment for thrills, for him, Mathias or anyone else.

'Was Alexandra there at lunchtime yesterday?'

'Yes.'

'Did you tell her about Dompierre's visit?'

'Yes. I didn't mean to, but she asked me. She was feeling down. So I chatted to her to cheer her up.'

'Don't worry, I'm not blaming you for that. It's sometimes a good thing to let out a bit of rope. Did you tell her where he was staying?'

Mathias thought for a few moments.

'Yes,' he said once more. 'She was afraid he would wait all day for Relivaux in the street. I reassured her and told her Dompierre was staying in the rue de la Prévoyance. I liked the name. I'm sure I said that, and I think I said the Hôtel du Danube too.'

'Why should it bother her if some stranger hung about all day waiting for Relivaux?'

'No idea.'

'Listen carefully, St Matthew. Dompierre was killed between eleven and two, with three stab wounds to the stomach. He had been tricked into meeting someone. It might have been Relivaux, who's off God knows where, as it happens; or it could be to do with Dourdan, or from somewhere else. Can you get away for five minutes, and find Marc? He's waiting for me at home. Tell him what I just told you, and ask him to get up to *Le Tonneau* and ask Lex where she was last night. In a friendly and calm way, if he's capable of that. And he should also discreetly try to ask Juliette if she saw or heard anything. Apparently she's a bad sleeper, so she might have heard something. It must be Marc who asks her, not you, understood?'

'Yes,' said Mathias, without taking offence.

'Your job is to be the waiter, you keep an eye on everyone as you do your rounds and you notice any reactions. And pray to God that Alexandra didn't budge from the house last night. Above all, not a word to Leguennec for now. He said he was going back to the station, but he's quite capable of going round to the garden house or to *Le Tonneau* without me. So be quick.'

Ten minutes later, Marc walked into *Le Tonneau* looking ill at ease. He kissed Juliette, Alexandra, and little Kyril who jumped up into his arms.

'Do you mind if I sit with you to have a bite?'

'Do,' said Alexandra. 'Move up, Kyril, you're taking all the space.'

'You know what's happened?'

Alexandra nodded. 'Mathias told us. And Juliette had heard it on the news. It's that same man, isn't it? There can't be any doubt?'

'No, unfortunately not.'

'It's just ghastly,' said Alexandra. 'He'd have done better to tell us everything that was on his mind. It looks as if they'll never be able to catch whoever killed Aunt Sophia now. And I don't know how I'm going to live with that. How was he killed? Do they know?'

'Knife in the stomach. Not instantaneous, but effective.'

Mathias was watching Alexandra, as he brought over Kyril's plate. She shivered.

'Keep your voice down,' she said gesturing towards Kyril with her chin. 'Please.'

'It must have happened between eleven o'clock and two in the morning. Leguennec is looking for Relivaux. You didn't hear anything, did you? A car perhaps?'

'No, I was asleep. Once I'm asleep, I don't hear a thing. You can check – I've got three alarm clocks on the bedside table to get me up in time to take him to school . . . And anyway . . .'

'Anyway?'

Alexandra hesitated, frowning a little. Marc felt uneasy, but he had his orders.

'Anyway just now, I'm taking stuff to help me sleep. So as not to lie awake thinking. So I've been sleeping more heavily than usual.'

Marc nodded. Reassured. Even if he did think Alexandra had rather overdone the explanation of her sleeping habits.

'But why are they going after Pierre?' Alexandra was saying. 'That's impossible. How could he have known that Dompierre came to see him?'

'Dompierre might have reached him by phone via the ministry. Don't forget he was on official business too. He seemed determined, you know. And in a hurry.'

'But Pierre's in Toulon.'

'There's such a thing as an aeroplane,' said Marc. 'There and back, quickly. Anything's possible.'

'I see,' said Alexandra. 'But they're really on the wrong track. Pierre would never have hurt a hair of Sophia's head.'

'He did have a mistress, though, and it had been going on some time.'

Her face darkened. Marc regretted his last remark. He had no time to think of anything intelligent to follow it with, because Leguennec walked into the restaurant. The godfather had been right. Leguennec had tried to pull a fast one on him. The *inspecteur* came up to their table.

'If you've finished your lunch, Mademoiselle Haufman, and if you could leave your son with one of your friends for an hour or so, I'd be glad if you would come with me. I have a few more questions I'm obliged to ask you.'

The bastard. Marc did not look at Leguennec. Still, he was simply doing his job, just as Marc had been a few minutes earlier.

Alexandra did not look troubled and Mathias confirmed with a nod that he would look after Kyril. She went out with the *inspecteur* and got into his car. His appetite gone, Marc pushed away his plate and went to the bar. He asked Juliette to serve him a large glass of beer.

'Don't worry,' she said. 'He won't be able to accuse her of anything. Alexandra didn't go out all night.'

'I know,' said Marc with a sigh. 'That's what she says. But he won't believe her. From the start he hasn't believed a word she's said.'

'That's his job,' said Juliette. 'But I can tell you she didn't move. That's the truth and I can tell him so.'

Marc grabbed her hand.

'Tell me, how do you know?'

'I could see,' smiled Juliette. 'At eleven o'clock, I finished my book and put out the light. But I couldn't sleep. I often can't. Sometimes I hear Georges snoring upstairs and that keeps me awake. But last night there wasn't even any snoring. So I went downstairs to get another book, and stayed down there reading until about half-past two. Then I thought I really ought to try and get some sleep. So I went back up and forced myself to take a pill and went off to sleep. But what I can tell you, Marc, is that between eleven o'clock and about half-past two, Alexandra didn't go out. There wasn't any sound of noise or cars. When she goes out at night, she takes the little boy with her. I don't like her doing that. Anyway last night Kyril's little nightlight was on. He's afraid of the dark, like any child.'

Marc felt all his hopes evaporate. He looked at Juliette, aghast.

'What's the matter?' said Juliette. 'You ought to be happy. Lex is out of trouble.'

Marc shook his head. Looking round the restaurant which was starting to fill up, he moved closer to Juliette.

'You're sure that at about two in the morning you heard absolutely nothing,' he whispered.

'I just told you,' said Juliette. 'So you've no need to worry.'

Marc drank off half the glass of beer and buried his face in his hands.

'Juliette,' he said softly. 'You're very kind.'

Juliette looked at him, puzzled.

'But you're lying,' Marc went on. 'You've just told me a pack of lies.'

'Keep your voice down!' Juliette told him. 'You don't believe me! Why not, for heaven's sake!'

Marc gripped Juliette's hand even more tightly and saw that Mathias was looking across at him.

'Listen, Juliette: you did see Alexandra go out last night and you know she's lying to us. So you're lying in turn to protect her. You may be trying to be kind, but you've just told me the opposite of what you wanted me to think. Because at two this morning, *I* was outside in the street myself. And I was in front of your gate, with Mathias, trying to get Lucien back in the house, he was drunk. And you were fast asleep with your sleeping pill, so you didn't hear the racket he was making? You must have been fast asleep. And you've made me remember, now that I think of it, that there wasn't a light in Kyril's window. None at all. Ask Mathias.'

Juliette's face fell. She turned to Mathias who nodded. Slowly.

'So, please tell me the truth now,' said Marc. 'It'll be better for Lex in the end if we're going to protect her intelligently. Because your little plan won't work. You're too naïve, you think the police are stupid.'

'Stop gripping my hand like that!' said Juliette. 'You're hurting me. The customers will see.'

'Come on, Juliette.'

Silently, her head bent, Juliette went back to washing glasses in the sink.

'All we have to do is agree our story,' she said suddenly. 'You didn't go out to fetch Lucien, and I didn't hear anything, and Lex didn't go out. Full stop.'

Marc shook his head. 'Lucien was shouting like crazy, any neighbour could have heard him. It won't work and it'll only make things worse. Tell me the truth, it will be for the best. After that we'll see how economical we need to be with the truth.'

Juliette remained undecided, twisting the tea towel in her hands. Mathias went over to her, put his big hand on her shoulder and whispered in her ear.

'Alright,' said Juliette. 'I went about it the wrong way. But how was I to know you were outside at two in the morning? Alexandra did go out in her car. She went out very quietly without putting on her lights, probably so as not to wake Kyril.'

'What time was it?' asked Marc, his throat dry.

'Quarter-past eleven. When I went down to fetch a book. That bit is true. I felt a bit cross seeing her go off, if you must know, because of the boy. Whether she'd taken him or left him behind on his own, it still upset me. I said to myself that I must pluck up courage to say something to her about it next day, though it isn't my business. The nightlight wasn't on, it's true. And no, I didn't stay downstairs reading. I went back up and took a sleeping pill, because I was upset. I went off to sleep straight-away. Then when I heard the news this morning at ten, I panicked. I heard Lex telling you just now that she hadn't left the house. So I thought the best thing to do would be . . .'

'To back her up?'

Juliette nodded sadly. 'I'd have done better to keep quiet,' she said.

'Don't reproach yourself,' Marc said. 'The police would have found out sooner or later. Because Alexandra didn't park her car in the same place when she got back. Now that I know, I remember that last night before supper, Sophia's car was parked a few yards up from your gate. I went past it – it's red, you notice it. This morning when I went to get the paper at about half-past ten, it wasn't there. The space was taken by a grey car, I think it belongs to the people up the road. Alexandra must have found the space taken when she got back, so she had to park some-where else. That'll be child's play for the police. This is a small street, everyone knows the cars, and other neighbours would probably notice that kind of thing.'

'That doesn't mean anything,' said Juliette. 'She might have gone out again this morning.'

'Well, they'll check that too.'

'But if she really had done what Leguennec suspects, she would have made sure to park it in the same place.'

'Juliette, don't be silly. How could she do that if someone else had parked there? She couldn't magic it away.'

'No, I'm sorry, I don't know what I'm saying. My head's all over the place. All the same, Marc, Lex did go out, but she was just going for a drive, that's all it was!'

'I think that too,' said Marc. 'But how do you think we can get that into Leguennec's head? What a night to choose to go for a drive. After all the fuss that's already caused, you'd think she'd stay put.'

'Keep your voice down,' said Juliette.

'Well, I'm getting bloody angry,' said Marc. 'Anyone would think she's doing it on purpose.'

'How was she to know Dompierre would be killed? Put yourself in her place.'

'In her place, I wouldn't have stirred from the house. She's really in a tight spot now, Juliette.' Marc banged his fist on the counter and finished his beer.

'What can we do?' asked Juliette.

'I'm going to Dourdan to see what's to be done there. I'm going to look for whatever Dompierre was after. Leguennec can't stop me. Siméonidis is free to let anyone see his archives if he wants to. The police can check that I haven't taken anything. Have you got her father's address?'

'No, but anyone will tell you over there. Sophia had a little house in the same street. She bought it so she could visit her father, without having to stay under the same roof as her stepmother. They didn't get on. It's a little way out of the town centre, rue des Ifs. Wait, and I'll go and check.'

Mathias came over, when Juliette went into the kitchen to get her handbag.

'Are you off now?' said Mathias. 'D'you want me to come with you? It might be wise. Things are hotting up.'

Marc smiled at him. 'Thanks, Mathias. But I think you'd better stay here. Juliette needs you and so does Lex. And anyway you've got the little Greek to look after and you're very good at that. It makes me calmer to know you're here. Don't worry, there's nothing to be afraid of. If I need to contact you, I'll telephone here or to Juliette's house. Tell the god-father when he comes.'

Juliette came back with her address book. 'The street is the allée des Grands-Ifs. Sophia's house is number 12. The old man's is somewhere nearby.'

'OK, got it. If Leguennec asks, you went to sleep at eleven and didn't hear a thing. He'll work it out for himself.'

'Of course,' said Juliette.

'Tell your brother to say the same, just in case. I'm just looking in at our house then I'm off to get the train.'

A sudden gust of wind blew open a window that had not been closed properly. The storm was arriving, apparently a fiercer one than the *météo* had forecast. It seemed to invigorate Marc, who jumped down from his stool and hurried out.

Back home, he quickly packed a few things. He didn't know how long he'd be away, or if he would find anything. But he had to try and do something. That fool Alexandra could think of nothing better to do than go driving round at night again. The fucking idiot, how stupid could you get? Marc cursed as he threw a few things into his rucksack. He was trying to convince himself that Alexandra had indeed just been driving around. And that she had lied to him simply to protect herself. That was it, there couldn't be anything else behind it. It took a lot of concentration. He didn't hear Lucien coming in behind him.

'Are you packing?' asked Lucien. 'You're making a terrible mess of it. Look at your shirt!'

Marc glanced up at Lucien. Of course, there were no classes on Wednesday afternoons.

'Bugger the shirt,' he said. 'Alexandra is in deep trouble. She went out last night, like a complete idiot. I'm off to Dourdan. I'm going to search in the Siméonidis archives. At least they won't be in Latin or Old French, that'll make a change. I'm used to looking through papers quickly, perhaps I'll find something.'

'I'm coming with you,' said Lucien. 'I don't want you ending up with a knife in the guts too. Let's stick together, soldier.'

Marc stopped stuffing things into the rucksack and looked at Lucien. First Mathias, now him. Coming from Mathias, he understood it and was touched. But Marc had never believed that Lucien was interested in anything except himself and the Great War. Interested, and committed even. Well, perhaps he had been mistaken about a lot of things lately.

'Do you mind?' said Lucien. 'You look surprised.'

'I was thinking of something else.'

'I can guess what you were thinking. But forget it, it's better to work in pairs. Vandoosler and Mathias here, you and me over there. Wars don't get won single-handedly, look what happened to Dompierre. So, I'm coming with you. I'm used to archives too, and we'll be quicker if there are two of us. Let me just pack a bag and let the school know I've got another dose of flu.'

'OK,' said Marc, 'but hurry. The next train's at 14.57 from the Gare d'Austerlitz.'

# XXIX

JUST UNDER TWO HOURS LATER, MARC AND LUCIEN WERE PROSPECTING the allée des Grands-Ifs. A gale was blowing in Dourdan and Marc took deep breaths of the north-westerly. They stopped in front of number 12, which was surrounded by protective walls either side of a high wooden door.

'Give me a leg-up,' Marc said. 'I'd like to take a look at Sophia's place.'

'What's the point?' Lucien asked.

'Just curious.'

Lucien put his bag down carefully, checked that nobody was around in the street and linked his hands.

'Take your shoe off,' he told Marc. 'I don't want muck on my hands.'

Marc sighed, pulled off one shoe and, holding on to Lucien, climbed up to peer over the wall.

'Can you see anything?' Lucien asked.

'There's always something to see.'

'Well, what?'

'It's a big place. Sophia was very rich, of course. The garden goes down in a slope behind the house.'

'What's the house like? Ugly, I guess?'

'No, not at all,' Marc replied. 'It looks a bit Greek, but with a tiled roof. It's long and white, single-storey. She must have had it built. That's odd, the shutters aren't even closed. Wait, no, there are wrought-iron bars on the windows. That's Greek too. There's a garage and a well. It's all modern, the only thing that's old is the well. Nice place in summer.'

'Can you come down?'

'Why? Are you getting tired?'

'No. But someone might come.'

'Yes, you're right, I'll come down.'

Marc put his shoe back on and they walked along the street noting the names on doors or letterboxes, when there were any. They preferred not to ask anyone, so as to be as discreet as possible.

'There,' said Lucien, after about a hundred yards. 'That smart little house with flowers round it.'

Marc made out the name on a tarnished brass plate: K. and J. Siméonidis. 'Right,' he said. 'Remember what we agreed.'

'I'm not stupid,' said Lucien.

'OK, OK.'

A rather fine-looking elderly man opened the door. He looked at them without speaking, waiting for an explanation. Since his daughter's death, he had had to open the door to many people: police, journalists, Dompierre.

Lucien and Marc took it in turns to explain the reason for their visit, trying to put it as kindly as possible. They had agreed on this in the train, but the great sadness on Siméonidis' face made it come naturally. They spoke very gently of Sophia. By the time they had finished, they almost believed their story, which was that Sophia, as their neighbour, had entrusted them with a personal mission. Marc told the story of the tree. It's always best to have an element of truth in a made-up story. After the tree incident, Sophia had still been anxious. One evening when chatting to them in the street, she had made them promise that if anything happened to her, they would try to find out what had happened. She was not confident in the police, because they have so many missing persons. But she would trust them not to give up. That was why they were there, out of respect and friendship for Sophia, and feeling they should carry out her wishes.

Siméonidis listened attentively to this story, which started to sound more and more clumsy to Marc as they went on with it. He invited them in. A uniformed policeman was in the sitting-room, asking questions of a woman who must be the second Madame Siméonidis. Marc did not dare to look hard at her, especially since their entrance had interrupted the session. He noted out of the corner of his eye a woman of about sixty, rather plump, with her hair in a chignon, who only made the vaguest of greetings towards them. She was concentrating on the policeman's questions and had that energetic look of people who wish to be considered energetic. Siméonidis crossed the room briskly, taking Marc and Lucien with him and being deliberately careless of the policeman who was occupying his sitting-room. But the policeman brought all three of them up short, jumping to his feet. He was young, with that obstinate, closed look, typical of the worst kind of short-sighted idiot who obeys orders without thinking. They were out of luck. Lucien sighed in an exaggerated way.

'I'm sorry, M. Siméonidis,' said the policeman, 'but I can't allow you to let any persons into your property without telling me their names and addresses and the reason for their visit. Those are orders and you've been told about them.'

Siméonidis gave a fleeting malicious smile. 'This isn't my property, it's my house,' he said in a resounding voice, 'and these are not persons, they are my friends. And let me tell you that a Greek born in Delphi, half a mile from the Oracle, doesn't take orders from anyone. So put that in your pipe and smoke it.'

'Nobody is above the law, monsieur,' replied the policeman.

'You know where you can put your law,' said Siméonidis evenly.

Lucien was delighted. Exactly the kind of cussed old bugger with whom they could have had a good laugh, if only circumstances hadn't left him so unhappy.

The palaver went on for a few more minutes, while the policeman took down their names and quickly identified them from his notebook as neighbours of Sophia's. But since there was no rule to stop them going to look at someone's papers, if he was prepared to give them permission, he had to let them pass, not without informing them that he would have to search them when they left. No document was to be taken out of the house for the time being. Lucien shrugged and followed Siméonidis.

Suddenly, in a moment of fury, the old Greek turned back and gripped the *flic* by his lapels. Marc thought he was going to punch him, and that that would be interesting, but the old man hesitated.

'No,' said Siméonidis after a moment. 'It's not worth it.'

Letting go of the policeman, as if he were some grubby object, he left the room to join Marc and Lucien. They went upstairs, along a corridor, and the old man used a key hanging from his belt to unlock the door to a poorly lit room, with bookshelves full of files.

'Sophia's room,' he said quietly. 'I presume that's what interests you?'

Marc and Lucien nodded.

'Do you think you're going to find anything?' asked Siméonidis. 'You really think so?'

He was looking at them intently, with pursed lips and sadness in his eyes.

'What if we don't?' asked Lucien.

Siméonidis banged his fist on the table. 'You'd better find something!' he ordered. 'I'm eighty-one years old, I can't get about as well as I could, and I can't always get the hang of things these days either. You might be able to. I want this killer caught. We Greeks never give up, that's what my dear old Andromache used to say. Leguennec is blinkered by his job. I need someone else to work on it, someone with an open mind. I don't care whether or not Sophia really asked you to carry out any "mission". Whether that's true or false – I think maybe it's false?'

'Well, yes, it's not quite true,' Lucien admitted.

'That's better,' said Siméonidis. 'Now we know where we stand. But why have you come poking about?'

'It's our job,' said Lucien.

'Why, are you detectives?' said Siméonidis.

'No, historians,' said Lucien.

'I don't see what that has to do with Sophia.'

Lucien gestured towards Marc. 'It's because of him. He doesn't want your granddaughter Alexandra Haufman to be charged with this murder. He's prepared to point the finger at anyone else, even an innocent party, rather than at her.'

'Excellent,' said Siméonidis. 'If it helps, Dompierre didn't stay long. I think he only looked at one file, and he knew exactly where to go. You can see, the files are arranged by year.'

'Do you know which one he looked at?' asked Marc. 'Did you stay in the room with him?'

'No, he was anxious to be left alone. I brought him a cup of coffee. I think he was looking around the year 1982, but I'm not sure. I'll leave you. You haven't much time to lose.'

'One more thing,' said Marc. 'How has your wife taken all this business?'

'Jacqueline didn't shed any tears. It's not that she's hard-hearted, but she always wants to "face up to things". "Facing up to things" for her is a great sign of character. And it's become such a habit with her, you can't get round it. Above all, she's concerned to protect her son.'

'And what about him?'

'Julien? He's not up to much. A murder would be way beyond him. Especially since Sophia was kind to him and helped him when he didn't know what to do with himself. She got him a few walk-on parts. He never made anything of them. He did shed a few tears over Sophia. He used to like her a lot back then. He had photos of her in his room when he was younger and used to listen to her records. But not these days.' Siméonidis was getting tired. 'I'll leave you,' he said again. 'A little siesta before dinner is no disgrace at my age. And my wife rather likes to see me give in to it. Go on, you don't have much time. It's quite possible that flatfoot downstairs will find some way to stop me letting anyone consult my archives.'

He went away and they heard him open a door further along the corridor.

'What d'you think of him?' asked Marc.

'He's got a good voice, must have passed it on to his daughter. He's argumentative, bossy, intelligent, entertaining and dangerous.'

'And his wife?'

'Just a stupid woman,' said Lucien.

'You're ruling her out pretty quickly.'

'Stupid people can kill, there's no rule against it. Especially people like her, putting on some kind of silly show of being strong. I was listening to her when she was talking to the policeman. She's so sure of everything she says, and she's very pleased with her own performance. Self-satisfied idiots are quite capable of killing.'

Marc nodded and walked round the room. He came to a box-file labelled 1982, looked at it without touching, and went on examining the shelves.

Lucien was fumbling inside his bag. 'Get down the box for 1982,' he said. 'The old man's right. Maybe we don't have much time before the law puts a stop to us.'

'It wasn't 1982 that Dompierre consulted. Either the old man made a mistake, or else he wasn't telling the truth. It was 1978.'

'The dust has been disturbed in front of that one, is that it?' asked Lucien.

'Yes. None of the others has been moved for ages. The *flics* haven't had time to come nosing round here.'

He took down the file for 1978 and carefully spread the contents onto the table. Lucien leafed through it quickly.

'It's all about one opera,' he said. '"Elektra", in Toulouse. Doesn't mean anything to us. But Dompierre must have been looking for something there.'

'Let's get on with it, then,' said Marc, who was a little discouraged by the mass of old newpaper cuttings, some with handwritten commentaries probably by Siméonidis, photographs and interviews. The press cuttings were carefully held together with paperclips.

'Look for any paperclips that have been moved,' said Lucien. 'This room's a bit damp. They've probably left rust-marks. It might help us see which articles Dompierre looked at in this pile.'

'Yes, that's what I'm doing,' said Marc. 'These reviews are all favourable. Sophia was good. She said she was only so-so, but she was better than that. Mathias was right. What are you doing, come on, help me!'

Lucien was putting something back into his bag.

'Look,' said Marc, raising his voice. 'Five bundles where the paperclips have been moved.'

He took three and Lucien took two. They read quickly and silently for a while. The articles were long.

'Did you say all the reviews were good?' said Lucien. 'Here's one that isn't very kind to Sophia.'

'I've got one too,' said Marc. 'He's really nasty. That won't have pleased her – or her father. He's written in the margin "stupid bastard". Wonder who the stupid bastard was.'

Marc looked for the signature. 'Hey, Lucien,' he said, 'the "stupid bastard" critic, he's called Daniel Dompierre. What d'you make of that!'

Lucien picked up the review. 'So, our Dompierre, who's dead, must have been some relation? Nephew, cousin, even son perhaps? Was that why he knew something about this opera?'

'Something like that, I suppose. We're getting warm. What's the name of your reviewer who didn't like Sophia?'

'René de Frémonville. Doesn't ring any bells. But I don't know anything about music anyway. Oh, wait, this is really something!'

Lucien started reading again, with a changed expression. Marc looked hopeful.

'Well?' he asked.

'No, don't get excited, it's nothing to do with Sophia. It's on the back of the review. Another article by Frémonville, but about a play, a real flop, a totally incoherent piece about the inner life of a guy in the trenches in 1917. A monologue nearly two hours long and boring as hell, it seems. Bother, the end of the article's missing.'

'Oh, for fuck's sake, Lucien, don't start doing this to me. We didn't come all the way to Dourdan to read about that stuff, d'you hear me.'

'No, shut up, listen. Frémonville says here that he's kept his own father's war diaries and that the author of the play would have done better to consult some real documents, instead of making up imaginary stuff. Do you realise what this means? Authentic diaries, written at the time from August 1914 to October 1918, seven notebooks! My God, it's fantastic. A whole series. Oh, if only the father was a peasant, please let him be. It would be a goldmine, Marc, it's so rare. Oh, please God, let Frémonville's father be a peasant. Oh, wow, what a good thing I came with you!'

Elated and hopeful, Lucien had got to his feet and was walking round the dark cramped room, reading and rereading the torn piece of old newspaper. Exasperated, Marc went back to the documents Dompierre had consulted. Apart from all the favourable reviews, there were three bundles containing more gossipy pieces about a serious incident which had affected the performances of 'Elektra' for several days.

'Listen,' said Marc.

But it was pointless. Lucien was completely oblivious, unreachable, so full of his discovery and unable to think of anything else. And yet he had been equally full of goodwill to start with. What bad luck that he'd found that reference to the war diaries. Marc sat down crossly and read to himself what had happened. Sophia Siméonidis had been in her dressing-room on the night of June 17, 1978, an hour and a half before the performance, when she had been attacked and an attempt had been made at a sexual assault. According to her, the attacker had fled on hearing a noise. She could not provide a description. He had been wearing a dark jacket, a blue woollen balaclava, and had punched her, forcing her to the ground. He had taken off the balaclava, but she was too dazed to be able to identify him and he had turned off the light. Sophia Siméonidis, badly bruised and in a state of shock but not seriously injured, had been taken to the hospital for observation. In spite of that, she had refused to lodge a formal complaint, and there had been no police enquiry. Reduced to conjecture, the press had supposed that the attack had been by someone from the chorus, since the theatre was closed to the public at that hour. The five principal singers had immediately been ruled out. Two of them were well known, and all of them had arrived at the theatre later, as had been confirmed by the janitors, who were elderly men and also not suspects. Reading between the lines, it was also clear that the sexual preferences of the five male singers eliminated them more certainly than their renown or their time of arrival. As for the many members of the cast with walk-on parts, since Sophia had not been able to provide a clear description, nothing in particular pointed to any one person. Nevertheless, reported one journalist, two of them had not reported for work next day. But he admitted that this was not unusual in the world of part-timers, where extras were paid daily rates and might disappear now and again for an audition somewhere else. And he also granted that the technicians could not be ruled out.

The number of possible suspects was large. Marc frowned and returned to the reviews written by Daniel Dompierre and René de Frémonville. They were both music critics and did not go into details about the attack, but did report that Sophia Siméonidis, who had been the victim of an incident, was replaced for three days by the understudy, Nathalie Domesco, whose dreadful imitation had really finished off the production. The show was not rescued by Sophia's return: the singer, once out of hospital, had yet again demonstrated her inability to sing this great dramatic soprano role. They concluded that the interruption could not excuse the inadequacy of her technical performance and that she had indeed been most unwise to tackle the demanding role of Elektra in the first place, because it was beyond her vocal talents.

Marc felt exasperated. Sophia had told them herself that she was no Callas. Maybe she should not have attempted Elektra. Maybe. He knew no more about music than Lucien. But the devastating hostility of these two critics infuriated him. No, Sophia had not deserved this. Marc pulled down a few more box-files and looked through other operas. The critics were generally favourable, or flattering, or satisfied, but there was invariably a hostile and barbed review from both Dompierre and Frémonville, even when Sophia stayed within the repertoire of a lyric soprano. These two had really had it in for Sophia, from the very beginning. Marc put the boxes back and thought, his head in his hands. It was almost dark and Lucien had lit the two desk-lamps.

Sophia had been attacked. She had not made a formal complaint, despite suffering grievous bodily harm. He returned to 'Elektra' and leafed through all the other articles on the opera, which all said more or less the same thing: the staging was mediocre, the sets were unimpressive, Sophia had been attacked, she was expected back, with the difference that the other reviewers all appreciated Sophia's performance, compared to the demolition jobs by Dompierre and Frémonville. He really did not know what to make of the 1978 file. Perhaps he ought to compare and check over the reviews which Christophe Dompierre had singled out.

But that would mean transcribing each one. At least those which Dompierre appeared to have read. It would mean hours and hours of work.

Just then, Siméonidis came back into the room.

'You're going to have to hurry up,' he said. 'The police are looking for some way of stopping me opening my archives to people. They haven't got time to look at them themselves, and they're afraid of being beaten to it by the murderer. I heard that idiot downstairs telephoning while I was taking my siesta. He wants seals put on the room. It sounds as if he's getting his way.'

'Don't worry,' said Lucien. 'We'll be finished in another half-hour.'

'Good. Are you making progress?'

'Can I ask you something?' said Marc. 'Did your stepson have a part in "Elektra"?'

'The Toulouse production? I think so,' said Siméonidis. 'He was in all her shows between 1973 and 1978. It was later that he gave up. But don't waste time on him, it's not worth it.'

'When Sophia was attacked that time, during "Elektra" did she say anything to you?'

'Sophia didn't like talking about that,' said Siméonidis after a silence.

When the old Greek had gone downstairs again, Marc looked at Lucien, who had flopped into a battered armchair with his legs stretched out in front of him, fiddling with his press cutting.

'Half an hour?' he cried. 'You're doing bugger all, you're dreaming of your war diaries, there are masses of things to copy out, and you think you'll be away in half an hour?'

Without stirring, Lucien pointed to his rucksack. 'In my bag,' he said, 'I have two-and-a-half kilos worth of laptop, nine kilos of scanner, some aftershave, spare underclothes, heavy-duty string, a duvet, a toothbrush and a baguette. Now do you see why I wanted to take a taxi from the station? Get your documents ready, I'll scan anything you like, and we can take them back to the house with us. See.'

'How did you manage to think of all that?'

'After what happened to Dompierre, it was foreseeable that the *flics* would want to stop anyone else copying the archives. To anticipate the actions of the enemy, my friend, is the secret of successful warfare. The official order will come soon, but we'll be out of here. So get a move on.'

'I'm sorry,' said Marc. 'I'm very jumpy just now. So are you, in point of fact.'

'No, I get carried away, in one direction or another. It's not the same.'

'Is all that stuff yours?' asked Marc. 'Is it valuable?'

Lucien shrugged. 'It's on loan from the university. I've got to give it back in four months. Only the cables belong to me.'

He laughed and switched on the machines. As they copied the documents, Marc started to breathe more easily. Perhaps there wouldn't be anything to find in them, but the idea that he could consult them at his leisure, in his medieval study on the second floor was comforting. They copied most of what was in the file.

'Copy the photos,' said Lucien with a wave of his hand.

'Do you think so?'

'Yes, send them through.'

'They're all just of Sophia.'

'No general view of the company on parade, or after their dress rehearsal?'

'No. Just Sophia. I told you.'

'OK, we won't bother.'

Lucien wrapped his machines in the old duvet, and tied it all up firmly with string, leaving one long end. Then he opened the window and lowered the fragile bundle carefully to the ground.

'Every room has an outlet,' he said, 'and where there's an outlet there must be some kind of surface underneath. This one is the yard with the dustbins in, which is better than the street. It's reached the ground now.'

'Someone's coming up,' said Marc.

Lucien let go of the string and closed the window without a sound. He returned to his armchair and took up his nonchalant pose once more.

The policeman came in with the satisfied air of one who has just shot a brace of pheasants.

'It's forbidden to make copies of anything or to consult any of these papers,' said the policeman. 'New orders. Bring your things and leave this room.'

Marc and Lucien obeyed, grumbling, and followed him. When they went into the sitting-room, Mme Siméonidis had laid the table for five. So they were expected to stay for dinner. Five, thought Marc, the stepson must be coming too. It would be good to set eyes on him.

They expressed their thanks. The young policeman frisked them before they sat down, and emptied the contents of their bags, which he turned inside out and examined every which way.

'Alright,' he said. 'You can pack it all up again.'

He left the room and went to station himself in the hall.

'If I were you,' said Lucien, 'I would stand in front of the door to the archives until we leave. We might go back up again. Aren't you taking a bit of a risk, officer?'

Looking annoyed, the policeman went upstairs and posted himself right inside the archive room. Lucien asked Siméonidis to show him the way to the yard with the dustbins and retrieved the bundle, which he stuffed back inside the rucksack. Dustbins seemed to be looming large in his life just now.

'Don't worry,' he said to his host. 'All your originals are still up there, I give you my word.'

The son arrived rather late to take his place at the table. A slow-moving, plump forty-year-old, Julien had not inherited his mother's anxiety to appear indispensable and efficient. He smiled nicely at the two guests, but looked unprepossessing and indeed rather pathetic. This seemed a pity to Marc. He felt sorry for this so-called useless and indecisive character, stuck between his busy-busy mother and his patriarchal stepfather. Marc was easily impressed when people smiled nicely at him. And after all, Julien had cried when he heard about Sophia. He was not ugly, but his face was rather puffy. Marc would have preferred to feel distaste or hostility for him, or at least some more convincing emotion, to turn him into a murderer. But since he had never seen any murderers, he told himself that a malleable person, dominated by his mother and smiling sweetly, might very well be the type. Shedding a few tears was neither here nor there.

The mother might also be the type. She was fussing about, far more than was necessary to serve the meal, and was more talkative than necessary trying to make conversation. Jacqueline Siméonidis was tiring. Marc took in her neat chignon, her busy hands, her artificial voice and manner, her stupid insistence as she served everyone with their chicory and ham, and thought that this woman might stop at nothing to acquire more power, and more capital to help resolve her son's precarious finances. She had married Siméonidis – out of love? Because he was the father of a famous singer? Because that would help Julien get on in the theatre? Yes, either one of them might have a motive for killing, and possibly a good opportunity. Not the old man though. Marc watched him cutting up his food with firm gestures. His authoritarian ways would have made him a perfect tyrant, if Jacqueline had not been well able to defend herself. But the patent distress of Sophia's father ruled out any suspicion they might have. Everyone could agree on that.

Marc hated ham and chicory unless it was very well cooked, which was not often the case. He watched Lucien wolf it down, while he toyed with the bitter slimy vegetables that nauseated him. Lucien had taken a leading role in the conversation, which was now turning to Greece in the early twentieth century. Siméonidis was replying with short answers, and Jacqueline was showing an exaggerated interest in everything.


Marc and Lucien caught the 22.27 train home. Siméonidis took them to the station, driving fast and competently.

'Keep me informed,' he said as he shook their hands. 'What's that in your bundle, young man?' he asked Lucien.

'A computer with all we need on it,' said Lucien, smiling.

'Well done,' said the old man.

'By the way,' Marc said. 'It was the file for 1978 that Dompierre looked at, not 1982. I thought I should let you know, in case you find something we missed.'

Marc watched the old man for a reaction. It was offensive of him, a father doesn't kill his daughter, unless he's Agamemnon.

Siméonidis did not respond. 'Keep me informed,' was all he said.

The journey back took an hour, during which neither Marc nor Lucien spoke. Marc was thinking that he liked being in a train late at night, and Lucien was thinking about the war diaries of Frémonville senior, and how he might get hold of them.

# XXX

GETTING BACK TO THE HOUSE AT ABOUT MIDNIGHT, MARC AND LUCIEN
found Vandoosler waiting for them in the refectory. Exhausted and incapable of classifying the data he had collected, Marc hoped the godfather
was not going to keep them up too long. Because it was obvious he was
expecting a report. Lucien, on the other hand, was in fine form. He had
carefully unloaded his rucksack, with its twelve kilos of equipment, and
poured himself a drink. He asked where the Paris phone books were.

'In the basement,' said Marc. 'Be careful, they're holding up the
workbench.'

They heard a crash from the basement and Lucien appeared, looking
delighted, with a directory under each arm.

'Terribly sorry,' he said. 'Everything collapsed.'

He settled down with his drink at the end of the large table and started
going through the phone book.

'There can't be all that many René de Frémonvilles,' he said. 'And with
a bit of luck, he lives in Paris. That would make sense, if he's a theatre
and music critic.'

'What are you two looking for?' asked Vandoosler.

'It's just him that's looking, not me,' said Marc. 'He wants to find a
theatre critic whose father kept a lot of diaries during the Great War.
He's completely obsessed. He's praying to all the gods past and present
that the father was a peasant. It seems this would make it very rare. He
was praying all the way back in the train.'

'Can't it wait?' asked Vandoosler.

'You know perfectly well,' said Marc, 'that for Lucien nothing to do with the Great War can wait. You wonder sometimes if he knows it's over. Anyway he's been in this state since this afternoon. I've had it up to here with his bloody war. He only likes violent action. Are you listening, Lucien? It's not history, it's sensationalism.'

'My friend,' said Lucien without looking up, as his finger ran down the columns of the directory, 'investigation of the paroxysms of human activity obliges us to come face to face with the essentials that are usually hidden.'

Marc, who was a serious person, took in this statement. It quite rattled him. He wondered whether his own preference for working on the everyday aspects of medieval history, rather than on its most sensational moments, was blinding him to the hidden essentials. He had always thought hitherto that little things were revealed in big things and vice versa, in history as in life. He had started to think about religious crises and devastating epidemics from another perspective, when his godfather interrupted his train of thought.

'Your historical reflections can wait too,' said Vandoosler. 'Did you or did you not find anything at Dourdan?'

Marc jumped. He came back across nine centuries and sat down in front of Vandoosler, visibly somewhat stunned by the time-travel. 'What about Alexandra? How did the questioning go?'

'As well as it could do, of a woman who wasn't home at the time of the murder.'

'So Leguennec knows?'

'Yes. The red car wasn't parked in the same place this morning. Alexandra had to withdraw her first statement, and got a serious talking-to. Then she admitted that she had been out between eleven last night and three in the morning. More than three hours, quite a spin, eh?'

'That's bad,' said Marc. 'And where did she go?'

'Out along the motorway towards Arras, according to her. She swears she went nowhere near rue de la Prévoyance. But since she had already been caught out in a lie . . . They've narrowed down the time of the murder. Between half-past twelve and two o'clock. Right bang in the middle of the time she was out.'

'Oh God, that's bad,' Marc repeated.

'Very bad. It wouldn't take more than a smidgeon now to make Leguennec wrap up the investigation and send his conclusions to the examining magistrate.'

'Well, take care he doesn't get his hands on that smidgeon.'

'You don't have to tell me. I'm holding him back by his braces as it is. But it's getting difficult. So, have you come up with anything?'

'It's all on Lucien's laptop,' said Marc, indicating the rucksack. 'He scanned a whole lot of papers.'

'Good thinking,' said Vandoosler. 'What papers would those be?'

'Dompierre consulted the file on a production of Strauss' "Elektra" in 1978. I'll fill you in on it. There are some interesting aspects.'

'Got it!' said Lucien, closing the directory with a bang. 'R. de Frémonville is listed. Not ex-directory. That's a stroke of luck. Victory in sight.'

Marc carried on with his explanations, which took longer than expected, because Vandoosler kept interrupting him. Lucien had had another drink and gone to bed.

'So,' Marc finished, 'the most urgent thing is to find out whether Christophe Dompierre was related to this critic, Daniel Dompierre, and if so how. You can do that, first thing tomorrow. If he was, the answer might be that the critic had found out something unsavoury about this production, and told his family about it. But what? The only thing out of the ordinary was the attack on Sophia. We need to check the names of the bit players who didn't turn up for work next day. But that's virtually impossible. Since she refused to lodge a formal complaint, there was no police enquiry.'

'That's very odd. That kind of refusal is nearly always for the same reason: the victim knows the attacker – husband, cousin, boyfriend – and doesn't want a scandal.'

'Why would Relivaux want to attack his own wife in her dressing-room?'

Vandoosler shrugged.

'We don't know who it was. It could be anyone. Relivaux, Stelios . . .'

'But the theatre was closed to the public.'

'No doubt Sophia could let in someone if she wanted to. And then there was Julien. He was in the show, wasn't he? What's his surname?'

'Moreaux, Julien Moreaux. He looks like an old sheep. Even fifteen years ago, I can't see him as a wolf.'

'You don't know much about sheep, I see. You told me yourself that Julien followed Sophia around in her productions for five years.'

'Sophia was trying to get him launched. He was her father's stepson, after all, and her stepbrother. Maybe she was fond of him.'

'Or he of her, more likely. You said he pinned photographs of her up in his bedroom. Sophia was about thirty-five then, she was a beautiful woman and famous. That'd be enough to turn the head of a young man of twenty-five. A smouldering passion, but frustrated. One day, he ventures into her dressing-room . . . Why not?'

'Do you think Sophia invented the balaclava?'

'Not necessarily. This Julien character might have wanted to hide his face when he followed his sexual urges. But it's quite possible that Sophia, who already knew he had a crush on her, recognised the attacker, balaclava or no balaclava. A police enquiry would have caused a major scandal. Better if she wiped out the incident and refused to talk about it. And as for Julien, he gave up playing walk-on parts from that point.'

'Yes,' said Marc. 'It's possible. But it still doesn't explain why someone should murder Sophia.'

'He might have had another go, fifteen years on, but this time it went wrong. So Dompierre's arrival would have panicked him. And he decided to strike first before Dompierre could speak to anyone.'

'That doesn't explain the tree.'

'Still on about the tree?'

Marc was standing by the fireplace leaning on the mantelshelf and looking into the dying embers.

'There's another thing I don't understand. If Christophe Dompierre read the articles written by this relation, maybe his father, I can see why. But why did he read Frémonville's articles too? The only thing they had in common was that they both slated Sophia's performance.'

'Perhaps they were friends, or confided in each other. That would explain their having the same opinions about music.'

'I'd really like to know what got them started in their vendetta against Sophia.'

Marc went over to one of the tall windows and looked out into the night.

'What are you looking at?'

'I'm trying to see if Lex's car is there.'

'Don't worry,' said Vandoosler. 'She won't be going anywhere tonight.'

'Did you persuade her not to?'

'I didn't try. I clamped her car.' Vandoosler smiled.

'A clamp? You could get hold of one?'

'Of course. I'll remove it first thing tomorrow. She won't know it was there – unless she tries to go out, that is.'

'Christ, you really do think like a policeman,' said Marc. 'And if you'd thought of that yesterday, she'd be off the suspect list. You're a bit late in the day with your bright idea.'

'I did think about it, actually,' said Vandoosler. 'But I didn't do it.'

Marc turned round, but his godfather stopped him with a wave of his hand before he could get launched.

'Don't get worked up. I've already told you it's a good thing sometimes to let out a bit of rope. Otherwise we might just get stuck, learn nothing at all, and the whaler will go down with all hands.'

He smiled as he pointed to the coin nailed to the beam. Preoccupied, Marc watched him go out of the room and heard him climb his four flights of stairs. He still did not understand what his godfather was up to and he was not even sure they were on the same side. He took the shovel, and collected a little pile of ash to cover the embers. However much you cover them, they still go on glowing underneath. If you put out the light, you can see that at once. That was what he did, and sat on a chair watching the glow of the red-hot cinders. He fell asleep in this position. At four in the morning, stiff-limbed and cold, he went up to his room. He did not have the willpower to get undressed. At about seven, he heard Vandoosler going downstairs. Ah yes, the clamp. Sleepily he sat up and switched on the laptop Lucien had left on his desk.

# XXXI

THERE WAS NO-ONE ELSE IN THE DISGRACE WHEN MARC SWITCHED THE
computer off at about eleven o'clock. Vandoosler had gone off to find
out whatever he could. Mathias had disappeared and Lucien had gone
in pursuit of his seven notebooks. For four hours, Marc had passed all
the press cuttings across the computer screen, reading and rereading every
article, memorising each detail, each turn of phrase, observing their
convergences and differences.

The June sunshine was steady and, for the first time, it occurred to
him to take a bowl of coffee out into the garden and sit on the grass,
hoping that the morning air would get rid of his headache. Marc trod
down a square metre of so of long grass, found a wooden plank and sat
on it cross-legged, facing the sun. He could not see where to go next. He
knew the documents by heart now. His memory was good and capa-
cious, and it collected everything, uncritically, including odds and ends
and the memory of past despairs. The trip to Dourdan had not produced
very much in the end. Dompierre was dead and had taken his story with
him, and it was hard to see how to go about resurrecting it. It was not
even clear that it would be of any interest.

Alexandra went past in the street, carrying a shopping bag and Marc
waved to her. He tried to imagine her as a murderer, but that pained
him. What the hell had she been up to, driving her car around for three
hours?

Marc felt useless, impotent, and sterile. He had the feeling there must be something he was not picking up. Ever since Lucien had come out with that sentence about the essential being revealed in the investigation of paroxysms, he had been ill at ease. It bothered him. Both in his research on the Middle Ages and when it came to the business in hand. Tired of having such vague and inconsequential ideas, Marc got up from his plank and observed the Western Front. It was curious how Lucien's way of talking had got under their skin. Now they would never dream of calling that house anything except the Western Front. Relivaux was probably not back yet or the godfather would have said something. Had the police been able to account for how he spent his time in Toulon?

Marc put his bowl down on the plank and went noiselessly out of the garden. From the street, he studied the Western Front. As far as he had observed, the cleaner only came on Tuesdays and Fridays. What was it today? Thursday. The house seemed quite still. He considered the tall gate, which was well maintained and not rusty like theirs, and which had sharp and efficient-looking spikes along the top. The problem would be to climb up there without being seen by a passer-by, and then, with luck, to be agile enough not to get impaled on the way over. He looked up and down the street. He was fond of this little street. He went over to the big refuse bin, and as Lucien had the other night, he climbed on top. Holding onto the railings, he managed after a few false starts to reach the top of the gate and climb over it without getting snagged.

His agility pleased him. He dropped down on the other side, thinking that after all he might have made a good gatherer, if not a hunter, wiry and nimble. Feeling satisfied with himself, he adjusted his silver rings, which had twisted on his fingers during the climb, and walked lightly over to the beech tree. What was he hoping for? Why was he going to all this trouble to see this dumb tree? No reason, just that he had promised himself he would, and because trying to save Alexandra was becoming a more doubtful project every day. That stupid girl with her pride was doing all the wrong things.

Marc put one hand, then the other, on the tree's cool trunk. It was still small enough for him to be able to encircle it with two handspans.

He felt like strangling it, wringing its neck until it told him, between choking sounds, just what it thought it was doing in the garden. He let his arms fall, discouraged. You can't strangle a tree. A tree just keeps quiet, it's as silent as a fish, and doesn't even make bubbles. All it produces are leaves, wood and roots. Yes, it makes oxygen too, that's quite practical. Apart from that, nothing. Deaf and dumb. As silent as Mathias, who tried to make his flint fragments and bones speak to him: a silent guy conversing with silent objects. Yes, they suited each other. Mathias swore he could hear them speaking, that you just had to learn their language and listen to them. Marc, who only liked what texts had to say, his own or other people's, couldn't understand this silent conversation. And yet Mathias did end up finding things out, that was certain.

He sat down by the tree. The grass had not yet grown back properly around it because it had twice been dug up. There was just a little covering of new grass which he touched with the palm of his hand. Soon it would be more plentiful and there'd be nothing to see. People would forget about the tree and the earth it stood in. Angrily, Marc pulled up a few tufts. Something was odd. The soil was dark, heavy, almost black. He remembered very well the two days they had spent digging and then filling in that pointless trench. He could see Mathias standing up to his thighs in the trench, saying that that was enough, they could stop because the lower layers of earth were undisturbed. He saw once more Mathias' feet, bare in sandals, covered with earth. But the earth had been yellowish-brown, light soil, the same as in the stem of the white clay pipe he had picked up, muttering, 'eighteenth century'. Light-coloured crumbly soil. And when they had filled it in, they had mixed leafmould with the same light soil. Not at all like the stuff he was kneading between his fingers. Was it new leafmould already? He scratched away some more. Black earth again. He walked round the tree, examining the topsoil the whole way round. No, there was no doubt, someone had disturbed the earth beneath the surface. The layers of soil were not as they had left them. But the police had come digging after them. Perhaps they had dug deeper, reaching a layer of black earth that was lower down. That must be it. Not being archaeologists, they had not been able to distinguish the layers and had dug into the black earth and then spread it around on the surface. No other explanation. Nothing to get excited about.

He stayed there a few moments more with his fingers furrowing the soil. He picked up a little piece of pottery that looked more sixteenth than eighteenth century to him, though he didn't really know much about it, and put it in his pocket. He got up, patted the tree trunk to tell it he was leaving and went back to climb over the gate. He had just touched down on the dustbin when he saw his godfather arriving.

'Very discreet,' said Vandoosler.

'Any objection?' said Marc, wiping his hands on his trousers. 'I only hopped over to look at the tree.'

'And what did the tree tell you?'

'That Leguennec's men dug much deeper than we did, right down to the sixteenth century. Mathias is not altogether wrong, you know, the earth can talk. What about you?'

'Come down off that dustbin so I don't have to shout. Christophe Dompierre was indeed the son of the critic Daniel Dompierre. So we've sorted that one out. As for Leguennec, he's started going through Siméonidis' archives, but he's as baffled as we are. His only satisfaction is that the eighteen missing Breton fishing boats are all safe back in port.'

Crossing the garden, Marc found his coffee bowl with a few cold drops left in it, which he drank.

'Almost midday,' he said. 'I'm going to get the mud off and then to have a bite at *Le Tonneau*.'

'That's a luxury,' said Vandoosler.

'Yes, I know, but it's Thursday. Out of respect for Sophia.'

'Are you sure it isn't to see Alexandra? Or perhaps the veal casserole tempts you?'

'That's not what I said. Do you want to come?'


Alexandra was at her usual table, trying to get her son to eat his lunch, but he was in an unco-operative mood. Marc ran his fingers through

Kyril's hair and let the boy play with his rings. Kyril liked St Mark's rings. Marc had told him that they had been given him by a magician, and that they had a magic secret, but he had never been able to find it. The magician had flown away out of the playground without telling him. Kyril had rubbed them, turned them, blown on them but nothing happened. Marc went over to say hullo to Mathias, who seemed to be stuck behind the counter. 'What's the matter?' said Marc. 'You look paralysed.'

'I'm not paralysed, I'm stuck. I got changed in a rush and put on my shirt, waistcoat, bow tie, and everything, but I forgot to put on proper shoes. Juliette says that I can't serve at table in sandals. It's funny, she's very fussy about it.'

'I can see her point,' said Marc. 'I'll go and fetch them for you, if you like. Can you organise me a veal casserole?'

Marc came back a few minutes later with the shoes and the white clay pipe.

'Remember this pipe and the earth it was in?' he asked Mathias.

'Of course.'

'This morning I went to see the tree. The soil on the surface isn't the same. It's much darker and more sticky.'

'Like there is under your fingernails?'

'Exactly.'

'Well it means the police were much more thorough than we were.'

'Yes. That's what I thought.'

Marc put the clay pipe back in his pocket and felt the little piece of pottery. He was always transferring bits and pieces from one pocket to another without getting rid of them. His pockets were like his memories, they would never leave him in peace.

Having put his shoes on, Mathias laid places for Marc and Vandoosler at Alexandra's table: she had said that was alright. Since she did not bring the subject up, Marc avoided asking her any questions about what the police had said to her the day before. Alexandra asked instead how the trip to Dourdan had gone, and how her grandfather was. Marc glanced at the godfather who nodded imperceptibly. Marc was cross with himself for asking Vandoosler's approval before talking to Lex, and realised that doubt had crept further into his mind than he had suspected. He told her in detail about the contents of the file for 1978, not knowing now whether he was doing so with sincerity or whether he was 'letting out rope' to watch her reactions. But Alexandra, looking pretty much at a low ebb, was not reacting at all. She simply said she ought to go and see her grandfather that weekend.

'I don't advise it at the moment,' said Vandoosler. Alexandra frowned, and stuck out her chin.

'Is it really that bad? Are they going to arrest me?' she asked, in a soft voice, so as not to upset Kyril.

'Let's say Leguennec is suspicious. Don't go away anywhere. Stick to the house, the school, *Le Tonneau*, the park, nowhere else.'

Alexandra looked sulky. Marc guessed that she didn't like taking orders from anyone, and it made him think for a moment of her grandfather. She was capable of doing the opposite of what Vandoosler asked, for the sheer pleasure of disobeying.

Juliette came over to clear their table, and Marc stood up to kiss her. He described what had happened at Dourdan in a few words. He was getting tired of the wretched 1978 file, which had only made things more complicated without making anything clearer. Alexandra was getting Kyril ready to go back to school when Lucien burst into the restaurant, out of breath, and letting the door slam behind him. He took Alexandra's place at table without seeming even to notice her leaving, and asked Mathias to fetch him a large glass of wine.

'Don't worry,' Marc told Juliette. 'It's the Great War that winds him up like this. It comes and goes. You have to get used to it.'

'Give it a rest!' said Lucien, still panting.

From Lucien's tone of voice, Marc realised that he was mistaken. It wasn't the Great War. Lucien did not have that delighted expression he ought to have if he had discovered the war diaries of a peasant in the trenches. He was in a state of high anxiety and running with sweat. His tie was crooked, and two red spots had appeared on his forehead. Still panting, he looked round at the customers eating their lunch, and motioned to Vandoosler and Marc to come closer.

'This morning,' he said between two deep breaths, 'I tried René de Frémonville's number. It had changed, different number, different address, so I went over there.'

He drank a large gulp of wine before going on.

'His wife was there. "R. de Frémonville" was the wife, Rachel, a lady of about seventy. I asked if it was possible to speak to her husband. Really put my foot in it. Hold on, Marc, wait till you hear this. Frémonville has been dead for years.'

'Well, what of it?' said Marc.

'He was murdered, that's what! Shot twice in the head, one night in September 1979. And, wait for this, he wasn't alone. He was with his old friend, Daniel Dompierre. Also shot twice. Bang bang, two theatre critics, final curtain.'

'No shit!' said Marc.

'You may well say that, because my war notebooks disappeared in the commotion after that, what with moving house and so forth. Frémonville's wife wasn't bothered about them. She's no idea what became of them.'

'And was he a peasant, the soldier?' Marc asked.

Lucien looked at him in surprise. 'Do you really want to know?'

'No, but you've gone on about it so much . . .'

'Well, yes, he was,' said Lucien getting even more excited. 'He really was a peasant. See? Isn't that fantastic? If only . . .'

'Never mind about the war diaries,' ordered Vandoosler. 'Carry on with the story. There must have been a police investigation, surely?'

'Yes, of course,' said Lucien. 'Rachel de Frémonville didn't want to talk about it, but I was very persuasive and wormed it out of her. Frémonville kept the Parisian theatre world supplied with cocaine. And his friend Dompierre too, no doubt. The police found a packet under the floorboards in Frémonville's house, just where the two men had been shot. The investigation concluded that it must have been gang warfare between dealers. The evidence was clear in Frémonville's case, though less obvious for Dompierre. All they found in his place was a few sachets of coke stuffed up the chimney.'

Lucien drained his glass and asked Mathias for another. Instead, Mathias brought him some veal casserole.

'Eat,' he said firmly.

Lucien looked at Mathias' expression and started on the food.

'Rachel told me that at the time, Dompierre's son, Christophe, refused to believe his father could be mixed up in anything like that. The mother and son both made a big fuss to the police, but it got them nowhere. The double murder was filed under drug dealing. They never caught the killer.'

Lucien was calming down and his breath was becoming regular. Vandoosler had his *commissaire*'s face on, a thrusting nose and narrowed eyes under lowered eyebrows. He was tearing apart pieces of bread from the basket Mathias had put on the table.

'In any case,' said Marc, who was rapidly trying to get his ideas into some kind of order, 'that has nothing to do with our business. These two guys were shot over a year after "Elektra". And drugs were involved as well. I presume the police knew what they were talking about there.'

'Don't be stupid, Marc,' said Lucien impatiently. 'Young Christophe Dompierre didn't believe that. Was it just out of loyalty to his father? Maybe, but when Sophia gets killed fifteen years later, he reappears and starts looking for new clues. Do you remember what he said about his pathetic "little sliver of belief"?'

'If he was wrong about it fifteen years ago,' objected Marc, 'he could still be wrong three days ago.'

'Except,' said Vandoosler, 'that he got himself murdered. People who are wrong don't usually get killed. It's people who are on to something who get killed.'

Lucien nodded agreement and mopped his plate energetically with his bread. Marc sighed. He felt his brain was slowing down recently and that bothered him.

'So Dompierre was on to something,' Lucien continued in a low voice. 'Therefore he was already on to something fifteen years ago.'

'And what was that?'

'That one of the extras had attacked Sophia. And if you want my opinion, his father knew who it was, and had told him. Maybe he had seen the man running out of the dressing-room with his balaclava off. So that would explain why the extra didn't come back next day. He was scared of being recognised. That must have been the only thing Christophe knew: that his father had seen who Sophia's attacker was. And if Frémonville was a dealer, it certainly wasn't the case for Daniel Dompierre. Three sachets stuffed up the chimney is a bit obvious, isn't it? The son told the *flics* all about the attack on Sophia. But this old story about the theatre didn't interest the police. The drugs squad was running the investigation and the Sophia incident didn't have a drugs angle. So Dompierre's son had to let it drop. But when Sophia in turn was killed, he got back on the case. The affair was still alive. He had always believed that his father and Frémonville had been killed not because of the cocaine, but because somehow their paths had crossed that of the attacker. And that he'd shot them to stop them talking. It must have been terribly important for him.'

'Your story doesn't make sense,' Marc said. 'Why didn't this attacker shoot them straightaway afterwards?'

'Well, because he probably had a stage name. If you were called Roger Prune for instance, you'd probably change it to something like Franck Delmer, or some fancy-sounding name that might appeal to a director. So he disappears under his stage name, his real identity can't be traced and he's out of danger. Who's going to connect Franck Delmer with Roger Prune?'

'Well, so what? I still don't bloody get it!'

'You're on edge today, Marc. Well, imagine that a year later, the guy meets Dompierre under his real name and is recognised. Then he has no choice. He shoots them both, him and his friend, who almost certainly knows too. He knows that Frémonville deals in cocaine and that suits him fine. He plants the sachets at Dompierre's, the police buy the story and the case is referred to the drugs squad.'

'And why would your Prune-Delmer kill Sophia fourteen years later, since Sophia didn't even identify him?'

Lucien, looking excited once more, produced a plastic bag which he placed on the chair. 'Don't move, pal, don't move.'

He fished around in it and pulled out a roll of paper held by a rubber band. Vandoosler was looking at him, visibly impressed. Luck had favoured Lucien, but he had also very skilfully harpooned his lucky chance.

'After our talk,' Lucien said, 'I was a bit shaken. And so was the old lady. It had upset her to dredge up her memories. She didn't know that Christophe Dompierre had been murdered and as you can guess, I didn't tell her. We had a cup of coffee at ten o'clock to restore ourselves. And then, that was all very well, but I was still thinking about my war diaries. I'm only human after all, you can understand that.'

'OK, I understand,' said Marc.

'Mme de Frémonville had a good look for the war diaries, but she couldn't find them anywhere, they really were lost. But while she was drinking her coffee, she gave a little cry. You know the kind of thing, like in old movies. She remembered that her husband, who was very attached to these war diaries, had had them photographed by his magazine's photographer because the paper was fragile and starting to disintegrate. She told me that with a bit of luck, the photographer might have kept the negatives or proofs of the photographs, because he had taken a lot of trouble over them. The diaries were written in pencil and not easy to reproduce. She gave me the photographer's address, in Paris luckily, and I rushed straight over there. And there he was, making prints. He's only about fifty and still in business. And get this, Marc. He had kept the negatives and he's going to print a set for me. I kid you not.'

'Great!' muttered Marc crossly. 'But I was talking abut Sophia's murder, not your notebooks.'

Lucien turned to Vandoosler and pointed to Marc. 'He's really edgy, isn't he? Too impatient.'

'When he was little,' Vandoosler said, 'if he dropped a ball from the balcony into the courtyard, he would stamp and cry until I fetched it. It was all that mattered to him. The number of times I went up and down the stairs. Just for those little cheap plastic balls with holes in, you know.'

Lucien laughed. He was looking pleased again, but his brown hair was still dark with sweat. Marc smiled as well. He had entirely forgotten about those plastic balls.

'Listen,' said Lucien, still in a whisper. 'This photographer, as you might expect, accompanied Frémonville on his assignments. He did the press photos for shows they covered. So I thought he might have kept some old prints. He knew about Sophia being killed, but he hadn't heard about Christophe Dompierre. I told him about it and he thought this sounded so serious he went to look for his file on "Elektra". And here,' said Lucien, waving his roll under Marc's nose, 'we have a set of press photographs. Not just of Sophia. Of the whole company.'

'Come on then, show us!' said Marc.

'Patience, patience,' said Lucien.

Slowly he unrolled the photos, and took out one picture which he laid on the table.

'The whole company on parade the first night,' he said, using wine-glasses to press down the corners of the photograph. 'Everyone's on it. Sophia in the middle, with the tenor and the baritone either side of her. They're all made up and in costume of course. But can you recognise anyone? *Commissaire,* do you recognise anyone else?'

Marc and Vandoosler leaned over the photo. The faces were made up, small but clear. It was a good photograph. Marc who had been feeling himself falling way behind, as Lucien became more and more ebullient, felt all his strength draining away. His brain was muddled and confused. He looked at the little white faces, but none of them rang any bells. No, wait a moment, there was Julien Moreaux, looking young and thin.

'Yes, of course,' said Lucien, 'but that's hardly surprising. Look again.'

Marc shook his head. He felt almost humiliated. No, he couldn't see anything. Vandoosler equally baffled, pulled a face. However, he pointed to one face with his finger.

'That one,' he said in a low voice, 'but I can't put a name to it.'

Lucien nodded. 'Quite right,' he said. 'But *I* can put a name to it.'

He looked quickly towards the bar and round the rest of the room, then drew even closer to Marc and Vandoosler.

'It's Georges Gosselin, Juliette's brother,' he whispered.

Vandoosler clenched his fists.

'Pay the bill, St Mark,' he said curtly. 'We're going home at once. Tell St Matthew to join us as soon as his shift's over.'

# XXXII

MATHIAS RAN HIS HANDS THROUGH HIS MASS OF BLOND HAIR GETTING it even more tousled, if that was possible. The others had told him everything and he was shattered. He had not even changed out of his waiter's costume. Lucien, who felt he had done more than his bit for the time being, had decided to let the others get on with it and to move on to something else. While waiting to go and meet the photographer at six o'clock to pick up the first prints of the promised notebooks, he had decided to polish the big dining table. He had brought the refectory table into the house when they moved in, and did not want it spoilt by cavemen like Mathias or careless people like Marc. He was putting beeswax on it now, lifting the elbows in turn of Vandoosler, Marc and Mathias to get under them with his bulky cloth. Nobody protested, because they knew it would have no effect. Apart from the sound of the cloth polishing the wood, the silence lay heavy over the refectory as each of them tried to sort out and digest recent events.

'If I've got it right,' Mathias said at last, 'Georges Gosselin attacked Sophia and tried to rape her in her dressing-room fifteen years ago. Then he ran off and Daniel Dompierre saw him. Sophia didn't say anything, because she thought it must have been Julien – is that right? A year or more later, the critic met Georges Gosselin and recognised him, so Gosselin shot him along with his pal Frémonville. But the way I see it, it's far worse to kill two guys in cold blood than to be charged even with assault and attempted rape. A double murder is out of all proportion.'

'The way you see it maybe,' said Vandoosler. 'But for a weak, secretive sort of person, to be put in prison for assault and rape might seem like the end of the world. He'd lose his image, his reputation, his work, and his peace of mind. What if he couldn't bear to be seen for what he was, a brute, a potential rapist? He panics, acts instinctively, and shoots the two men.'

'How long has he been living in rue Chasle?' Marc asked. 'Do we know that?'

'Must be about ten years, I reckon,' said Mathias. 'Ever since the old grandfather with his beet fields left them his money. Juliette has been running *Le Tonneau* about ten years, so I guess they bought the house at about the same time.'

'Well, that would make it five years after "Elektra" and the attack,' said Marc, 'and four years after the murder of the two critics. So why, after all that time, should he come and live near Sophia. Why was he so keen to stick close to her?'

'Obsession, I suppose,' said Vandoosler. 'He was obsessed. He wanted to be close to the star he had tried to beat up and rape. Return to the scene of his crime, call it what you like. He wanted to come back, to watch and wait for her. Ten years waiting, with his secret violent thoughts, then one day he would kill her. Or have another go, and then kill her. A maniac, under the guise of an unobtrusive nobody.'

'Does that actually happen?' asked Marc.

'Oh yes, it happens, alright,' said Vandoosler. 'I've caught at least five guys of that type. The slow killer, who chews over his frustration, and puts off the moment, calm as can be on the surface.'

'Excuse me,' said Lucien, lifting Mathias' huge arms.

Now he was shining the table with a soft cloth, and barely listening to the conversation. Marc thought that he really would never understand Lucien. They were all sitting there intensely, with the murderer only a few yards away, and all Lucien could think of was polishing his table. And yet without him, they would have got nowhere. It was practically all his own work, but he didn't give a damn.

'Now I understand something,' said Mathias.

'What?'

'Nothing. Why I felt warm. I understand now.'

'Well, what should we do next?' Marc asked his godfather. 'Tell Leguennec? If something else happens, and we haven't told him, he'd have us for aiding and abetting.'

'Yes, and concealing information from the agents of the law,' said Vandoosler, with a sigh. 'We'll tell Leguennec, but not straightaway. There's one little detail missing in this scenario that bothers me a bit. St Matthew, would you be so good as to ask Juliette to come over? Even if she's cooking for tonight, ask her to come. It's urgent. As for the rest of you,' he said sternly, 'not a word to anyone, do you understand. Not even to Alexandra. If a whisper of all this gets to Gosselin, I wouldn't give much for your chances. So not a word until further notice.'

Vandoosler interrupted himself and grasped Lucien by the arm. Lucien was still polishing the table with wide sweeps, and stooping to the surface to take a view of how it was coming up.

'Do you hear me, St Luke?' said Vandoosler. 'That means you too. Not a word. I hope you didn't hint at any of this to your photographer?'

'No, of course not,' said Lucien. 'I may be polishing the table, but I can hear what you're saying.'

'That's just as well,' said Vandoosler. 'Sometimes you give the impression of being half-genius and half-idiot. It's infuriating, take it from me.'

Mathias went off to change his clothes before going to fetch Juliette. Marc looked down at the table in silence. It was true that it was beautifully polished now. He ran his finger over it.

'Feels good, huh?' said Lucien.

Marc shook his head. He did not really want to talk about the table. He was wondering what Vandoosler had in store for Juliette, and how she would react. The godfather was good at breaking things, he had got it down to to a fine art. He always cracked nuts with his bare hands, never deigning to use a nutcracker. Even when they were fresh, which makes it harder. But that had nothing to do with this.

Mathias brought Juliette in and seemed to help her onto the bench. Juliette didn't look at ease. It was the first time that the old *commissaire* had so formally asked her to come. She saw the three evangelists sitting round the table with their eyes fixed on her and that didn't make her look any more comfortable. Only the sight of Lucien, carefully folding his polishing cloth, seemed to relax her a little.

Vandoosler lit one of the shapeless cigarettes he always had loose in his pockets, no-one knew why.

'Marc told you about Dourdan, did he?' said Vandoosler, looking hard at Juliette. 'The production of "Elektra" in 1978, in Toulouse, and the attack on Sophia?'

'Yes,' said Juliette. 'He said that complicated things without making them any clearer.'

'Well, now, they're becoming a bit clearer. St Luke, pass me the photo.'

Muttering, Lucien fished about in his bag and gave him the photograph. Vandoosler placed it in front of Juliette.

'Fourth on the left, fifth row down, recognise him?'

Marc stiffened. He would never have gone about it this way.

Juliette glanced at the photograph but without concentrating.

'No,' she said. 'How am I supposed to recognise anyone? It's an opera Sophia was in, isn't it? I've never seen an opera in my life.'

'It's your little brother,' said Vandoosler. 'And you know that as well as we do.'

Bang goes the nut, thought Marc. Single-handed. He saw the tears come into Juliette's eyes.

'Alright,' she said with a trembling voice, her hands shaking. 'It's Georges. But what about it? What's wrong?'

'There's so much wrong with it that if I call Leguennec, he'll have him down at the station in an hour. So tell us about it, Juliette. You know it will be better in the end. It might avoid people jumping to conclusions.'

Juliette wiped her eyes, took a deep breath, but said nothing. As he had in *Le Tonneau* the other day to Alexandra, Mathias came up to her, put his hand on her shoulder and whispered something in her ear. And as the other day, Juliette made up her mind to talk. Marc promised himself he would ask Mathias what kind of 'open sesame' he was using. It could be useful in all sorts of ways.

'There's nothing wrong with it,' said Juliette. 'When I came to live in Paris, Georges followed me. He's always followed me. I started doing cleaning jobs and he didn't do anything. He wanted to work in the theatre. You might laugh now, but he was quite good-looking then, and he'd had a bit of success acting at school.'

'Any success with the girls?' asked Vandoosler.

'Not much,' said Juliette. 'Well, he looked around and he got a few walk-on parts. He said you had to start that way. Anyway we didn't have enough money for him to go to drama school. Once you are an extra, you get to know your way around. Georges managed quite well. He was an extra several times in operas where Sophia was the lead singer.'

'Did he know Julien Moreaux, Siméonidis' stepson?'

'Yes, of course. In fact he used to hang around him, hoping he would get a bit of help. But in '78, Georges gave up the stage. He'd been at it for four years and it wasn't going anywhere. He got discouraged. Through a friend in a theatre company, I can't remember which one, he got a job as a courier for a firm of publishers. He stayed there, and now he travels for them. And that's all.'

'No, it's not all,' said Vandoosler. 'Why did he come and live in rue Chasle? And don't tell me that it was a fantastic coincidence, as I won't believe you.'

'If you think Georges had anything to do with the attack on Sophia,' said Juliette, getting indignant, 'you're completely on the wrong track. It upset him and he was quite shaken, I remember very well. Georges is a timid, mild man. Back in the village, I had to push him to make him go and talk to girls.'

'He was shaken? Why was he shaken?'

Juliette sighed, looking unhappy and hesitating to go on.

'Tell me the rest before Leguennec gets it out of you,' said Vandoosler gently. 'You can give the police an edited version. Just tell me everything and we'll sift it all afterwards.'

Juliette glanced at Mathias. 'Alright' she said. 'Georges had fallen for Sophia. He didn't tell me about it, but I wasn't so stupid I couldn't see it. It was just obvious. He would have turned down any walk-on part that was better paid, if it meant missing a chance to be in Sophia's opera season. He was mad about her, absolutely mad. One night I got him to tell me about it.'

'What about her?' asked Marc.

'Sophia? Oh she was happily married, and a million miles from suspecting that Georges worshipped her. And even if she had known, I don't think she would have been attracted to him, he was so clumsy and awkward and unsure of himself. He didn't have much success, no. I don't know how he managed it, but women never noticed that he was quite good-looking in fact. He always walked about staring at the ground. In any case, Sophia was in love with Pierre and she still was, up to the time of her death, whatever she might say.'

'So what did he do?' asked Vandoosler.

'Who, Georges? Nothing,' said Juliette. 'What could he do? He suffered in silence as they say, that's all.'

'And what about your house?'

Juliet winced.

'When he stopped acting I thought he was going to forget this opera singer and meet other women. I was relieved. But I was wrong. He bought her records, he went to see her at the Paris Opéra when she was singing there, and even to towns in the provinces. I can't say I was happy about it.'

'Why?'

'It was just making him sad, and it was going nowhere. And then one day, our grandfather fell ill. He died some months later, and we inherited. Georges came to see me, looking at the ground as usual. He said that there was a house that had been on the market for three months, in central Paris, but with a garden. That he'd often been past it, doing his rounds on his scooter. I was tempted by the garden. If you come from the country, you miss the grass. I went to see the house with him, and we decided to buy it. I was keen, especially because I had seen a place nearby where I could set up with my restaurant. That is, I was enthusiastic until I found out who our neighbour was.'

Juliette asked Vandoosler for a cigarette. She hardly ever smoked. She looked tired and sad. Mathias brought her a glass of cordial.

'Of course, I had it out with Georges,' said Juliette. 'We quarrelled. I really wanted to sell it. But by that stage we couldn't. We'd already started to have work done on the house, and in *Le Tonneau*. There wasn't really any way we could pull out then. He swore to me that he wasn't in love with her any more, or almost not, that he just wanted to be able to see her from time to time, maybe even become friends. I gave in. Anyway I didn't have much choice. He made me promise not to tell anyone, especially Sophia.'

'Why? Was he afraid?'

'He was ashamed. He didn't want Sophia to guess he had followed her here, or for people round about to know and laugh at him. It was only natural. We decided to say that I'd found the house, if anyone asked us. Nobody did. Anyway. When Sophia recognised Georges in the street, we laughed and said what a coincidence.'

'And she believed that?' asked Vandoosler.

'Apparently,' Juliette said. 'Sophia never seemed to suspect anything. When I saw her for the first time, I understood why Georges was so keen on her. She was really beautiful. She charmed everyone. At first she wasn't here much, always going off on tour. But I tried to meet her often, and to get her to come to the restaurant.'

'What for?' asked Marc.

'Well, I was hoping to help Georges, to get her to notice him a bit. I was sort of matchmaking, I guess. It wasn't the right thing to do, no, I know, but he is my brother. Anyway it didn't work. Sophia would say hello nicely to Georges when she met him in the street, and that's as far as it ever went. He began to get the message. So his idea of buying the house was turning out OK after all. And gradually, I became very friendly with Sophia.'

Juliette finished the cordial and looked round at them. Their faces were silent and preoccupied. Mathias was wriggling his toes in his sandals.

'Tell me, Juliette,' said Vandoosler. 'What was Georges doing on the night of Thursday June 3? Was he here, or was he away somewhere?'

'June 3? When they found Sophia's body? Why do you want to know?'

'I'd just like to know.'

She shrugged and picked up her handbag. She took out a little diary.

'I make a note of all his trips,' she said. 'So as to know when he'll be back and get a meal ready for him. He left here on the morning of the third, and came back at lunchtime next day. He was in Caen.'

'So the night of the second to the third, he was here?'

'Yes, that's right,' she said, 'and you know that as well as I do. I've told you everything now. You're not going to stir things up about this, are you? It's just a sad story of unrequited love that went on too long. There's nothing more to say about it. And he certainly didn't attack her. He wasn't the only man in the cast, for heaven's sake!'

'But he was the only one who kept following her for several years after that,' said Vandoosler. 'And I don't know what Leguennec will make of that.'

Juliette stood up abruptly.

'He worked under a stage name!' she cried. 'If you don't tell Leguennec, he'd never know Georges was in the cast that year.'

'The police have ways and means,' said Vandoosler. 'Leguennec will check the cast list.'

'He won't be able to find him!' cried Juliette. 'And anyway, Georges didn't do anything wrong!'

'Did he go back on the stage after the attack?' Vandoosler asked.

Juliette looked upset. 'I don't remember,' she said.

Vandoosler got up in turn. Feeling desperate, Marc stared at his knees and Mathias had gone to look out of the window. Lucien had disappeared without anyone noticing. Off to fetch his war diaries.

'You *do* remember,' said Vandoosler. 'You know he didn't go back to acting. He came back to Paris, and he told you that he had been too upset by the attack, didn't he?'

Juliette looked panic-stricken. Yes, it was obvious that she remembered. She ran out, slamming the door.

'She's cracking up,' said Vandoosler.

Marc was gritting his teeth. Georges was a murderer, he had killed four people, and Vandoosler was a brute and a bastard.

'Are you going to tell Leguennec?' he hissed.

'We have to. See you this evening.'

He took the photograph and left.

Marc didn't feel like seeing his godfather that evening. If Georges was arrested, it would get Alexandra off the hook. But he was feeling ashamed. My God, one doesn't crack nuts with one's bare hands.


Three hours later Leguennec and three policemen arrived at Juliette's house to arrest Gosselin. But he had fled, and Juliette couldn't tell them where he had gone.

# XXXIII

MATHIAS SLEPT BADLY. AT SEVEN IN THE MORNING, HE PULLED ON A sweater and trousers and slipped out quietly to knock at Juliette's door. The door was wide open. He found her sitting on a chair, looking shattered, three policemen round her turning the house upside down, hoping to find Georges Gosselin hiding in a cupboard. Others were doing the same thing at *Le Tonneau*. Cellars, kitchens, every room was subjected to the same search. Mathias stood with his arms dangling, looking at the unimaginable mess the police had managed to make in just an hour. Leguennec, who arrived at about eight o'clock, gave the order for the house in Normandy to be searched as well.

'Shall we help you clear up?' Mathias asked when the police had left.

'No,' said Juliette. 'I don't want to see the others. They shopped Georges to Leguennec.'

Mathias pressed his big hands together.

'You'll be paid for the day, but the restaurant won't open,' Juliette said.

'So I can help you clear up?'

'Yes, as long as it's just you,' she said. 'You can give me a hand.'

While he was sorting things out, Mathias tried to talk to Juliette, to explain a few things, to prepare her and calm her down. It seemed to comfort her somewhat.

'Look,' she said. 'Leguennec's taking Vandoosler away with him. Now what else is that old man going to say to him?'

'Don't worry, he'll pick and choose. That's how he is.'

\* \* \*

From his window, Marc watched Vandoosler going off with Leguennec. He had managed to avoid meeting his uncle that morning. Mathias had gone to Juliette's, he must be talking to her, choosing his words. He went up to see Lucien. Completely absorbed in transcribing the pages from war diary number one (September 1914 to February 1915), Lucien motioned to Marc not to interrupt him. He had decided to take another day off work, judging that to have flu for only forty-eight hours was not convincing. As he watched Lucien working, totally oblivious to the world outside, Marc told himself that perhaps in the end that would be the best thing for him to do too. The war was over. So he had better harness himself up to his medieval plough, even though nobody was asking him to. He'd work for nobody and for nothing, as he got back to his lords and peasants. Marc went back downstairs and opened his files without enthusiasm. Gosselin would be caught sooner or later. There would be a trial, and that would be it. Alexandra had nothing more to fear, and would go on giving him a little wave from the street. Yes, it was better to plunge into the eleventh century than to wait for that.

Leguennec waited until they were in his office with the door shut before exploding.

'So,' he bellowed. 'I hope you're pleased with yourself!'

'That'll do,' said Vandoosler. 'You've got your man, haven't you?'

'I *would* have him, if you hadn't allowed him to get away. You're corrupt, Vandoosler, through and through!'

'Let's just say that I gave him three hours' thinking time. That's the least one could give him.'

Leguennec slammed both hands onto the desk. 'Why for crying out loud did you do that?' he shouted. 'What's this guy to you? Nothing. Why did you do it?'

'To see what would happen,' said Vandoosler nonchalantly. 'One shouldn't obstruct the course of events. That's always been your weakness.'

'You know what your little game might cost you?'

'Yes, I know. But you won't do anything to me.'

'That's what you think?'

'Yes, that's what I think. Because you'd be making a very big mistake, let me tell you.'

'You're well placed yourself, to talk about mistakes, don't you think?'

'What about you! If it hadn't been for Marc, you would never have linked Sophia's death and the murder of Christophe Dompierre. And if it hadn't been for Lucien, you would never have connected all this to the murder of the two theatre critics, and you would never have identified Georges Gosselin as the bit player in the opera!'

'And if it hadn't been for you, he'd be in this office, right now!'

'Just so. Shall we play cards while we wait?' said Vandoosler.

A young assistant inspector opened the door in a hurry.

'You could knock!' yelled Leguennec.

'No time, sir,' said the young man. 'We've got someone here who wants to see you urgently. It's the Siméonidis–Dompierre case.'

'The case is wrapped up. Get him out of here.'

'At least ask who it is?' suggested Vandoosler.

'Who is it?'

'A guest who was staying at the Hôtel du Danube at the same time as Christophe Dompierre. The one who drove off in the morning without noticing there was a body in the car park.'

'Get him in,' hissed Vandoosler through clenched teeth.

Leguennec gestured, and the young man called into the corridor.

'The cards will have to wait,' said Leguennec.

The man came in and sat down without being invited to. He was in a state of high excitement.

'What's all this about?' asked Leguennec. 'Hurry up. I've got a man on the run. Your name, occupation?'

'Eric Masson, section head at SODECO Grenoble.'

'As if I care, really,' said Leguennec. 'What's your business?'

'I was staying at the Hôtel du Danube,' said Masson. 'It's not very grand, but I'm used to it and it's near SODECO Paris.'

'As if I care,' Leguennec repeated.

Vandoosler gestured to him to take it easy. Leguennec sat down, offered a cigarette to Masson and lit one himself.

'OK, I'm listening,' he said, less irritably.

'I was there the night Monsieur Dompierre was killed. The awful thing was, I drove my car out in the morning without suspecting a thing, and the body was just beside it, they told me afterwards.'

'Go on.'

'It was a Wednesday morning. I went straight to SODECO and parked in the underground car park.'

'So bloody what?' said Leguennec.

'I'll tell you so bloody what!' said Masson, suddenly angry. 'If I'm telling you these details, it's because they're extremely important!'

'I'm sorry,' said Leguennec. 'I'm having a hard day. Go on.'

'Next day, Thursday, I did exactly the same. I was on a three-day training course. Put the car in the car park, came back to the hotel at night, after dining with the other people on the course. My car's black, I have to tell you. It's a Renault 19, with a very low chassis.'

Vandoosler made a sign once more to Leguennec to stop him saying 'so bloody what?' again.

'The course finished last night. This morning all I had to do was settle up and leave for Grenoble, no hurry. I left the hotel, and stopped at the first garage to fill the tank. It was the kind of garage where the pumps are out in the open.'

'Calm down for God's sake,' Vandoosler whispered to Leguennec.

'So *that's* why,' Masson continued, 'for the first time since Wednesday morning, I went round the car in daylight to take the cap off the petrol tank. It's on the right, of course. And that's when I saw it.'

'What?' said Leguennec, suddenly taking notice.

'Writing. In the dust on the front wing, low down, someone had written something with their finger. At first I thought it must be kids. But they usually do it on the windscreen and write PLEASE CLEAN ME or something. So I knelt down and read it. My car's black, as I said, so the dust and mud show up on it and the writing was very clear, like on a blackboard. Then I suddenly understood. It must have been him, Dompierre, writing on my car as he lay dying. He didn't die straightaway, is that right?'

Leaning forward, Leguennec was genuinely holding his breath. 'No,' he said. 'He would have taken several minutes to die.'

'Well, lying there, he had time and just enough strength to stretch out his arm and write. He wrote the killer's name on my car. Lucky it hasn't rained since.'

Two minutes later, Leguennec was telephoning the police photographer and rushing out into the street where Masson had parked his dusty black Renault.

'A few more minutes,' Masson was shouting as he ran along behind him, 'and I would have taken it through the carwash. Funny old world, eh?'

'You must be crazy, leaving a piece of evidence out in the street. Anyone could have come past and rubbed it out.'

'Well, Monsieur, they wouldn't let me park it in your courtyard. Those were their orders they said.'

The three men were now kneeling down beside the front wing of the car. The photographer asked them to get back so that he could get on with his job.'

'I want a copy,' Vandoosler said to Leguennec. 'Get me a copy as soon as you can.'

'What for?'

'You're not running this case unaided, as you very well know.'

'Don't I know it. OK, you'll get your picture. Come back in an hour.'


At about two o'clock, Vandoosler was getting out of a taxi in front of the disgrace. Taxis cost money, but right now minutes counted. He hurried into the refectory and seized the broom handle, still not capped. He banged loudly seven times on the ceiling. Seven bangs meant 'All evangelists downstairs'. The usual code was one for St Matthew, two for St Mark, three for St Luke, and four for himself. Seven for everyone all together. Vandoosler had devised the system because everyone was fed up with coming downstairs and back up again for nothing.

Mathias who had come home after lunching quietly with Juliette, heard the seven bangs and repeated them for Marc, before going down. Marc in turn passed the message to Lucien, who tore himself from his reading, muttering, 'Ordered to the Front. Reporting for duty'.

A minute later, they were all in the refectory. The broom handle system was efficient, except that it made a mess of the ceiling and didn't allow you to communicate with the outside world as a telephone would.

'Is it all over?' Marc asked. 'They've caught Gosselin, or he's killed himself?'

Vandoosler swallowed a glassful of water before replying.

'Say you've got someone who's been stabbed and knows he's dying. If he still has the strength and the means to leave a message, what will he write?'

'The murderer's name,' said Lucien.

'All agreed?' asked Vandoosler.

'Yes, it's obvious,' said Marc.

Mathias nodded.

'Right,' said Vandoosler. 'I share your view. And I've seen a few cases in my career. The victim, if there's time, and if they know the murderer's name, always writes it. Unfailingly.'

Looking preoccupied, Vandoosler pulled out of his jacket pocket the envelope containing the photograph of the black car.

'Christophe Dompierre wrote a name in the dust on the body of a car before he died,' he told them. 'The name has been driving round Paris for three days. The driver has only just noticed the writing.'

'Georges Gosselin,' said Lucien.

'No,' said Vandoosler. 'What Dompierre wrote was "Siméonidis S".'

Vandoosler threw the photograph onto the table and sat down heavily on a chair.

'Dead and alive,' he murmured.

Wordlessly the three men approached the photograph to look at it. None of them dared to touch it, as if they were frightened. The writing was wobbly and irregular, and Dompierre must have had to raise his arm to reach the car. But there was no doubt about it. It looked as if the writer had tackled it in spurts, as if summoning up his final strength. The only odd thing about it was that the last capital S was the wrong way round, so that it looked more like a 2.

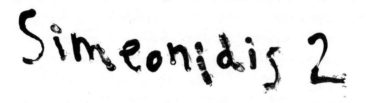

Devastated, they all sat back in silence, shying away from the terrible accusation in black and white. So Sophia Siméonidis was alive, and had murdered Dompierre. Mathias shivered. For the first time, fear and distress settled on the refectory early that Friday afternoon. The sun was shining in through the windows, but Marc felt his fingers growing cold and a prickling in his legs. Sophia still alive, arranging a false death, having somebody else burnt in her place, leaving her piece of basalt as evidence. Sophia, the beautiful singer, prowling in Paris by night, in rue Chasle. Dead yet alive.

'What about Gosselin?' Marc asked in a low voice.

'It can't have been him,' said Vandoosler, also speaking low. 'I knew that already yesterday.'

'You knew?'

'Remember those two hairs of Sophia's that Leguennec found in the boot of Lex's car?'

'Of course,' said Marc.

'Well, those hairs weren't there the day before. When we heard about the fire at Maisons-Alfort, I waited for nightfall and I went out to vacuum Lex's car. I've kept a little gadget from my police days. It's a battery-operated vacuum cleaner, with clean bags. There was nothing in the boot, no hair, no nails, not a shred of cloth. Only sand and dust.'

Dumbfounded, the three men stared at Vandoosler. Marc remembered now. It was the night when he had been sitting on the seventh step, thinking about tectonic plates. The godfather had gone outside to take a leak, carrying a plastic bag.

'It's true,' said Marc. 'I thought you were just going out for a pee.'

'Well, that too,' admitted Vandoosler.

'I see,' said Marc.

'So,' Vandoosler went on, 'when Leguennec requisitioned the car the next day and said he had found these hairs, it made me laugh. I had proof that Alexandra was not responsible. And proof that somebody had gone to the car, after me, in the night to put this bit of evidence in the boot to implicate the niece. And it couldn't have been Gosselin, because Juliette said he only came back at Friday lunchtime. And that's quite true, because I checked.'

'But for Christ's sake, why didn't you say anything?'

'Because I was operating outside the law and I needed to keep in with Leguennec. And also because I wanted the murderer, whoever it was, to know that his plan was working. I wanted to let out as much rope as possible, and to see where the beast would go if it was let free without being tied up.'

'Why didn't Leguennec take the car in on the Thursday?'

'He did waste some time, that's true. But cast your mind back. We didn't think it was Sophia's body until quite late on that day. And the initial suspect was Relivaux. It's simply not possible to think of everything, impound everything and so forth on the first day of an investigation. Actually Leguennec knew he hadn't been quick off the mark. That's why he didn't charge Alexandra. He wasn't absolutely sure about those hairs.'

'But what about Gosselin?' asked Lucien. 'Why did you tell Leguennec to bring him in for questioning, if you knew he was innocent?'

'Same idea. Let things run their course. And see what the real murderer would do. You have to leave murderers free, so that they make some mistakes. You will have noticed that I allowed Gosselin to get away by warning Juliette. I didn't want him to be questioned about the ancient history of the attack in the dressing-room.'

'That was him?'

'Must have been. You could tell, from Juliette's face. But not the murders. In fact, St Matthew, you could go and tell Juliette that she can tell her brother now.'

'D'you think she knows where he is?'

'Yes, bound to. I guess he's somewhere in the south of France, Nice, Toulon or Marseille, ready to be off across the Mediterranean at a word from her, with false papers. You can tell her about Sophia Siméonidis too. But everyone should be very careful. She's still alive and still out there somewhere. But where? I've no idea.'

Mathias tore his eyes away from the black and white photo on the polished table and went out quietly.

Marc felt weak and shattered. Sophia dead, Sophia back from the dead.

'When the dead awaken,' murmured Lucien.

'So,' Marc said slowly. 'It was Sophia who killed the two theatre critics. Because they were both so vicious about her, because they were destroying her career? But things like that don't happen, do they?'

'With singers, who knows, anything's possible,' said Lucien.

'She killed them both? . . . And then later someone found out . . . and she preferred to disappear rather than face arrest?'

'Maybe not some*body*,' said Vandoosler. 'It might have been the tree. She was a killer but at the same time, superstitious, anxious, perhaps living in fear that one day she would be found out. Maybe the tree that appeared in her garden so mysteriously sent her over the edge. She thought it was a threat, a blackmailer perhaps. She got you to dig underneath it. But the tree wasn't concealing anything or anybody. It was just there to send her a message. Did she receive a letter? We don't know. But she must have chosen to disappear.'

'But then all she had to do was stay disappeared. She didn't need to burn someone else in her place!'

'She certainly meant to stay disappeared. To have people think she'd gone off with Stelios. But when she planned her flight, she'd forgotten all about Alexandra. She only remembered too late, and knew that her niece would think it impossible she had vanished without telling anyone, so would surely start enquiries. So she would have to provide a corpse, in order to be left in peace.'

'And Dompierre? How did she know he was asking about her?'

'She must have gone to earth in her house in Dourdan. She saw Dompierre coming to visit her father's house. She must have followed him. But then he wrote her name.'

Suddenly Marc cried out. He felt frightened and feverish. He was trembling. 'No! No!' he cried. 'Not Sophia! Not Sophia! She was beautiful. It's horrible, it's too horrible.'

'The historian cannot close his ears to anything,' said Lucien.

But Marc had left, telling Lucien to get stuffed with his history, and had run out into the street with his hands over his ears.

'He's over-sensitive,' said Vandoosler.

Lucien went back up to his room. To forget. To work.

Vandoosler remained alone with the photograph. His head was aching. Leguennec must be checking homeless people in various sectors of Paris. He was looking for a woman who had disappeared on June 2. When Vandoosler had left the station earlier that afternoon, there was already a trail that looked promising: an old woman called Louise, who lived under the Pont d'Austerlitz, who refused to move out of her little archway, furnished with cardboard boxes, and who was well known for her outbursts at the Gare de Lyon. Apparently she had gone missing a few days ago. It seemed likely that the beautiful Sophia had tempted her away, and that she had been incinerated in the car.

Yes, he had a headache alright.

# XXXIV

MARC RAN A LONG WAY, UNTIL HE COULD RUN NO MORE, AND HIS LUNGS
were aching. Panting for breath, with his sweat-soaked shirt sticking to
his back, he sat down on the first milestone he found. Dogs had pissed
all over it. He didn't care. His head was ringing as he sat there with his
hands squeezing his temples, and trying to think. Sickened and distracted,
he was trying to calm down sufficiently to get his thoughts in order. He
must avoid stamping his foot as he used to over the plastic balls. Or letting tectonic plates wander round his head. He would never manage to
clear his brain, sitting on a stone that stank of piss. He needed to walk,
slowly, just to walk along. But first he needed to get his breath back. He
looked around to see where he was. On the avenue d'Italie. Had he really
run that far? He got up carefully, mopped his brow and went towards the
nearest Métro station: Maison-Blanche, the white house. That reminded
him of something. Ah yes, the white whale. Moby Dick. The five-franc
coin nailed up in the refectory. That was typical of the godfather, playing
games, when everything was ending in horror. He must go back up the
avenue d'Italie. Walking with careful steps. Get used to the idea. Why
didn't he want Sophia to have done all this? Because he had met her one
morning, in front of the gate? And yet Christophe Dompierre's dying
accusation was there, blindingly clear. 'Siméonidis S', even if the S was the
wrong way round. Marc suddenly froze. He started walking again. Stopped.
Went into a café for a cup of coffee. Took up his walk again.

It was nine that evening by the time he got home, with an empty stomach and a heavy head. He went into the refectory to get himself a piece of bread. Leguennec was there, talking to his godfather. Each of them had a deck of playing cards in his hands.

'There's this old *clochard*, Raymond, hangs around the Pont d'Austerlitz,' Leguennec was saying. 'He's a pal of Louise's. He says a la-di-da lady came to find her about a week ago, on a Wednesday. He's absolutely sure it was a Wednesday. This woman was well dressed, and when she talked, she kept putting her hand to her throat. Spades.'

'She made some kind of proposition to Louise?' asked Vandoosler, putting three cards down, one of them face up.

'Yes. Raymond doesn't know what it was, but Louise was secretive about having a date with someone, and she was "bloody pleased with herself". What a business! She was about to get bumped off in a car in Maisons-Alfort. Poor old Louise. Your call.'

'No clubs. I'm discarding. What does the police doctor have to say?'

'He thinks it fits, because of the teeth. He would have thought the teeth would have survived better. But the ancient Louise had hardly any left. So that explains it. Maybe that was why Sophia picked her. I'm taking your hearts, and I'm harpooning the jack of diamonds.'

Marc pocketed the bread and put a couple of apples in his other pocket. He wondered what strange game the two policemen were playing. But he didn't care. He hadn't finished walking yet. Nor had he got used to the idea yet. Going out again, he went down the other side of rue Chasle, passing the Western Front. It would soon be dark.

He walked around for another two full hours. He left one apple core on the parapet of the Saint-Michel fountain, and the other on the plinth of the Belfort Lion on the place Denfert-Rochereau. It was hard getting close to the lion and climbing up onto the plinth. There's a little rhyme that says that the Belfort Lion comes down at night and pads around Paris. At least you can be sure that that really *is* a fairy story. When Marc jumped down again, he felt a lot better. He came back to rue Chasle, with his head aching a bit still, but calmer. He had digested the idea. He knew where Sophia was now. He had taken some time to work it out.

He came into the darkened refectory, feeling composed. Half-past eleven. Everyone must be asleep. He put on the light and and picked up the kettle. The horrible photo was no longer on the table. Instead there was a bit of paper with a message from Mathias: 'Juliette thinks she knows where she is. I'm going to Dourdan with her. I'm afraid she might be going to help her run away. I'll call Alexandra if I need to. Caveman greetings. Mathias.'

Marc put the kettle down with a bang. 'Oh God, the idiot!' he muttered. 'The bloody idiot.' He ran up to the third floor, four steps at a time. 'Lucien, get dressed!' he shouted, shaking his friend by the shoulder.

Lucien opened his eyes, ready to retort something.

'No, don't ask, don't start talking. I need you! Hurry!'

Marc rushed up to the fourth floor and shook Vandoosler awake.

'She's going to get away!' Marc said, panting. 'Quick! Juliette and Mathias have gone! That idiot Mathias doesn't realise the danger. I'm going with Lucien. Go and get Leguennec out of bed, and make him bring his men to Dourdan, number 12 allée des Grands-Ifs!'

Marc rushed out again. His legs ached from all the walking he had done. Lucien was coming downstairs, drowsy from sleep, pushing his feet into his shoes, a tie in his hand.

'Come and find me in front of Relivaux's house,' said Marc, pushing past him.

Hurtling down the steps, he ran across the garden and shouted up at Relivaux's house. Relivaux appeared at the window, looking wary. He was only lately returned, and the news about the name Dompierre had written on the car had apparently left him in a state of collapse.

'Throw me the keys to your car!' yelled Marc. 'It's a matter of life and death!'

Relivaux did not stop to think. A few seconds later, Marc caught the keys as they sailed over the gate. Say what you like about Relivaux, he was good at throwing.

'Thanks,' Marc yelled.

He turned on the ignition, moved off, opening the passenger door to pick up Lucien. Lucien tied his tie carefully, put a small flat bottle on his thigh, adjusted the angle of his seat backwards and settled comfortably.

'What's in the bottle?' asked Marc.

'Cooking rum. Just in case.'

'Where d'you get that?'

'It's mine. Got it to make cakes.'

Marc shrugged. That was Lucien for you.

Marc drove fast, gritting his teeth. In Paris at midnight you could generally get through very quickly. But it was Friday night and the traffic was heavy. Marc was sweating with anxiety, overtaking, jumping traffic lights. Only when he got out of Paris and onto the empty main road did he feel able to talk.

'What the hell does Mathias think he's playing at?' he exclaimed. 'He believes he can manage a woman who's already liquidated tons of people. He doesn't realise. He's worse than a bison!'

As Lucien didn't reply, Marc glanced across at him. The dope was fast asleep again.

'Lucien!' Marc shouted. 'Come on, look lively!'

But there was nothing to be done. Once he had decided to go to sleep, you couldn't wake him if he didn't want you to. Same as with the Great War. Marc put his foot down even harder.

He braked to a halt in front of number 12 allée des Grands-Ifs at one o'clock in the morning. The big wooden gate to Sophia's house was closed. Marc hauled Lucien out of the car and propped him up.

'Atten-shun!' he shouted at him.

'OK, OK, don't shout so loud,' said Lucien. 'I'm awake. I always wake up if I know I'm really needed.'

'Hurry up,' said Marc. 'Give me a leg-up like the other time.'

'Take your shoe off then.'

'Good grief, Lucien! We may be too late already. Just help me up, never mind the shoes.'

Marc put his foot on Lucien's linked hands and hauled himself to the top of the wall. He had to make an effort to get astride it.

'Your turn,' he said. 'Bring that dustbin over, and stand on it and grab my hand.'

Lucien found himself alongside Marc, astride the wall. The sky was cloudy and it was pitch dark. Lucien jumped down, with Marc behind him. Once on the ground, Marc tried to find his bearings. He thought of the well. He had been thinking about the well for some time. The well, water. Mathias. The well, the place where so many medieval crimes were committed. Where was the fucking well? Over there, a pale patch. Marc ran towards it, with Lucien behind him. He couldn't hear anything, no sound except his own footsteps and Lucien's. He was beside himself with fear. Frantically, he pulled away the heavy planks across the coping. Shit, he hadn't brought a torch. Anyway, it was ages since he had owned a torch. Two years? Yes, about two years. He leaned over the coping and called Mathias' name.

No reply. Why was he so sure about the well? Why was he not going to the house or the wood behind it? No, he was absolutely certain it had to be the well. It's easy, it's clean, it's medieval, and nobody ever finds out. He lifted up the heavy zinc bucket and lowered it gently down. When he heard it touch the surface of the water, far below, he wedged the chain and put one leg over the coping.

'Make sure the chain stays in place,' he told Lucien. 'Don't move away from the goddamn well. And, whatever you do, take care. Don't make a sound, don't alert her. Four, five, six corpses, she's past counting. Give me the rum.'

Marc began the descent. He was scared. The well was narrow, dark, slimy and cold, like all wells. But the chain was strong. He thought he had gone down about six or seven metres when he felt the bucket, and icy water on his ankles. He let himself slide in up to his thighs and his skin almost burst with the cold. He felt the inert mass of a body against his legs and wanted to scream.

He called him, but Mathias didn't reply. Now that Marc's eyes were used to the darkness, he lowered himself further into the water, up to the waist. With one hand, he felt the body of the hunter-gatherer, who had allowed himself to be tipped into the well, like a complete cretin. His head and knees were still above water. Mathias had managed to press his long legs against the walls of the well. It was lucky the well was so narrow. He had succeeded in wedging himself in place, but how long had he been in this freezing water? How long had he been here, sliding, centimetre by centimetre, downwards, till he was swallowing that black water?

He couldn't haul Mathias to the top if he was a deadweight. Mathias would have to be able to hold on.

Marc wrapped the chain round his right arm, and pressed his legs against the bucket, confirmed his grip, and began to pull Mathias up out of the water. He was so big and heavy. The effort was exhausting. Gradually Marc managed to pull him clear, and after a quarter of a hour's effort, Mathias' head and shoulders were resting on the bucket. Marc held him up with his leg, by bracing it against the wall, and with his left hand managed to pull the bottle of rum out of his jacket pocket. If Mathias still had some life left in him, he certainly wouldn't like the cooking rum. He poured it as best he could into his friend's mouth. It was going everywhere, but Mathias spluttered. Not for a second had Marc allowed himself to think that Mathias would die. Not the hunter-gatherer. Marc gave him a few clumsy slaps and tipped more rum into him. Mathias groaned. He was coming up from the depths.

'Can you hear me? It's Marc.'

'Where are we?' asked Mathias in a croaking voice. 'I'm freezing. I'm going to die.'

'We're in the well. Where do you think?'

'She pushed me in!' stammered Mathias. 'She hit me and pushed me in. I didn't hear her coming.'

'I know,' said Marc. 'Lucien is at the top. He's going to pull us up.'

'He'll rupture himself,' muttered Mathias.

'Don't worry about him. He's good at front-line jobs. Come on, drink this.'

'What the fuck is this stuff?' Mathias was almost inaudible.

'It's cooking rum for cakes, it's Lucien's. Is it warming you up?'

'Have some yourself. This water's paralysing.'

Marc swallowed a few mouthfuls. The chain around his arm was biting and burning into his flesh.

Mathias had closed his eyes again. He was breathing, that was as much as you could say for him. Marc whistled and Lucien's head appeared in the little circle of light far above.

'The chain!' said Marc. 'Start hauling it up, but very gently, and whatever you do don't let it go down again. If it jerks, I'll have to let go.'

His voice sounded echoing and deafening in his ears. But perhaps his ears were frozen.

He heard a clanking sound. Lucien was releasing the chain, while holding on so that Marc did not fall lower. Lucien was a trooper, alright. The chain started to go up, slowly.

'Pull it up link by link,' Marc called. 'He weighs as much as a bison.'

'Has he drowned?' Lucien called down.

'No! Haul away, soldier!'

'What a bloody shambles!' came the reply.

Marc was holding onto Mathias by his trousers. Mathias kept his trousers up with a thick cord which was handy to grip on to. That was the only advantage that Marc could see for the time being of Mathias' rustic habit of holding his trousers up with string. The hunter-gatherer's head banged from time to time against the walls, but Marc could see the parapet approaching. Lucien heaved Mathias out and laid him on the ground. Marc climbed over the parapet and let himself fall to the grass. He unwound the chain from his arm, pulling a face. The arm was bleeding.

'Take my jacket to put round that,' said Lucien.

'Did you hear anything?'

'No, but here comes your uncle.'

'He took his time! Slap Mathias on the face, and rub his limbs. I think he's lost consciousness again.'

Leguennec was the first to arrive, at a run, and knelt down by Mathias. He did have a torch.

Marc got up, nursing his arm, which seemed to have turned to stone, and went to meet the six policemen.

'I'm sure she's hiding in the copse,' he said.

They found Juliette ten minutes later. Two men brought her over, holding her by the arms. She appeared exhausted, and was covered in scratches and bruises.

'She . . .' panted Juliette. 'I ran away . . .'

Marc rushed at her and grabbed her shoulder.

'Shut up!' he shouted at her. 'Just shut up, d'you hear!'

'Should I stop him?' Leguennec asked Vandoosler.

'No,' whispered Vandoosler. 'There's no danger. Let him alone. This was his discovery. I suspected something like this, but . . .'

'You should have told me, Vandoosler.'

'I couldn't be sure. But medieval historians have special ways of thinking. When Marc gets his mind in gear, he gets straight to the answer. He takes it all in, important stuff and rubbish, and then all at once he goes for it.'

Leguennec looked at Marc, who was standing stiff and pale, his hair soaking wet, and still gripping Juliette's shoulder with his left hand, covered in shining rings, a large hand close to her throat and looking dangerous.

'What if he does something stupid?'

'He won't do anything stupid.'

Leguennec, all the same, motioned to his men to stand close around Marc and Juliette.

'I'm going to see to Mathias,' he said. 'It looks as if he had a close shave.'

Vandoosler remembered that when Leguennec had been a fisherman, he had also been in offshore rescue. Water, water everywhere.

Marc had let Juliette go now and was staring straight at her. She was ugly, she was beautiful. He felt sick. Maybe it was the rum? She wasn't moving a muscle. Marc was shaking. His wet clothes were clinging to him and turning his body to ice. Slowly he looked around for Leguennec among the men clustered together in the darkness. He saw him further off, alongside Mathias.

'*Inspecteur,*' he said hoarsely, 'give orders to have the tree dug up back in rue Chasle. She's underneath it, I think.'

'Under the tree?' said Leguennec. 'But we've already dug there.'

'Exactly,' said Marc. 'The place we've already searched, the place nobody will open up again. But that's where Sophia is.'

Now Marc was shivering all over. He found the little bottle of rum and drank what remained in it. He felt his head swimming and wanted Mathias to make a fire for him, but Mathias was lying on the ground. He wished he too could lie down, and scream perhaps. He wiped his forehead with the wet sleeve on his left arm, which was still functioning. The other arm was hanging limp, and blood was running onto his hand.

He looked up. She was still staring at him. Of all her plans, now in ruins, all that remained was that rigid body and the bitter resistance of her gaze.

Feeling stunned, Marc suddenly sat down on the grass. No, he didn't want to look at her any longer. He even regretted what he had already seen.

Leguennec was hoisting Mathias into a sitting position.

'Marc . . .' Mathias was saying.

His croaking voice reached Marc, shaking him into speech. If Mathias had had more strength he would have said: 'Tell them, Marc.' That's what he would say, the hunter-gatherer. Marc's teeth were chattering and the words came out in fragments.

'What Dompierre wrote . . .' he said.

Head down, cross-legged, he was pulling out the grass in tufts, as he had under the beech tree. He scattered the tufts all round him.

'He wrote Sophia's name in a funny way: Siméonidis S. We thought he had written that last S the wrong way round, because he was trying to summon up strength. We said it looked a bit like a 2, and we were right, it wasn't an S at all, it *was* a figure 2.'

Marc shivered. He felt his uncle pulling off his jacket and his dripping wet shirt. He didn't have the strength to help him. He was still pulling up grass with his left hand. Now someone was wrapping him in a coarse blanket, which he felt against his skin, one of the blankets from the police van. Mathias was draped in one as well. It was scratchy, but warm. He relaxed a bit, huddled himself into it, and his jaw became less clenched. He kept his eyes fixed on the grass, instinctively so as not to have to look at her.

'Go on,' came Mathias' voice.

Now his voice was coming back, he could speak more easily and compose his thoughts more clearly as he went along. But he still couldn't say her name.

'I worked out that Christophe didn't actually mean to write "Sophia Siméonidis". But what the hell did he write? He'd written Siméonidis 2, Siméonidis number 2, the double of Siméonidis. His father, in the review of "Elektra", had written a rather odd phrase, something like "Sophia was replaced for three days by her understudy, Nathalie Domesco, whose pathetic *imitation* finished off the opera": and imitation was an odd choice of word, as if the "double" was not just replacing Sophia, but imitating her, mimicking her, with hair dyed black and cut short, red lipstick, and a scarf round her neck – that's how she did it. Sophia's "double". And "the double" was the nickname that Dompierre and Frémonville gave the understudy, probably to mock her, because she was overdoing it. And Christophe knew that, he knew her nickname, but not her name, and he found out – but too late – who she was, and I guessed it too, but almost too late.'

Marc looked towards Mathias who was sitting on the ground between Leguennec and another policeman. He also saw Lucien, who had taken a position standing behind the hunter-gatherer, providing him with a support to lean on, Lucien with his tie in shreds, his shirt filthy from the parapet of the well, his childlike face, his parted lips and frowning eyebrows. A closely knit group of four silent men, clearly outlined by the light from Leguennec's torch. Mathias seemed dazed, but Mathias was listening. Marc had to go on talking.

'Will he be OK?' he asked.

'He'll be OK,' said Leguennec. 'He's starting to move his feet now in his sandals.'

'Ah, he'll be OK, then. Mathias, did you go to see Juliette this morning?'

'Yes,' said Mathias.

'And you talked to her?'

'Yes. I'd felt warm, remember, when we were out in the street, the night when we found Lucien out there wandering about drunk? I didn't have any clothes on, but I wasn't cold, I felt some warmth on my back,

I thought about it later. It must have been the engine of a car. I'd felt the warmth of her car, parked in front of her house. I understood then, when Gosselin was accused. But what I thought was that he'd taken his sister's car out, the night of the murder.'

'So you were in the shit, if you told her that. Because sooner or later, once Gosselin was exonerated, there would have to be some other explanation of why you felt warm. But when I came back to the house tonight, I knew all about her, I knew why she did it, I knew everything.'

Marc was scattering grass all round him, tearing up the little patch of ground he was sitting on.

'Christophe Dompierre had tried to write "Siméonidis number 2" or Siméonidis' double. Why? Georges had certainly attacked Sophia in her dressing-room and somebody benefited from that. Who? The understudy, of course, the stand-in, who would replace her on stage – in other words number 2. I remembered then . . . the music lessons . . . she was the stand-in, for years – under the name Nathalie Domesco. Only her brother knew about it, her parents thought she was doing cleaning jobs. Perhaps she was out of touch with them, or had quarrelled with them, or something. And I remembered something else, yes Mathias, Mathias who didn't feel cold that night when Dompierre was murdered, Mathias who was standing in front of her gate, just by her car . . . and I remembered the police when they were digging under the tree, I could see them from my window, and they were only up to their thighs in the trench . . . so they didn't dig any deeper than we did . . . someone else *had* dug after them, and had gone down deeper to the layer of black earth . . . and then I knew enough to plot the course of events, like Ahab with the whale, and like him I knew the route she had taken – and the one she would take.'

Juliette looked at the men posted around her in a semi-circle. She threw back her head and spat at Marc. Marc let his head fall onto his chest. The fair Juliette, with her smooth white shoulders, with her welcoming body and welcoming smile. The pale body in the moonlight, soft, round, heavy, and spraying foam. Juliette, whom he used to kiss on the forehead, the white whale, the killer whale.

Juliette spat again, at the two policemen holding her, then nothing came from her but loud hoarse breathing. Then a short cackle of laughter, then the breathing again. Marc could imagine her gaze fixed on him. He thought of *Le Tonneau*. How happy they had all been there . . . the cigarette smoke, the beers at the counter, the sound of clinking coffee cups. The veal casseroles. And how Sophia had sung just for them, that first night.

Pull up more grass. By now he had made a little pile on his left.

'She planted the tree,' he went on. 'She knew that the tree would worry Sophia and that she would talk about it. Who wouldn't be worried by it? She sent the card, supposedly from Stelios. She intercepted Sophia that Wednesday night, as she was going to the station, and brought her back to the damned restaurant with some pretext or other, I don't know what, and I don't care how she did it, I don't want to hear anything from her! She probably said she'd heard from Stelios, got Sophia inside, took her to the basement, killed her, trussed her up like a side of beef, and that night she drove her to Normandy, where I'm sure she put her in the old freezer down in the cellar.'

Mathias was wringing his hands. Oh God, how he had wanted that woman, in the cosy proximity of the restaurant at night when the last customers had left, or even that very morning when he had brushed against her as he helped her tidy the house. A hundred times, he had wanted to make love to her, in the cellar, in the kitchen, in the street. He had wanted to tear off the clothes that constricted him. He wondered now what obscure prudence had somehow always held him back. He also wondered why it was that Juliette had never seemed attracted to any man.

A rasping sound made him jump.

'Make her shut up,' shouted Marc, still looking down at the grass.

He drew breath. There was no grass left in reach of his left hand. He shifted position. To make another pile.

'Once Sophia had disappeared,' he went on, in a shaky voice, 'everyone began to get worried, and she was the first to raise the alarm. Like a loyal friend. The police were sure to dig under the tree. So they did, and found nothing there, so they filled it in again. And then everyone ended up thinking Sophia had gone off somewhere with Stelios. So the . . . the place was ready. Now she could really bury Sophia where nobody, not even the police, would ever look for her, because they'd already done it once. Under the tree. And nobody would be looking for Sophia any more, they all thought she'd gone swanning off to some Greek island. Her body, sealed in by a beech tree nobody would touch, would never come to light. But she needed to be able to bury her unobserved, without any nosy neighbours around – without us there to see.'

Marc stopped again. It was taking him so long to tell all this. It seemed to him he wasn't telling things in the right order, the proper sensible way. Well, the proper sensible account would have to come later.

'She took us all off to Normandy. And that night, she got into her car, with her frozen bundle, and drove back to rue Chasle. Relivaux was away, and we like complete nitwits, were sleeping peacefully in her country cottage, a hunded kilometres away! Then she did her disgusting job, and buried Sophia under the beech tree. She's a strong woman. In the early morning, she came back to the cottage, on tiptoe . . .'

Thank goodness. He'd got past the worst bit. The bit about Sophia being buried under the tree. He needn't pull up any more grass now. It was passing. And this was Sophia's grass anyway.

He got up and walked about slowly, wrapping the blanket around him with his left hand. Lucien thought he looked like a Sioux with his dark straight hair damp from the water and his blanket over his shoulders. He walked to and fro, without going near her, turning without letting his eyes move in her direction.

'So she wasn't best pleased after that, to see this niece turn up with the little one. She hadn't expected it. Alexandra had arranged to meet her aunt, and she didn't accept that she had just disappeared into thin air. Alexandra was determined and headstrong, the police took it up, and they started looking for Sophia again. It was impossible and risky to try to recover the corpse from under the tree. This time she would have to produce a body, to halt the investigation before the cops started digging up the entire neighbourhood. So the woman who went to find poor old Louise under the Pont d'Austerlitz, that was her. She dragged Louise off to Maisons-Alfort and set fire to her!' Marc was shouting again. He forced himself to take deep breaths from down in his stomach, and started again. 'Of course, she had Sophia's little travelling bag. She put the gold rings on Louise's fingers, put the bag beside her in the car and started the fire. A very big fire. Because there had to be no sign left of Louise's identity, and the police mustn't be able to tell which day she died. It was an inferno but she knew that the basalt would survive. And the basalt would point straight to Sophia. It would talk.'

Suddenly Juliette began to scream. Marc stood still and blocked his ears, the left with his hand, the right with his shoulder. He could hear only snatches of what she was screaming: basalt, Sophia, filth, deserved to die, Elektra, fucking critics, singing, nobody, Elektra . . .

'Make her shut up!' Marc shouted. 'Make her shut up, take her away, I can't stand to hear her any longer.'

There were more noises, more spitting sounds and the footsteps of the policemen who, at a sign from Leguennec, were leading her away. When Marc gathered that Juliette was no longer there, he let his arms fall. Now he could look at anything he liked, his eyes were free. She had gone.

'Yes. She did sing,' he said, 'but only as a stand-in, an understudy, a second-best, and she couldn't bear it, she needed her big break. She was mortally jealous of Sophia. So she pushed her luck, she got her poor benighted brother to attack Sophia, so that she would be able to take her place on stage, a simple idea.'

'What about the attempted rape?' said Leguennec.

'The attempted rape? Well, that must have been something his sister told him to do as well, to make the attack look more convincing. The attempted rape was really nothing of the sort.'

Marc stopped speaking, and went over to Mathias, examined him, nodded and went on walking round, with long, unnatural paces, and his arm still hanging down. He wondered whether Mathias found the police blanket scratchy, as he did. Probably not. Mathias was not the sort of person to make a fuss about scratchy wool. He wondered how it was he could go on talking like this, when his head was hurting so much, when he felt so sick, how he could both know all this and tell them about it? How was it? It was because he had been quite unable to swallow the story that Sophia had killed anyone. That had to be the wrong conclusion, he was sure of that, it was an impossibility. And that meant going back to the beginning, looking at all the evidence again. If it wasn't Sophia, it had to be someone else, there had to be another history of how things had happened. And that history was what he had been telling himself in bits and pieces earlier that day, little bit by bit, working out the path of the whale, its instincts, its desires . . . By the Saint-Michel fountain . . . its favourite haunts, its feeding grounds . . . By the Denfert-Rochereau Lion, that comes down from its plinth at night . . . the lion that walks by night, that does lion-type things without anyone seeing it, the bronze lion, like her, coming back and lying down on its pedestal in the morning, turning back into a statue once more, stable, reassuring, far from any suspicion . . . back in the morning on her pedestal, back behind the counter, as usual, smiling, but without having any real affection for anyone, no little pang of the heart, no, not even for Mathias, nothing . . . But at night, it was a different story; at night, he knew her route now, now that he was on her back. Hanging on like Ahab, gripping the back of the whale that had taken his leg.

'Let me see that arm,' whispered Leguennec.

'Leave him be, for Christ's sake,' said Vandoosler.

'She only sang for three nights,' Marc said, 'after her brother had made sure Sophia went to hospital. But the critics either ignored her or, which was worse, two of them, Dompierre and Frémonville, demolished her quite definitively. After that, Sophia changed understudies. It was all over for Nathalie Domesco. She had to give up opera, give up singing, and her fury and pride, and I don't know what other emotions, stayed with her. After that, she just lived to take her revenge on those who had broken her career: she was intelligent, she was musical, she was mad, beautiful, and demonic, she looked so beautiful on her pedestal – like a statue, untouchable.'

'Let me see that arm,' Leguennec was saying again.

Marc shook his head.

'She waited a year, so that people would have forgotten about "Elektra," then months later, in cold blood, she killed the two critics who had massacred her. And to get Sophia, she waited fourteen years. She wanted a long time to pass, so that the murder of the two critics would be forgotten and no link found. And she waited, perhaps savouring the wait – I don't know. But she followed her, and observed her, from the house she had bought close by, a few years later. Perhaps she even persuaded the previous owner to sell it to her, yes, it's quite possible. She didn't leave things to chance. She had let her hair grow back to its natural colour, which was blonde, changed her hairstyle, the years passed, and Sophia didn't recognise her, any more than she recognised Georges. There wasn't much risk. Top singers hardly know their understudies, and as for the extras . . .'

Leguennec had taken firm hold of Marc's right arm without asking him again, and was putting on some powerful-smelling antiseptic. Marc let him do it; he couldn't feel the arm any more.

Vandoosler was watching him. He would have liked to interrupt and ask questions, but he knew one shouldn't interrupt Marc at a time like this. You don't wake up a sleepwalker, because apparently it will make them fall over. Whether that was true or false he didn't know, but it was certainly true of Marc. You shouldn't wake Marc up when he was launched, trance-like, into his research. Or he too would fall over. He knew for certain that since Marc left their house that night, he had flown like an arrow directly to the target. It was just like when he was a child, and couldn't accept something: he would run off somewhere. And when that happened, he knew from experience that Marc could travel very quickly, and become as taut as a wire until he found what he was after. Earlier in the evening, his nephew had come into the house and picked up a couple of apples, he remembered quite well. Marc hadn't said a word. But his intense gaze, his far-off expression, his mute violence, all that had warned him. And if he hadn't been deep in his game of cards, he should have noticed that Marc was in the process of searching, finding and homing in on his target, that he was engaged in unpicking Juliette's logic, uncovering it . . . and that he knew. And now he was telling them. Leguennec probably thought that Marc was telling them all this with incredible calm. But Vandoosler knew that this unstoppable flow, some-times smooth, but always driven onwards like a vessel by a squally wind, had nothing to do with being calm. He was sure that by now his nephew's thigh muscles would be feeling stiff and painful, so that they would need to be wrapped in hot towels as he had often done for him when he was a boy. Everyone else thought Marc was moving normally, but Vandoosler could tell that he was as if made of marble from his hips to his ankles. If he interrupted him, he would stay paralysed like that, and that was the reason he should be left in peace to finish, to reach harbour after this infernal mental chase. His leg muscles would only be able to relax at the end.

'She told Georges never to say a word to Sophia, because he was in trouble too,' Marc was saying. 'And Georges would do whatever she said. Perhaps he was the only person she ever really loved, a bit, but I'm not even sure of that. Georges believed her. She may have told him she wanted to try again to be Sophia's understudy. He has no imagination, he never dreamed she wanted to kill Sophia, or that she had shot the two critics. Poor old Georges, he was never in love with Sophia. That was a lie, a filthy lie. And that cosy little world of *Le Tonneau* was built on lies. Juliette was watching Sophia; she wanted to know everything about her and become her bosom friend in the eyes of the world, and then she was going to kill her!'

He was certain of himself. It would be easy to find the evidence now, and witnesses. He looked at what Leguennec was doing. He was putting a dressing on the arm. It wasn't a pretty sight. His legs were hurting terribly, much worse than the arm. He forced them to carry him, auto-matically. But he was used to that, it had happened before and he knew it was inevitable.

'And fifteen years after "Elektra", she laid her trap. She killed Sophia, she killed Louise, put two of Sophia's hairs in Alexandra's car, killed Dompierre. She pretended to protect Alexandra's alibi for the night of the murder. In fact, of course, she had heard Lucien yelling his head off in the street at two o'clock in the morning, because she had just got back from the Hôtel du Danube after stabbing that poor guy. She was sure that the alibi for Alexandra wouldn't hold water, and that I would be bound to realise it was a lie. So she could "admit" that Alexandra had gone out, without seeming to betray her. It was disgusting, in fact worse than disgusting.'

Marc recalled the conversation at the bar: 'You're very kind, Juliette.' Not for a moment had the thought crossed his mind that Juliette was manipulating him in order to incriminate Alexandra. Yes, worse than disgusting.

'But then suspicion fell on her brother. It was getting too close for comfort. She persuaded him to run away, so that he couldn't give anything away under questioning. And then it was an extraordinary piece of luck for her that they found the message from the man she'd killed. She was safe! Dompierre seemed to be accusing Sophia, who was dead, but was then believed alive! It was too perfect. But I just couldn't swallow that. Not Sophia, no, Sophia would never have done those things. And what about the tree? It didn't explain the tree. No, I couldn't swallow it.'

'Oh, what a dirty war,' murmured Lucien.


When they reached the house again at about four in the morning, the beech tree had been dug up, Sophia Siméonidis' body had already been exhumed and taken away. This time the tree had not been replanted.

The three evangelists, worn out, didn't feel like going to bed. Marc and Mathias, still wrapped in blankets instead of clothes, were sitting on the little wall. Lucien was perched up on the big dustbin opposite them. He was growing fond of it. Vandoosler was smoking a cigarette and walking up and down. It felt warm. At least compared to the well, Marc thought. The chain would leave a scar on his arm in the shape of a coiled snake.

'It'll go well with your rings,' said Lucien.

'Wrong arm.'

Alexandra came round to say good night. She had not been able to get back to sleep after the police had been to dig up the beech tree. And Leguennec had been round. To give her the piece of basalt. Marc looked at her. He would have been so glad if she could have fallen in love with him. Just like that, to see what happened.

'Tell me, Mathias,' he said, 'when you whispered in her ear to make her talk, what did you say?'

'Nothing. I just said "Go on, Juliette, talk to them".'

Marc sighed. 'I might have guessed there wasn't any magic trick. It would have been too good to be true.'

Alexandra kissed each of them and went away. She didn't want to leave her son on his own. Vandoosler followed her slim figure with his eyes as she walked away. Three little dots. The twins, the woman. Shit. He looked down and stamped out his cigarette.

'You should get some sleep,' Marc said.

Vandoosler started off towards the house.

'Does your godfather usually do what you tell him?' asked Lucien.

'No, never,' said Marc. 'Look, he's coming back.'

Vandoosler tossed the five-franc piece into the air and caught it. 'Let's chuck it away,' he said. 'Anyway, we can't cut it into twelve.'

'There aren't twelve of us,' Marc said. 'Only four.'

'Ah, that would be too simple,' said Vandoosler.

He swung his arm and the coin tinkled to the ground a long way off. Lucien had climbed onto the dustbin to follow its trajectory.

'Company dismissed!' he cried.